The
Lucky Dog
Matchmaking
Service

ALSO BY BETH KENDRICK

The Bake-Off

Second Time Around

The Pre-nup

Nearlyweds

Fashionably Late

Exes and Ohs

My Favorite Mistake

The
Lucky Dog
Matchmaking
Service

·····································

BETH KENDRICK

DOUBLEDAY LARGE PRINT HOME LIBRARY EDITION

 NEW AMERICAN LIBRARY

NEW AMERICAN LIBRARY
Published by New American Library, a division of Penguin Group (USA) Inc., 375 Hudson Street, New York, New York 10014, USA

Penguin Books Ltd., Registered Offices: 80 Strand, London WC2R 0RL, England

First published by New American Library, a division of Penguin Group (USA) Inc.

ISBN 978-1-61793-895-5

Printed in the United States of America

For Will
I'm so lucky to have you in my life

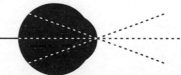

This Large Print Book carries the
Seal of Approval of N.A.V.H.

The
Lucky Dog
Matchmaking
Service

Chapter 1

"I'm short, I'm balding, and I've put on twenty pounds since my fiancée left me for her personal trainer. You're my last hope for love."

Lara Madigan froze in the drugstore parking lot, one hand on the door handle of her Oldsmobile station wagon. She didn't recognize the wheezy male voice behind her and so she hoped, for a moment, that perhaps he was addressing someone else.

But the guy made a deep, phlegmy noise in his throat and persisted: "You're the matchmaker, right?"

Lara turned around slowly, pulling up the collar of her coat to shield her neck from the chilly winter wind. "Yes, I am. Pleased to meet you." She offered her right hand, and the man grabbed it like a lifeguard's buoy, both of his sweaty palms engulfing her fingers.

"Peter Hoffstead. You have to help me." He tightened his grip. "I'm desperate."

Lara's mind automatically whirred into assessment mode. The first thing she noticed about Peter was that his outfit didn't match his personality. Though his complexion looked pasty and his remaining hair was graying, he was attired in visible designer labels: Cartier watch, Rock & Republic jeans, Burberry belt. From the neck up, he was Bill Gates, but from the neck down, he was P. Diddy. Someone else had clearly picked out his wardrobe—someone who wanted him to be more of a debonair playboy and less of a middle-aged homebody.

She gently but firmly pulled away from his grasp and rummaged through her shoulder bag for her business card.

As she handed it to him, she cautioned, "I'm always looking for promising prospects, but you have to understand that I can't match just anyone. All my prospective clients undergo a rigorous screening process, and my standards are very high. I have to consider the long-term happiness of everyone involved."

"One of your previous clients can vouch for me." Peter rubbed at his nose with a clean but wrinkled handkerchief. "Mark Heston—he's my neighbor. He said you hooked him up with Amelia."

"Amelia!" Lara softened at the name. "What a sweetheart. How's she doing these days?"

Peter shrugged. "Great, I guess. Mark never shuts up about her. I need you to do for me what you did for him." He stuffed his hand into the pocket of his black leather jacket and offered up a stack of cash. "I'll pay whatever you ask. I'll double your usual fee."

Lara made no move to accept the folded green bills. "What I do isn't about money. It's about finding a true soul connection. I want all my pairings to last a lifetime, so I need to figure out exactly what your needs are and who best meets them."

Peter nodded, and as he stuffed the money back into his pocket, he sighed with resignation. He stopped the posturing and name-dropping and gave her a glimpse of the raw loneliness festering beneath all those designer labels. "Look." He spread out his hands. "I know I'm not the most appealing guy, physically. My fiancée made that very clear before she left me. But I've got a lot to offer: love, stability, all that stuff."

Lara tilted her head and took in his body language. Years of trial and error had taught her that it didn't really matter what a prospective client said. People used words to manipulate and evade, to justify their mistakes and prejudices. The truth was in the tone of their voices and the light in their eyes.

"When I make a commitment, I keep it," Peter continued. "I own my own business, I work at home. . . ."

"You do?" Lara's eyebrows shot up. "Do you have a yard?"

"Half an acre," Peter assured her, puffing up with pride. "Fenced. Backs up to a nature preserve." He beckoned her closer. "With hiking trails. I've started jogging four days a week. Well, I do a fifteen-minute mile, which I guess doesn't really qualify as jogging. But I'm trying. And it's easier to get motivated to exercise when you have a partner, you know?" He looked at her with a mixture of hope and chagrin. Clearly, he was bracing himself for her refusal.

She started compiling a profile in her head: *attentive, outdoorsy, willing to learn . . .*

"I'll do whatever you tell me. You won't be sorry. I just need help meeting women. I've tried going to bars, signing up for Internet dating sites, but nothing's working. I need a wingman—someone to break the ice. Will you help me? Please?"

He gazed at her through his smudged, crooked glasses, and she started to smile. This was a good man, with a good heart, who just needed a little boost to his confidence. A carefully chosen companion to help him rediscover his sense of self-worth without flaunting pricey logos or stacks of cash.

"I think I have the perfect match for you."

His whole body tensed with anticipation. "You do?"

Lara nodded. "Cute, charismatic, and virtually irresistible. Guaranteed to draw a crowd wherever you go." She brought up a photo on her cell phone and showed Peter the snapshot of a scrappy, scruffy yellow terrier. "Meet Murphy."

Chapter 2

Lara could smell vanilla and lemon as soon as she stepped into the house. Two steps later, she could sense turmoil brewing, too.

She braced herself for the wildly enthusiastic canine greeting committee, but the hallway remained empty. Her boyfriend, Evan, had bought this house last year, but Lara had moved in only a few weeks ago, and the place retained the bare-walled, sparsely furnished feel of a stereotypical bachelor pad. Lara had been no help in adding a homey "woman's touch" to the place—her interior decorating contributions began and ended with setting up a doggie wading pool on the back patio and pulling all the potentially poisonous shrubbery out of the landscaping.

Oh, and the piles of her boxed-up belongings helped to balance out the lack of furniture.

"Hello?" The sound of her flip-flops echoed off the tile floor as she headed toward the kitchen. "Where is everyone?"

"In lockup." Evan stood in the middle of the breakfast area, his hair wet, his light blue shirt unbuttoned, and his expression grim as he scrubbed the counter with a damp dish towel. Tall and lanky, with reddish brown hair and a head full of brilliant business sense, Evan had intrigued Lara from the day they first met. He taught economics in a prestigious MBA program, but at home he always looked like he was a pair of Converses and a few swipes of a razor away from playing ultimate Frisbee on the quad. He wasn't into status symbols, but he'd worked hard for everything he had and he took good care of his investments—including his house.

"Uh-oh." Lara put her bag down on a wrought-iron chair and approached him with a conciliatory smile. "Should I even ask what their crime was this time?"

Evan leaned back against the counter and crossed his arms over his chest. "My afternoon meeting got canceled, so I came home early to bake a cake for your birthday tomorrow. While it was cooling, I ran upstairs for a two-minute shower, and your dogs—"

She went up on tiptoe and gave him a kiss. "*Our* dogs, darling. Remember?"

"—ate the entire thing."

Lara's eyes widened with alarm. "It wasn't chocolate cake, was it?"

"No, it was banana sour cream, and those bastards ate every crumb. I made lemon icing, too. We're going to have to stick a candle in that and eat it with spoons."

She exhaled and relaxed. "That's good. I mean, it's not *good*, but if the dogs ate a chocolate cake, the theobromine could cause serious heart problems."

"I made that cake from scratch." He thumped the cookbook next to the sink. "With actual flour and eggs and butter."

"And I appreciate every granule of sugar you put into it. I'm sure it was delicious."

"They also ate the flowers I bought you." Evan pointed to a shard of glass by the patio door. "Watch your step. I'm still cleaning up the vase."

"That must've been Zsa Zsa. She has a bizarre craving for greenery." Lara grabbed the front of his shirt and pulled him down for another kiss. "Flowers and cake? A girl could get used to this."

He frowned. "Well?"

"Well, what?" She took off her jacket and got the broom out of the pantry.

He nodded toward the door of what used to be a spare bedroom and was now known as "the dog room." "Aren't you going to punish them?"

"No."

"Why the hell not? They're a bunch of conniving cake thieves."

Lara shooed him away from the counter and got to work sweeping up the broken glass. "First of all, discipline has to be immediate to be effective. If I correct them now, they'll have no clue what I'm correcting them for."

"They ate my banana sour cream cake. They must pay."

"Second of all, they're not conniving. You're giving them way too much credit. They saw a cake within striking distance, so they struck. Maverick was probably the ringleader. We're working on his counter-surfing tendencies, but if you leave a cake out and don't crate him . . ."

Evan grabbed an apple out of the refrigerator and took a big, angry bite. "So you're saying it's my fault for leaving the cake on my kitchen counter instead of in a bank vault? That's bullshit. It's *my* counter in *my* house, and he should—" He saw her expression change and hurriedly corrected himself. "I mean, *our* counter in *our* house."

Lara stopped sweeping and took a long, analytical look at her boyfriend. He was usually calm and levelheaded to a fault. "I've never seen you so angry. Are you mad at the dogs or at me?"

He made her wait through another

bite of apple before he responded. "You're a dog trainer, right? So shouldn't your dogs be, I don't know, *trained*?"

Her grip on the broom handle tightened. "I'm a trainer who takes on dogs after other people have instilled a lifetime of bad habits in them. It's not magic. It takes time and patience. And I've got news for you: If you want a houseful of well-behaved dogs, you need to help out with the training. They're adjusting to the new living situation, too, and they need structure and consistency from both of us."

He muttered something under his breath that sounded suspiciously like "And a shock collar."

Lara's eyebrows shot up. "I'm sorry—what was that?"

Evan set his jaw and returned her stubborn stare.

"What exactly do you want me to do here?" she demanded. "Do you want me to move out?"

His expression went from irritated to stunned. "Who said anything about moving out?"

Lara looked away.

"Why is leaving always your first line of defense?" He nodded toward the mountain of boxes in the living room. "I'm still trying to get you to actually move in. You've been here over a month and you haven't unpacked."

"I don't want to get settled until I'm sure you can handle the reality of living with me. I mean, if a counter-surfed cake is going to upset you this much . . ."

"I'm allowed to be upset that they ate your birthday cake," he said. "That doesn't mean I don't want to be with you. I love you."

"I love you, too." Lara brightened, hoping this would wrap up the argument.

But then Evan asked the question that could never be unasked: "But do you love me more than the dogs?"

Lara got a wineglass out of the cabinet, poured herself a splash of Shiraz, and took a long, deliberate sip before answering. "Must I remind you of our contract? The contract that you yourself drew up and signed on the night you asked me to move in?" She glanced over at the cocktail napkin stuck to the refrigerator door with a magnet. Scribbled in pen on the napkin was Evan's solemn vow: *I, Evan Walker, do hereby promise to become a "dog person" and never complain about shedding or slobbering, so help me God.*

"This is life with rescue dogs." A note of defiance crept into her voice. "Things get messy. Things get eaten. You're going to get to know the vet on a first-name basis."

From the dog room, they heard barking and the scrabble of claws against the wooden door.

"They've scratched the hell out of the drywall." Evan rubbed his forehead.

"I'll call a contractor and have it repaired," Lara offered. "That's what I want for my birthday—new drywall."

"No, no, I'll take care of it." He blew out a breath. "It's my house, and besides, you already spent how much at the vet this month?"

"About twenty-three hundred dollars." Lara paused. "And it's *our* house. Right?"

He opened his arms to her, and as he held her, she could feel both of their bodies relax. "Our house." He rested his chin on the top of her head. "I'm sorry. It's just . . . all these dogs . . . I don't understand why you feel the need to take on other people's problems."

Lara pressed her cheek into the warmth of his chest, willing him to understand. "They're not 'problems.' Each of these dogs has a purpose. They're not just pets; they're lifelines. I've seen it, Evan. I've lived it."

Lara had been sixteen when she first fell in love with a rescue dog. She'd come home from high school on the Friday before spring break, waterlogged from the rainstorm outside and frazzled from a week of studying for midterms and trying to blend in with the other students in her class. Not *fit* in—she knew she would never feel at ease with the kids at the exclusive private school her mother insisted she attend. She just wanted to *blend* in, render herself invisible so that no one would notice all her flaws and insecurities.

But she could never escape her mother's notice.

"Honestly, Lara, just look at those nails," was her mother's greeting when she walked through the door. As the work-obsessed owner of a chain of local salons, Justine usually didn't come home until well after dinnertime, but apparently she'd decided it was her maternal duty to say good-bye before Lara headed off for vacation. "So sloppy and trashy."

Lara opened her mouth, tempted to retort that if Justine hadn't practically forced her to get a manicure over the weekend, chipped polish wouldn't be a problem. But all she said was, "I must've peeled it off during my pre-calc exam. I didn't even realize I was doing it."

Justine sighed as she slipped off her light tan Burberry raincoat and hung it in the hall closet. "What am I going to do with you?"

Lara bit the inside of her cheek, forced herself to silently count to ten, then glanced at the clock. Fifteen minutes before her father arrived to take her camping up in the northern Arizona mountains. She had to endure fifteen more minutes of criticism, and then she would have a whole week of freedom, far away from her mother's demands and disapproval. She could wear sweatpants, forgo washing her hair, and spend all day with mud lodged under her fingernails. Most of the girls in her class were jetting off to exotic locales—surfing in Hawaii, skiing in Aspen—but Lara wasn't envious. Any break from the pressure of prep school and Justine's impossible standards was a dream vacation.

She turned her back on her mother and clicked on the TV to derail the conversation. "I'm all packed."

Justine stepped out of her high-heeled pumps and carefully wiped the raindrops off the Italian leather shoes. "Good. I'll expect you back by six o'clock on Sunday. Do you have any homework you need to get done for next week?"

Lara ignored her and turned up the TV. Thirteen more minutes, twelve more minutes . . .

The phone rang in the kitchen, and her mother answered on the second

ring. Justine's voice dropped immediately after she said hello, and Lara
grabbed the remote and turned the TV
way down so she could eavesdrop.

"You cannot keep doing this, Gil.
She's counting on you. . . . I'm well
aware she's not a little kid anymore.
She's sixteen, and adolescence is a
very tough stage. . . . No, absolutely
not . . ."

Careful not to rustle the cushions,
Lara got up off the couch and tiptoed
over to the kitchen door. She held her
breath.

Justine's tone went glacial. "Well, I
guess you have to do what you have to
do, but you're going to tell her yourself. . . . I am sick and tired of always
being the bad cop. . . . No, *you* tell her."

Lara sprang away from the doorway
and tried to look innocent as Justine
charged into the family room, brandish-
ing the cordless phone at arm's length
as if it were a handgun.

"Your father would like a word with
you."

Lara knew what she was about to
hear, but she kept her tone upbeat as

she pressed the phone to her ear. "Hi, Daddy. What's up?"

All she heard in response was a dial tone.

She put the phone down. "He's not coming."

Justine sank down on the sofa. "I'm sorry."

"No, it's fine." Lara forced a smile. "He must've . . . Something must've come up, right?"

"That's what he said." Justine patted the cushion next to her, but Lara refused to sit down. During the silence that followed, she avoided her mother's pitying gaze and focused instead on the sound of cars splashing by in the puddles outside.

"You don't want to go camping, anyway," Justine said. "It's supposed to rain all week. You would have been miserable."

Lara finally snapped and lashed out at her mother. "No, *you* would be miserable. *You're* the one who hates camping. You're the one who's, like, physically incapable of having fun."

Her mother sat back, tilting her chin

up. "Here we go. Your dad gets to be the fun parent, and I'm stuck being the evil disciplinarian, right? The witch who pays your tuition and buys all your clothes and makes sure you have a roof over your head."

"Oh, so now I'm the reason you're a buzzkill ice queen? I didn't ask to be born!"

"Lara Madigan, you lower your voice this instant. If you're angry at your father, yell at him. Don't yell at me."

But Lara couldn't yell at her father; he wouldn't even stay on the phone long enough to tell her he was bailing on spring break. So she kept glaring at her mother, so glossy and remote in designer clothes and sleekly styled hair. She had never been able to reconcile this version of Justine with the giggling, windswept bride she'd glimpsed in a snapshot of her parents' wedding day. With every year, Justine became more guarded, more tightly wound. "You and Dad used to have fun together, right?"

Justine didn't reply, but her expression flickered for an instant.

Lara persisted. "You weren't always like this."

Her mother's lips were a hard white line. "Like what?"

"Like nothing's ever good enough for you." Lara's heart ached and she wanted to make her mother share some of that pain. "You used to be different. You wouldn't have married Dad if you hadn't thought he was your soul mate."

Justine let out a dry little laugh. "Don't be naive. Soul mates don't exist."

"Then why did you marry him?"

"I was nineteen and I thought I knew everything." Justine's voice dripped with contempt for her younger self. "I was 'in love.' And now I'm older and wiser, and I'm here to tell you: Love doesn't solve your problems. You have to take care of yourself. I don't want you to ever depend on a man, Lara. That's why I'm busting my ass to give you the best education, the best opportunities."

Lara started picking at her nail polish again.

"Stop that." Justine checked herself, taking a deep breath as she got to her feet. "Come on. Let's go to the salon and get you a fresh manicure. You'll feel better."

Lara brushed past her mother and grabbed the pristine Burberry trench coat from the closet on her way out the door. "I'm going for a walk."

"Don't you dare get that coat dirty!" Justine cried. "Get back here this instant, young lady!"

But Lara slammed the door behind her and ran down the driveway, turning her face up so that rain plastered her long dark hair against her cheeks.

All she wanted was to be left alone, she told herself as she splashed down the sidewalk toward the park. All she wanted was to be invisible.

She didn't realize she was crying until her nose started running. Burning with anger and rebellion, she wiped it on the sleeve of her mom's precious trench coat.

Justine would be furious.

Good.

Lara walked for almost an hour, wandering aimlessly until she ended up at the small commercial center on the outskirts of the upscale neighborhood. The bank, jewelry repair shop, and vet clinic were all closed at this hour on a Friday. A large cardboard box rested on the doorstep of the vet clinic. The seams were already starting to come apart from the water seeping up from the sidewalk. Scrawled on the side of the box in black ink was a single word: FREE.

Lara knew what she would find before she even looked inside and, sure enough, when she opened the top flap she discovered a tiny black puppy, shivering and huddled in the corner.

She was frozen in place. A thousand thoughts seemed to surface—first and foremost: *mine.* When the puppy peered up at her with pleading brown eyes, Lara's purpose became clear to her.

When she found her voice, she murmured, "Everything's going to be okay." And for once she truly believed that. She reached for the puppy. It scrambled into her hands, tumbling over its feet to get closer to her.

This lonely little creature *needed* her.

Almost as much as she needed it.

She picked up the dog and tucked it

underneath her coat, nestling the tiny trembling body next to her chest.

"Don't worry," she murmured. "You're safe now. I've got you."

The puppy whimpered at the sound of her voice. Then it peed on the lining of Justine's coat.

Lara ran all the way home and when she opened the front door, her mother commanded, "Change into dry clothes. You're going to catch pneumonia."

"In a second. I've got to take care of my dog first." Lara unbuttoned the coat and produced the shivering, skinny little pup. "Mom, meet Beacon."

"Oh no. No, no, no, no, no. You are not keeping that thing. *We* are not keeping that thing."

"Oh yes, we are. And you're wrong, Mom. Soul mates *do* exist."

Lara gazed up at her boyfriend with the same steadfast conviction she'd shown her mother all those years ago. "My dog Beacon saved my life in high school. He kept me sane through all the crazy drama of adolescence. He got me through college, my first jobs, a bunch of crappy apartments, and bad break-ups. My mom could never understand why I loved him so much, since he wasn't beautiful and he didn't have a fancy pedigree, but there was just something about him." She smiled wistfully, remembering the tiny, floppy-eared Chihuahua mix. "He died two years ago, and I'll probably never have that same connection with another dog. But I know it exists, and my job is to match people up with the dog that can save them the way Beacon saved me. This is my calling. Love me, love my dogs."

"I do love you." Evan cupped her cheek in his palm. "And I'm sure I'll start loving the dogs, too. Plus, they'll motivate me to learn how to install drywall."

"That's the spirit. Now give me five minutes to change, and let's go have dinner far away from the scene of the crime. And when we get home"—she slid her hands up his biceps and gave a saucy smile—"I have some interesting ideas involving nudity and that bowl of frosting."

Chapter 3

Lara white-knuckled the station wagon's steering wheel the next morning as she gunned the car down the quiet suburban street and screeched to a halt in front of her best friend's house. Not pausing to yank the keys out of the ignition, she dashed across the driveway and rang the bell.

"Thank God you're here," Kerry said when she opened the door. A tiny, square-jawed redhead with a huge personality, Kerry was the cofounder with Lara of their canine rescue group, Lucky Dog. Although she was in the final weeks of pregnancy, she had managed to maintain her wiry frame, and she looked like she'd tucked a volleyball under her maternity tank top.

Lara scanned her friend for signs of distress. "I couldn't even understand your voice mail. Are you in labor?"

"No, no, I'm fine, but we've got a mastiff on the loose. Titus got out of the yard somehow." Kerry opened the door wider to accommodate her belly, and a little yellow terrier streaked out between her feet. "Murphy, no! Not another one!"

Lara raised her hand, snapped her fingers, and commanded gently but firmly, "Come."

Murphy stopped in his tracks, pivoted, and trotted back with his mouth open in a naughty dog grin. He sat down at Lara's feet and looked up expectantly for his treat.

"Good boy." Lara reached down, put a hand on Murphy's collar, and motioned for Kerry to sit on the front stoop. "Calm down. Breathe."

"What the hell?" Kerry remained standing. "How come all the dogs listen to you and ignore me? I told Titus to come, and he galloped off like he didn't even hear me." She started toward the station wagon, bracing both hands on her lower back. "We have to find him. And we have to take your car, because there's no way Titus is going to fit into that stupid car Richard bought me."

"You mean the brand-new German-engineered convertible in your garage?" Lara said. "That 'stupid car'?"

"That's the one. German engineering doesn't do you any good when you're trying to squeeze your third-trimester belly behind the wheel and a mastiff in the passenger seat." Kerry scowled. "I'm trading it in for a minivan. Mark my words." She climbed into Lara's car. Murphy leapt in beside her and braced his front paws on the dashboard. "Hurry! Head toward that white house and then go around the block."

Lara started the car and eased into a five-mile-per-hour cruise. "Why the hysterical voice mail? This is a nice neighborhood; there's hardly any traffic. I'm sure Titus won't get hit."

"I'm not worried about traffic." Kerry

rolled down the window, listening for telltale barks. "Last time he got out, he dug up our neighbor's flower bed. She was furious, and her husband is a gun enthusiast."

The car crawled down the wide, empty street. As both women—and Murphy—searched for any sign of Titus, Lara recounted the previous night's birthday cake debacle.

"So basically, you distracted Evan with sex and sugar," Kerry summed up.

"Correct." Lara turned right as Murphy stuck his nose out the window and whined.

"But now everybody's happy?"

"Until the next canine crime spree." Lara scanned yards on both sides of the street. "That's the problem. I can't keep all five dogs out of trouble forever. And even if I could, there's always a new one coming down the pike. Jason from the Shayland Animal Hospital just left me a voice mail. He's got a Rhodesian ridgeback mix he wants me to evaluate this afternoon." Although she taught private obedience classes evenings and weekends, Lara's "real job" was being a veterinary drug rep. She visited local clinics on behalf of a pharmaceutical distributor. The job didn't offer great benefits and her salary consisted mainly of performance bonuses, but there were other perks. Such as substantially discounted medical care for the sick and injured dogs she and Kerry took in. "Apparently, this one's got some kind of funky skin condition. Evan's going to love that."

"Hang on a second." Kerry grimaced and pressed a hand to her stomach. "I swear this kid's doing the Worm in there."

Lara's eyes widened as Kerry winced again. "Listen to me. Do not start having contractions." She grabbed the stainless-steel water bottle from the cup holder. "Drink. Stop stressing."

"I'm fine. I have at least two more weeks to go. Plus I refuse to give birth until Richard gets back from Russia." Kerry's husband was a corporate trainer for an international company that sent him all over the world.

"Which will be . . . ?"

"Friday. Saturday at the very latest."

"Which way now?" Lara asked after they'd circled the block to no avail.

"Turn right. There's a playground a few blocks over, and you know Titus loves little kids." Kerry chugged some water. "I'm sorry about Evan and the cake, Lar. This is my fault, really. If I hadn't gotten married and moved out on you last year—"

"Eventually the landlord would have figured out we were in total violation of the two-pets policy and evicted us, anyway," Lara finished. "I should never have let Evan talk me into moving into his place. But you know how he gets. He made an actual PowerPoint presentation demonstrating how I couldn't swing the rent at the other house by myself much longer and how I could redirect a huge portion of my monthly income toward rescue expenses if I shacked up with him."

"You can't argue with his PowerPoint presentations."

"I know. He had pie charts and everything. And he signed a contract swearing to become a dog person." Lara paused at a stop sign. "Although it was written on a paper napkin and signed at a bar, so I'm not sure it's legally binding."

"Well, then, he better get with the program. Especially if he wants to get married."

Lara tapped the brake at the mention of the M word. "Slow down. I just moved in with him last month. No one's talking about marriage yet."

Her friend smiled knowingly. "Maybe *you* aren't."

"Meaning . . . ?"

"Last time he saw Richard, he asked for the name of the guy who designed my engagement ring."

"What?" The car came to a standstill. "When did this happen?"

"Right about the time you were moving in." Kerry paused for a few moments, then added, "You can keep driving, you know."

Lara pulled up next to a grassy neighborhood park, which was empty except for two young moms with strollers. "Excuse me," she called. "Did you see a giant brown dog run by?"

The women shook their heads, so

Lara turned left at the next corner and doubled back toward Kerry's house. She didn't realize her fingers had closed around the wheel in a death grip until Kerry reached out and patted her hand.

"Why are you freaking out? You love Evan, right? And he loves you."

Lara nodded, her throat dry.

"So why the panic attack? Diamond rings are delightful." Kerry stretched out her left hand and examined her bare fingers. "Although I had to take mine off last month since my fingers are so swollen."

"Marriage is just so permanent. I mean, that's a serious commitment."

"You'll commit unlimited time, money, and energy to any random stray dog off the street," Kerry pointed out.

"Committing to a dog is one thing. But committing to a guy . . . I just don't think I believe in happily-ever-after."

Kerry finished off the water, then declared, "That's your mother talking. Look, your family is totally jacked; I get it. But good marriages do exist, and Evan's a great guy. The man made you a cake from scratch. Lock him down and throw away the key."

"Evan doesn't want to marry me," Lara said. "He wants to marry the *image* he has of me. What's he going to do when he finds out what a lunatic I really am?"

Kerry closed her eyes and shifted in her seat. "*Oof.* It's like my uterus is a hotel penthouse and this baby is a rock star on a three-day bender."

Lara chose her words carefully. "Do you think Richard will be home more after the baby's born?"

Kerry stilled, but kept her eyes closed. "Nope."

"And you're okay with that?"

"I knew what his schedule was like when I married him. Besides, I'll manage just fine. I've provided round-the-clock care for entire litters of puppies. Taking care of one little human will be a breeze compared with that." She opened her eyes and glanced at Lara, almost daring her to contradict this. "What?"

"Nothing." Lara shrugged one shoulder. "You know, you might consider cutting down on the dogs until after you have the baby and get the new routine down."

"That's what Richard said, too." Kerry looked stricken. "But hear me now and believe me later: I'll never be one of those people who has a baby and forgets her dogs even exist." She sighed. "So you found a match for my sweet little Murphy, huh?"

"Murphy's match found me," Lara said. "And I've got a good feeling about this one." She provided a quick rundown of Peter's life circumstances. "This guy is committed, and he'll listen to my recommendations about nutrition and training. Most single men won't consider a little terrier; they insist on a 'manly' dog like a Rottie or a shepherd. But this guy melted as soon as he saw the pictures. I told him I'd talk to you and set up a meet and greet."

"But I love Murphy. He's special." Kerry basked in Murphy's look of infinite adoration. The same look he gave anyone who had food, toys, or a desirable spot on the sofa.

"They're all special," Lara reminded her. "And anyway, he has a greater purpose in life—to score chicks for the dumped and downtrodden."

"Well, if you think this is the guy, I'll take you at your word. You do have a one-hundred-percent success rate."

"Except for Mullet." Lara sighed. "Evan says that Mullet is nobody's soul mate, and as much as I hate to admit it, he may be right."

Half-blind, grouchy, and prone to digestive woes, Mullet was a shaggy white Shih Tzu mix that had been dumped at a county shelter with no explanation. Her coat had been so matted and snarled that Kerry's dog groomer had to completely shave her front legs and stomach, leaving a floppy cape of fur around her haunches that they affectionately started referring to as a mullet. Although her coat eventually grew out— sort of—no amount of grooming and training could change her grumpy, contrary disposition.

"Mullet's future owner is out there somewhere," Kerry predicted. "Probably waving his cane and yelling at kids to stay off his lawn."

Lara opened her mouth to reply, but

Murphy's whining suddenly intensified as the car headed up a hill.

"Oh no," Kerry breathed as they heard a series of booming barks. She pointed at the construction-paper sign taped to the light post on the corner:

BELLA'S BIRTHDAY PARTY THIS WAY!

Lara's stomach plummeted. Murphy started scratching at the car window.

The barking grew louder and louder.

And then Lara lunged for the door handle as she heard the sounds of children shrieking and balloons popping.

"Sorry I'm late." Lara used a crumpled tissue to wipe the sheen of sweat off her forehead as she met her friend Jason at the door of the vet clinic. "Titus crashed a preschool party."

Jason's jaw dropped. "The mastiff?"

Lara nodded as he led her back to the exam rooms. "He slipped past Kerry this morning and galumphed right into a Disney princess bounce house. Toddlers everywhere. Mass hysteria."

"Is everyone okay?" Jason handed her a Styrofoam cup of coffee.

"Well, there were a few tense moments when he spooked the pony, but
then Kerry put the saddle on Titus and
let the kids ride him instead. After that,
he was the life of the party. In fact, one
of the moms gave me her card. I think
he may have found a new family." She
took a sip of coffee. "Thank you."

Jason lowered his voice as he opened
the door. "No sudden moves. This poor
guy is practically catatonic."

Lara took one look at the scrawny,
scabby red mutt cringing in the corner
and started oohing and aahing. When
she offered her upturned palm for an
introductory sniff, the dog shrank back
and lowered its head.

"My neighbor found him abandoned
in the yard," Jason reported. "I guess
the renters there moved out and left
him behind. He's pretty young—I'd say
nine months to twelve months. Not neu-
tered, of course. I think he's spent most
of his life on a six-foot chain staked to
the ground."

"Yikes." Lara peered closer to inspect
the series of open, oozing puncture
wounds dotting the dog's flank. "I can't

tell if these are from an injury or a skin condition."

Jason leaned in next to her. "That's why I was thinking valley fever. We're running blood work, but the results won't come back for a few days."

Lara doled out a reassuring pat, stepped back, and announced, "Homeboy's a hot mess. Good thing I love a challenge."

The dog turned toward her and thumped his tail.

"Look who's in love already. Your pheromones must smell like bacon."

Lara laughed. "Stop—I'm blushing. He needs a name. Care to do the honors?"

They both cocked their heads and studied the dog, who refused to look back. Finally, Jason said, "Linus?"

"Sounds good. Linus it is."

Jason mirrored her furrowed brow. "You look worried."

Lara exhaled slowly, rocking back on her heels. "I'm not worried."

"Do you think you can take him? I know it's a lot to ask, but I couldn't dump him at the shelter. He'd never get adopted, looking the way he does."

"Really, it's no problem," she said firmly. "Are you kidding me? Remember the Dalmatian with the impacted tooth and the gangrene in his leg? Compared to that, this is nothing." She babbled for a bit, citing examples of starving, scarred, and deeply traumatized dogs they'd rescued together.

Jason waited patiently for his turn to speak. "Valley fever is a pretty big deal. If you're worried about your health—"

Lara petted the dog and confessed the truth. "Oh, I'm not worried about my health. I'm worried about my boyfriend."

"Why? Is he immunosuppressed?"

"No, but I think he might be at the end of his leash, so to speak." She gave Jason the rundown on Evan, Maverick, the cake, the drywall, and the phantom engagement ring. "He claims he's going to become a dog person, but I don't know."

Jason's eyebrows shot up.

"What?" Lara demanded.

"We get lots of husbands in here who got a puppy 'for the kids' or 'for my wife,' and most of them still see the dog as an expensive nuisance. Take it from me. Dogs, you can change. Men, not so much."

Chapter 4

"Happy birthday!" Evan met her at the door with a fresh bouquet of roses. He kissed her, then pulled away, frowning. "Why do you smell like cotton candy and dog poop?"

"Don't ask." Lara had a feeling the tale of Titus and the birthday party wouldn't put him in the right frame of mind to welcome a new rescue dog. "I just want to take a long shower and go to bed. But first . . ." She took his hand and led him out to the garage. "Are you ready to meet the new recruit?"

"Oh no." Evan shook his head ruefully when he saw the scabby, shedding dog curled up in the back of the station wagon. "Not another one."

Lara gave his fingers a squeeze. "This is Linus. He's a good boy."

Evan tugged his hand away and crossed his arms over his maroon Arizona Cardinals T-shirt. "So now we're up to how many dogs? Some people would say you're getting into hoarding terrltory."

"None of those people have ever worked in dog rescue." Lara popped open the car's back door and tried to coax the skittish red mutt out. "It's temporary. I'll find him a home in no time." She fished a treat out of her pocket and used it to enticc Linus to jump onto the garage floor.

Evan's expression softened. "Aw. He looks so dumb."

"Evan!"

"What? That's a good thing! The dumb ones don't make any trouble. The dumber, the better—that's my motto."

Lara shot him a filthy look. "Cut the poor baby some slack. A vet tech found him abandoned in a yard with no food, water, or shelter. He's had less than twelve hours to adjust to civilization."

Linus shrank back against a tire and whimpered pathetically. While Evan went back into the house and herded the other dogs into the yard, Lara offered Linus a metal bowl brimming with kibble and canned food. He scarfed the food down so quickly that he started to choke.

"Come on." Lara dragged a spare crate down the hall. "We'll let him rest in the office for a bit before we introduce him to the others." She stopped at the linen closet to grab a stack of old towels, which she used to pad the bottom of the crate. It took only a few minutes of sweet-talking and bribery to persuade Linus to duck inside the crate.

Finished, she sat back on her heels and turned her full attention to Evan. "Okay. How was your day?"

"Not as good as yours is going to be." He helped her to her feet, led her out of the office, and pointed toward two new cardboard boxes next to the front door. "The UPS guy just dropped off some birthday loot for you."

Lara ran the blade of Evan's pocket-knife along the seams of the smaller carton, revealing a perfectly packed, beautifully wrapped box topped with a bow and a card signed in unfamiliar handwriting:

Happy Birthday, Lara.
Love, Mom

"Looks expensive," Evan observed as Lara untied the wide satin bow and peeled off the floral-printed paper.

"I'm sure it is." She was equally sure that her mother had never laid eyes on the contents of this box; nor had she filled out the tag or tied the bow. Justine was a very busy woman who liked things to look a certain way—beautiful, flawless, and enviable. She had no doubt called up a sales associate in an upscale boutique, outlined her gift requirements, and tasked the employee with selecting and delivering the actual item.

Lara lifted the lid to reveal a buttery-soft calfskin handbag with brass hardware and a designer logo prominently displayed on one side.

It was lovely. It was classic. It was eerily similar to the bag her mother had sent her last year—the one Bugsy, a high-strung Weimaraner mix, had snatched off the hall table and gnawed to shreds in a bout of separation anxiety.

Justine gave people what she thought they should have, rather than what they wanted. And that went double for her daughter. For Christmases and birthdays, Justine sent hand-painted silk scarves, bejeweled stiletto sandals, and Italian cashmere. Lara stowed all of these luxuries in their original boxes on the very top shelf of her closet, for fear they'd be chewed up or desecrated by dog hair.

In return, Lara gifted her mother with generic, practical standbys like candles and cookbooks. Justine would accept these graciously, but they both knew that these items, too, would be relegated to a darkened closet shelf.

"You don't like it?" Evan prompted as

Lara blinked down at the bag nestled in tissue paper.

"It's gorgeous." She ran her palm along the smooth, cool leather. "But I wouldn't dare use it. This thing probably cost eighteen hundred dollars."

"For a *purse*?" He looked incredulous.

"My mom's bag collection could pay for a small house," Lara said. "The high-end stuff's pricey. And do you know what happened to the Prada she gave me last year?"

"Someone mauled it?" he guessed.

"Bugsy," Lara confirmed. "Two days after I got it. He ate half of it, then spent the rest of the night throwing up."

Evan glanced at the dogs milling around in the backyard, then shook his head. "For eighteen hundred dollars, you should be carrying that thing all day, every day. Heck, you should use it for a pillow at night. Maximize your cost-per-wear ratio."

Lara closed the box and set it aside. "I'll just take it out and wear it when we see her on Mother's Day." She turned her attention to the other package, a huge, heavy carton.

"Oh my God. Honey, look!" She gasped as the box flaps unfolded to reveal a purple plastic behemoth with cyclone technology and a HEPA filter. "The vacuum of my dreams."

The holy grail of pet hair removal. Not as expensive as the handbag, to be sure, but exactly what she wanted.

Then she came to the card:

Happy Birthday, La-la! You'll always be my little girl.

She dropped the paper as if scorched, and Evan picked it up, scanned the text, and returned her look of alarm.

"Oh no." She stood up and backed away from the vacuum. "What does he want this time?"

"Maybe he just wants to say happy birthday?" Evan suggested, but his voice lacked conviction.

"Yeah, right. 'You'll always be my little girl'?" Lara scoffed. "A Dyson? He definitely wants something. Something big."

Evan didn't refute this. He himself had grown up in an absurdly functional family: His mother packed his lunch every day, his father coached his Little League team, and everyone said grace at the dinner table before passing the potatoes and chatting about their days. When he and Lara first started dating, he'd urged her to take the initiative and call her father if she hadn't heard from him in a while. Then Lara's father, Gil, had started campaigning in August for Lara and Evan to come to his cabin in the mountains for Thanksgiving. He'd painted such a lavish, Norman Rockwell picture of communal family cooking and eating that Lara had finally agreed, rearranged her work schedule, and found a pet sitter for the dogs. Then, while she was packing her suitcase the night before, Gil called and apologized, explaining that he had decided to spend the holiday with his new girlfriend's family instead.

Evan had immediately driven to the grocery store, where he nearly resorted to hand-to-hand combat to secure the last frozen turkey, spent the next twelve hours cooking, and never again suggested that she call her father.

She left the vacuum in the box, staring down at the label. Evan came up behind her, put his arms around her, and rested his chin on the top of her head. He didn't say anything at first, just held her.

Lara leaned back against him and said, "It's exactly what I wanted—I just don't want it from him."

"I know." Evan kissed her temple. "But it's your birthday and I'm feeling generous. Tell me what else you want, and you might get lucky."

Lara nibbled her lower lip. "Well, the vet says that Linus may need surgery if he has valley fever."

There was a long pause before Evan said, "Dog surgery. That's what you want for your birthday."

"Yes."

"You know, most women would prefer jewelry and a candlelight dinner."

"I'm not most women."

Evan sighed and pulled away. "I'm starting to realize that."

Chapter 5

Lara woke up the next morning to the low rumble of snoring. She turned over and reached for Evan, but her hand connected with fur. Maverick, the huge black Rottweiler mix, was sacked out beside her, his blocky head resting on the pillow. Maverick usually slept on the carpet by the foot of the bed, but Evan must have gotten up early for work.

She pushed herself up to a sitting position, which incited Rufus and Raggs, the brown and white spaniels, and Zsa Zsa, the deeply neurotic white standard poodle, to leap up on the mattress and swarm around in a frenzy of anticipation.

"Okay, okay," she mumbled. "Breakfast is coming, you tyrants."

Linus was still sleeping in his crate in the office, but there was an empty bowl just inside the doorway. Evan must have fed him and let him out earlier this morning.

She closed the office door and let him nap. The last thing she needed was a Rhodesian ridgeback and a Rottweiler battling it out for dominance before she'd had her coffee.

As she stumbled down the hall, she yawned and tried to rub the last remnants of sleep from her eyes. The dogs finished breakfast in approximately 2.8 seconds, then looked at her expectantly for more.

"Forget it." She opened the sliding glass door and shooed them out. Then she herded everybody back into the bedroom and returned to the office to wake up Linus. After much coaxing, he finally got to his feet, followed her to the kitchen, and lumbered out onto the patio.

Lara leaned against the wall and observed him. The big red dog refused to venture past the border where the concrete ended and the grass began. Apparently the lawn freaked him out— either he wasn't used to the feel of grass on his paws or he assumed that venturing into the yard would mean another stake and chain to confine him.

Yes, Linus was going to need a lot of work. Training and surgery and plenty of affection.

Dog rescue could burn you out—and drain your bank account. But Lara always felt she was at her best when she was working with animals. It was the one thing she truly excelled at, much to her mother's dismay.

After putting Lara through one of Scottsdale's most prestigious prep schools, Justine had urged her to enroll in Pepperdine University, a pricey private college in California. The master plan called for Lara to major in business or accounting, then spend a few years sharpening her teeth in the corporate shark tank before pursuing an MBA at Stanford. After that she would return to apprentice under Justine at her chain of salons, which Lara would inherit and expand into a global beauty brand like Redken or Aveda.

Every summer, while Lara's college classmates took off for monthlong trips to Europe or signed on for cushy corporate internships, Lara reported for duty at the Coterie spa and salon. She dusted off the display bottles of hair product, made sure the floors and restrooms were clean, then settled in to answer phones and schedule appointments at the reception desk.

"The front desk is where you learn the business," Justine always said. "You meet the delivery people, talk to the product suppliers, get to know the clientele, and figure out how to accommodate a team of extremely talented, extremely high-maintenance employees."

So Lara had learned to juggle schedules, assess profit-and-loss statements, and politely but firmly insist on timely delivery from vendors. Although Justine very rarely made an appearance on the main floor, the rest of the staff treated

Lara like family—more specifically, like an awkward but endearing little sister. The hairstylists and aestheticians delighted in performing "practice facials" on Lara and trying to shock her with tales of their wild after-hours exploits. Yes, the salon employees were happy to embrace a hormonally volatile, coiffure-challenged college kid.

The customers were another story.

From the moment Justine opened the doors at her first salon, she targeted a very specific type of client: rich, fashion-forward, and prone to pretentiousness. Young trendsetters with bloated trust funds flocked in to enhance their tanned, taut bodies and long platinum hair. For the most part, they ignored Lara, but when their gazes flickered over her, they registered a mixture of annoyance and pity. Lara always smiled back, offering to store their cavernous designer bags and fetch a bowl of water for their tiny jewel-bedecked dogs.

Papillon, Coton de Tulear, Japanese Chin, Havanese. All these pups could comfortably fit inside a Louis Vuitton satchel, and most of them had been styled to complement their owners. The girls bought them on impulse, charmed by the cute little fluff balls and the novelty of painting their dogs' toenails the same shade as their own. But then, as the dogs aged and shed and started nipping or gnawing on the handles of that Louis Vuitton satchel, the owners' affections lapsed.

"Ugh. She keeps pooping in my closet."

"I'm going to Cabo for spring break and the resort doesn't allow pets."

"My new boyfriend doesn't like little dogs."

"Here," one freshly highlighted socialite said as she deposited a tan teacup poodle in Lara's lap. "Would you please watch Enzo for a second while I run next door and grab a latte?"

She never came back. At the end of the day, Lara tried unsuccessfully to convince one of the stylists to take the dog overnight. Finally, after she locked the doors and turned off the lights, she dialed her mother's office.

"Yes?" Justine sounded neither pleased nor displeased to hear from her daughter. As usual, she was all business.

And so Lara tried to be all business, too. She explained the situation as briefly as possible, keenly aware that for Justine, time was money.

Justine didn't bother with exclamations of outrage or surprise. "Where is the dog now?"

"Right here." The poodle sat at her feet, staring up intently as though he understood every syllable. "His name is Enzo."

"Who left it?"

Lara scanned the appointment book to find the name.

"Kristi Spillane."

"Do you have a contact number for her?"

"Yes. I've tried to reach her multiple times, but she didn't pick up, so I left voice messages."

"Kristi Spillane," her mother repeated. "How long has she been a client?"

"Today was her second time here, I think."

"And who referred her?"

Justine insisted on keeping meticulous social as well as financial records, so Lara could check this with the click of the keyboard. "Bianca Altisanti."

"Bianca's brought us a lot of new business over the last year," Justine said. "I'd hate to offend her over a misunderstanding."

"But, Mom, this girl went out for coffee and never came back for her dog."

"Maybe she's dealing with an emergency," Justine suggested. "Don't panic. Just put the dog in the stockroom overnight with some food and water. Everything will be fine."

Lara gasped. "I can't just leave him all night long."

"Fine, then come back before you go to bed and let him out to pee."

"Mom, no. That's inhumane."

"We're not dealing with a human—we're dealing with a dog." Her mother was clearly finished with the conversation. "Make him a little bed out of towels and be on your way."

"I can't do that."

"Why on earth not?"

"He'll be scared! He'll be lonely. He won't understand what's going on."

"Stop. If this dog is anything like Bianca, he's dumber than a bag of hair. It'll take him at least twelve hours just to figure out where he is."

"There is no way I'm leaving him in the stockroom overnight."

"Then what would you suggest?"

"He can stay with us tonight. Beacon loves other dogs; they can have a little slumber party."

"Absolutely not. I worked too hard to pay for our home and our furniture. I will not have it destroyed by some overbred, overindulged animal."

Lara understood and appreciated the full extent of her mother's sacrifices over the last two decades. Justine had given up everything—her youth, her social life, her sense of spontaneity—to build a life out of pampering others. But none of this was Enzo's fault. Enzo, like Lara, had been born into a life where he was compelled to look and behave a certain way, regardless of his own preferences.

Plus, he was totally adorable.

"Just one night," Lara vowed to her

mother. "You'll never even know he's there."

"Open your ears," Justine shot back. "*No* means *no*. I caved and let you keep Beacon in a moment of weakness, but this time I'm holding my ground."

Lara had no choice but to break out the heavy artillery. "Okay, but what if something happens to him in the storeroom overnight? What if he eats something or gets caught somewhere and gets hurt? What if he *dies*? How would we ever explain that to Kristi and Bianca? And all the girls they've referred?"

Justine didn't reply.

"Or what if they, like, sue? The publicity would be *awful*. One night, Mom. Think of it as an investment in the business."

Justine laughed dryly. "Your sales skills need some work." But she relented. Lara brought Enzo home to the tiny two-bedroom bungalow located just inside the desirable Paradise Valley zip code. Beacon welcomed the little poodle as if he'd finally found his long-lost brother.

Kristi never returned. And when Lara

finally got in touch with her two days and fifteen phone messages later, she mumbled something about moving, no pets allowed, before the connection conveniently cut out.

"And you're telling me all this, why?" Justine asked when Lara called to update her on the situation. "I said no to a second dog, and I absolutely meant it. Drop him at the shelter on your way home from work."

Lara gasped and clutched the poodle to her chest. "The pound?"

"Yes, the pound. He's little; he's pure-bred; he's cute. He'll be adopted before breakfast."

"I can't."

"You will."

"But, Mom—"

"This isn't how you get ahead in life, Lara. You can't take on other people's problems."

But when Lara looked at Enzo, she didn't see a problem; she saw potential. "I don't want to keep him. I just want him to go to a good home. Give me a few days to find him a family."

"Do not ask me for this. I give you

everything you need. Food, shelter, the very best clothes and education money can buy."

Lara swallowed hard. She couldn't deny the truth in her mother's words, but neither could she deny her own heart. "One week, Mom. Please?"

"Fine," Justine said, her voice clipped. "But this is it, young lady. I don't want you coming to me for another thing for the rest of the summer."

"I won't. Thank you." Lara hesitated. "I love you, Mom."

Justine didn't respond to this. "If I see so much as a single flea, I'm taking him to the pound myself." She hung up.

Three days later Lara was dialing the towel supply service when a middle-aged woman with limp brown hair and dark sunglasses walked in.

"I'm sorry." She apologized before Lara even said hello. "I don't have an appointment, but I was hoping . . . I was wondering if I might be able to get my hair cut."

Lara scanned the appointment book. Every employee was booked solid for the rest of the afternoon. "Of course. If you'll excuse me for one moment, I'll find someone to squeeze you in."

After five minutes of begging, bribery, and blackmail, Lara had persuaded one of the stylists to work in an extra client. "Good news." She smiled brightly at the woman. "Tasha will be with you in twenty minutes. What would you like to have done today?"

"Well." The woman tugged at the ends of her messy bob. "I don't know, exactly. I just need a change." A tear trickled out from beneath the sunglasses.

Lara immediately offered a box of tissues. "Tasha's a genius. You'll be in good hands."

"I'm sorry," the woman said again as she pulled out a few more tissues and dabbed at her eyes. "I just . . . My mother passed away last week and my daughter left for college yesterday, and I can't seem to stop crying."

"It's okay," Lara said in a soothing tone. "Lots of people cry at the spa. May I offer you some lemon water or green tea?"

"I just need a minute to collect myself. Is there a restroom?"

Before Lara could give directions, Enzo popped out from under the desk and darted around the corner. He ran right up to the woman and started sniffing her sandals.

"Oh, my goodness, aren't you precious?" She stopped crying and knelt down to say hello.

"Sorry." Lara jumped to her feet, but the woman scooped the little poodle up and cradled him like a baby. She started crooning high-pitched, singsong nonsense that made Enzo wriggle with delight.

"Is he yours?" The woman took off her glasses and looked at Lara with the beginnings of a smile. "I used to have a dog just like this when I was a little girl. A tan poodle named Taffy. Oh, how I loved that dog." She turned her attention back to Enzo, who lunged up to lick the tears from her cheeks.

Two hours later, that woman went home with a stunning auburn pixie cut and a newly adopted teacup poodle.

And Lara had a new identity: the dog matchmaker.

There must have been some kind of underground newsletter for gum-snapping, spray-tanning prima donnas, because all of a sudden, Lara was the go-to girl for fashionistas trying to unload pint-size pooches.

"My sorority sister is allergic."

"The breeder said he was only going to be eight pounds, but he's already up to twelve and he's taking up too much space in my bag."

"Could you please just watch her for the weekend? I'll come get her on Monday, swear to God."

At first Lara tried to reason with the owners. But she soon realized that any sentence beginning with "I love my little pookie so much, *but* . . ." was going to end with Lara opening up her arms to accept yet another high-strung pup whose paws had hardly touched the ground since birth.

She started volunteering on weekends at a no-kill animal shelter, bathing and walking the dogs that no one else had time for. She found a pet store that hosted obedience classes every Saturday morning.

Shawna, the trainer, taught Lara everything she needed to know to survive with a dog: Say it once and mean it; you get the behavior you're willing to tolerate; you can't show fear even if you're terrified on the inside. Lara had never had a mentor before. But she strove to reach the goals she set for her dogs—and, by extension, herself—and by the end of the summer she had placed five dogs and emptied her wallet.

And Justine's master plan imploded when Lara declared her major as biology and decided to stay in Los Angeles over school breaks, interning for movie studio animal trainers and studying marine mammal training techniques at SeaWorld instead of working at the Scottsdale salon. Her dog-handling skills improved exponentially. And her human-handling skills deteriorated.

"What exactly is your life plan?" Justine had demanded. "How are you going to make your fortune training dogs to eat Pedigree on command?"

"I'm not going to make a fortune. No one gets into this kind of work for the money," Lara countered. "But it's my calling."

"Who cares what your calling is?" Justine scoffed. "Do you think I get some deep-seated spiritual fulfillment out of providing eyebrow threading and blond highlights? Don't follow your calling. Follow the money."

By graduation, Lara had learned not to divulge any details of her internship or her dating life to her mother, because Justine would always say the same thing: "You cannot trust a man. You can only rely on yourself."

And yet here she was, living with a wonderful guy who wanted to marry her. Proving her mother wrong. She should feel happy and victorious. So why was she constantly edgy and anxious?

"Okay, okay." She took pity on Linus, who was standing on the other side of the glass door with a worried expression on his jowly face, desperate to get back inside. "You know, someday soon

you're going to beg to get out there.
Trust and believe."

The second she opened the door,
Linus bounded inside. It was the fastest
she'd ever seen him move. He returned
to his crate and immediately went back
to sleep with a contented sigh.

Maybe the key to happiness was having a short memory and the conviction
that all of life's problems could be solved
with a chew toy, a nap, and the occa-
sional belly rub.

She returned to the kitchen, checked
the clock, and determined that she still
had two hours before she had to be at
her first appointment of the day. So she
put on jeans and whispered, "Park," to
the dogs, setting off the canine equivalent of a prison riot.

With the exception of Linus, everyone
was leashed, out the door, and loaded
into the station wagon in less than sixty
seconds. The park was a three-mile
drive, during which all the dogs slobbered on the windows and Lara cranked
up the radio and sang along with the
Go-Go's at the top of her lungs. Rufus
howled along at the chorus.

Upon arrival, she was so busy untangling leashes that she didn't notice the woman approaching the car until the willowy blonde with the perfect makeup and the determined smile was within handshake distance.

"Are you Lara Madigan?"

Another parking lot ambush? Lara glanced past the woman, noticed the man with a video camera behind her, ducked back into her car, and grabbed her little metal canister of pepper spray before admitting, "Yes."

"It's wonderful to finally meet you. I'm Claudia Brightling, one of the anchors on the Channel Three morning show. We've been waiting for you all morning."

Chapter 6

"These must be your dogs." The impeccably attired anchorwoman managed to keep her poker face as Maverick wound his leash around her knees and Zsa Zsa sniffed at the crotch of her charcoal gray pants.

"Yes." Lara pointed to each furry head by way of introduction. "Maverick, Rufus, Raggs, and that's Zsa Zsa there, acting very unladylike." She gave the poodle's leash a quick tug. "Zsa Zsa. Sit."

Zsa Zsa sat.

Lara led the pack toward the fenced

dog run. "I'm not sure I understand. You said you've been waiting for me?"

"Your boyfriend didn't tell you?"

Lara was feeling more confused by the second. "No, Evan didn't mention anything about the Channel Three morning show." She looked over at the camera. "Is that thing on?"

Claudia shook her head. "Don't worry; we're not recording you. We just wanted to get a few exterior shots of the park for the show. And yes, I spoke with Evan this morning when I called your house. He said you come here every Friday morning, so we thought we'd kill two birds with one stone. I'm hoping you'll be willing to appear on the show next week." The interviewer's detached smile transformed into a genuine grin as she confided, "I got your contact information from Peter Hoffstead."

"Murphy's owner?"

"Yes." A faint blush seeped into Claudia's cheeks. "I met him on the jogging path over the weekend, and he described how you hooked him up with Murphy. He said you're famous all

around the city as 'the dog matchmaker.' "

Lara let the dogs through the gate
and unclipped the leashes. "Well, I don't
have an official title, but I do the best I
can."

"It's a terrific human interest story.
You could bring one of your dogs, explain what you do and how you match
people up with their canine soul mates."

"I've never been on TV."

"You'll do great," Claudia assured her.
"All you have to do is show up, prefer-
ably with a well-behaved dog, and be
yourself."

Lara envisioned herself walking onto
a television set, with bright lights and
cameras and lots of people staring at
her—not to mention thousands of home
viewers—and her throat closed up.

"Think of it as a chance to get some
free publicity for the rescue group you
work with. We could list the Web site
on-screen while we interview."

"I don't work with an official incorpo-
rated rescue," Lara confessed. "We're
kind of a grassroots operation. It's just

me, my friend Kerry, and way too many dogs."

"Perfect! Together, we'll find them all great homes." Claudia whipped out her smartphone and tapped the screen. "Shall we say Wednesday?"

"Um . . ."

"My producer will be in touch with all the details."

"Great. Thanks for the opportunity."

"Do we have the footage we need?" Claudia called to the camera guy. Then she turned back to Lara and said, "I've got to go home and throw on some spandex and sneakers. I'm going hiking with Peter."

Lara finally started to relax. "Murphy reeled you in, huh?"

Claudia nodded, laughing. "I couldn't say no."

"Watch yourself. Those terriers are trouble."

"What? No! He's just a lovable little bundle of scruff."

Lara couldn't suppress a triumphant smile as she watched Raggs and Rufus chase each other around. She might never be CEO material, and she was far from the ideal girlfriend, but as a dog matchmaker, she was a virtuoso.

"I got the blood work results," Jason reported when Lara walked into the vet clinic after her last appointment of the day.

Lara braced herself for the worst. Linus's extreme lethargy didn't bode well for his health. "And?"

"And everything came back normal. Kidney function looks good, liver function's fine, pancreas checks out. Red and white cell counts are within normal range." Jason scanned the sheet of paper, nodding. "No sign of pathology at all."

Lara frowned. Linus had been sleeping almost without interruption for two days straight. "So no valley fever, then."

"No valley fever."

"What about his thyroid?"

Jason glanced up. "Thyroxine and triiodothyronine are both fine. Why?"

Lara dropped her bag on the counter and rested her chin in her hand. "Well, he just seems exhausted all the time."

"Maybe he's traumatized."

"Maybe." But Lara sensed shenani-gans. "Or maybe he's just a big faker."

Lara crept down the hallway as silently as possible, tiptoeing on bare feet and holding her breath. Since Linus had seemed so mopey that morning, she'd left him in the kitchen with the crate door open so he could explore the room and help himself to a drink from the wa-ter bowl if he so desired.

She peeked around the corner to find the big red dog lying next to the patio door, gazing out at the backyard with his head lifted and his eyes open.

As soon as he saw her, his head dropped and his eyes snapped shut.

Then she noticed the faucet. A steady trickle of water dripped from the kitchen sink, almost as if someone had nudged the handle. And there were fresh nose prints on the window behind the sink. And wet paw prints on the countertop.

"Aha!" she cried, pointing at the sink. "You are so busted."

Linus remained immobile, but started

to snore in a very dramatic and unconvincing fashion.

"Give it up. You're not fooling anyone. You're totally hale and hearty, and I have the blood work to prove it. On your feet, private. We're going for a walk."

She gated the other dogs in the kitchen, put Linus on a leash, and led him out the front door. At first, he dragged along behind her with his head hung low and his tail curled under, but by the time they'd circled the block, he started to show signs of life. His gait picked up, he turned to look at the kids playing in driveways, and he began sniffing signposts and maiiboxes.

Once he'd cheered up enough to snatch a stick lying by the curb and wave it around in his jaws, Lara decided to hold a mini training session, just to gauge his potential and intellect.

Ten minutes later, Linus could sit on command and was well on his way to staying. Evan had been right—Linus was kind of dumb, which could actually be an asset, from a trainer's point of view. He didn't try to defy her or anticipate her next move. He just stared at her, his brow furrowed and his black eyes bright with concentration as he devoted all his brainpower to figuring out what she wanted. Lara felt the kind of high she imagined a shopaholic might get upon discovering the very last designer dress in her size tucked away at the back of the clearance rack.

This dog was a treasure. This dog was a bargain. This dog was going to be the type of companion that would forever set the benchmark for some lucky family. All their future pets would be compared to Linus—and would probably come up lacking.

"Good boy." She patted his head and broke into a slow jog. "Ready to go home? You can take another five-hour nap if you want."

Halfway home, her cell phone rang and her father's name flashed across the screen.

"Hey, La-la." She could hear the smile in her father's voice. "How's my girl?"

Lara hesitated for a moment, gathering her defenses. The problem wasn't that she didn't want to talk to her father; the problem was that she always *did* want to talk to him, no matter how long it had been since their last conversation, or how much had happened. She never, ever learned. "Fine," she answered. "Thanks for the vacuum."

"It's the least I could do. The sales guy said it's the top of the line, the best for picking up pet hair." He sounded sheepish. "And I had a year or two to make up for, right?"

"I'm a grown woman, Dad. I don't expect anyone to make a big deal about my birthday."

"Hang on. You're telling me you *don't* want me to buy you a pony?"

They both laughed, remembering the summer that Justine had signed Lara up for equestrian camp, despite Lara's protests. Justine had insisted that girls "of a certain background" needed to be comfortable with the English style of riding, while twelve-year-old Lara had maintained that horses were boring and the girls at horse camp would haze her mercilessly. Gil had stepped in at the last minute, allowing Lara to spend the weekend before camp at his house. On Sunday evening, he convinced Justine that Lara had come down with a stomach bug and needed to rest and recover. Father and daughter spent the entire week playing video games and splashing in the pool. That had been one of the happiest times of Lara's childhood—unstructured, uninterrupted time with a parent who didn't constantly demand that she look and behave like someone better than her true self.

She assured her father, "I love the vacuum, and I was really surprised."

"I've got another surprise for you." He sounded triumphant. "Want to have dinner?"

"Sure," she agreed. "When?"

"Half an hour?"

She slowed her pace, and Linus adjusted his gait to match hers. "Wait. You want to have dinner tonight?"

"There's a seafood place on Camelback called the Bluewater Grill. Let's meet there."

"Dad, I'd love to, but that's in the middle of downtown, and I already left work. I told my friend Kerry I'd watch *Teen Mom* with her tonight. She's nine months pregnant and she has a morbid fascination with that show."

"Oh." Her father paused. "I'm sorry, hon. I shouldn't have sprung this on you at the last minute." He sounded disappointed, but with himself.

"No, it's okay. Let me call Kerry and reschedule. She recorded it, so we can watch it whenever."

"Are you sure?"

"Of course. It's no problem. But it's going to take me more than half an hour to change and get all the way downtown. Be there in forty-five minutes?"

"Take your time. We can wait."

Lara blinked. "Who's we?"

When her father chuckled, she could picture the mischievous glint in his blue eyes. "That's the other surprise."

"Lara, this is Trina. Trina, this is my beautiful daughter."

"I'm so glad to finally meet you." A sweet-faced, dimpled brunette wriggled out of the booth and threw her arms around Lara. "Your father talks about you constantly."

Trina hugged like she meant it. She was relatively young—maybe seven or eight years older than Lara—but she was probably sensible and secure. Gil liked beautiful women, but he didn't go for bimbos. His girlfriends tended to be the nurturing type. They doted on him, took care of him in a way that Justine never could.

When everyone settled down and Lara slid onto the leather bench across the table, she noticed the engagement ring on Trina's left hand. Her eyes widened, and Trina and her father exchanged flustered, fluttery glances.

"We wanted to tell you in person," her father said.

"It just happened," Trina gushed. "Last weekend."

"I didn't know you were dating anyone," Lara blurted out. As soon as she said it, she knew she shouldn't have.

Trina turned to Gil, confused and slightly wounded. Gil reached across the table and covered Lara's hand with his.

"Sorry. It's my fault," Lara told Trina.

"I've been so swamped at work lately, I haven't returned any of his calls."

When the server arrived to take their drink orders, Gil said to Lara, "You look worn-out, honey. You know what you need? A root beer float."

One corner of Lara's mouth tugged up in a half smile. "I could definitely go for that." She asked Trina, "Has he made you one yet?"

"No." Trina gave Gil a little nudge.

"Well, he's holding out on you," Lara said. "He's worth marrying for the root beer floats alone."

Gil nodded in acknowledgment. "I hate to brag, but she's right."

"You?" Trina kept saying. "Mr. Herbal Tea and Mineral Water?"

"Just because I don't drink 'em doesn't mean I can't make 'em. Prepare to have your mind blown." Gil called the waiter over and gave him detailed in-structions—complete with diagrams scribbled on a cocktail napkin—for proper assembly and ice cream–to-soda ratio. Finally, the server invited Gil to come back behind the bar and oversee the operation himself, which Gil was happy to do.

While Gil manned the soda fountain, Trina stretched out her right hand, admired the little diamond sparkling away on her ring finger, and sighed with contentment. "You look just like him, you know."

Lara didn't argue. Although she'd inherited Gil's blue eyes and thick hair, her features were less pronounced, and she'd never had his charisma. She knew that Trina wasn't really seeing her right now—she was just seeing reflections of the man she adored.

Trina leaned in and confided, "I know it seems rushed. The engagement and all."

Lara shifted in her seat, not sure what to say. "Hey, as long as you're happy."

"We are. And we have plans, lots of plans, and you know, what's the point of waiting?"

"Right." Lara studied the skylights. "Good for you."

They heard the bar staff laugh at one of Gil's jokes, and Trina smiled. "He must've been a great dad."

"He was . . ." Lara searched for the right word. "Fun. I didn't have the most conventional upbringing, but he was fun, and he always let me be a kid. I needed someone like that in my life." Gil had been the dad who let her go to the movies instead of slaving away on her history paper, who signed the release form so she could have her belly button pierced when she was fifteen.

Of course, Justine had been the one who'd had to meet with the history teacher to deal with the repercussions of the late term paper. Grim-faced and silent, Justine had driven Lara to the emergency room on a Sunday evening when the belly button piercing she'd neglected to clean had started to blister and ooze.

When Gil returned with the root beer floats, he made a big show of swirling the metal serving cup and sniffing it, as though preparing to sample the finest vintage on the wine list.

They all unwrapped their straws and sipped. The moment the cool, bubbly drink hit her tongue, Lara was transported back to her childhood.

"Oh my God." Trina swooned. "You *have* been holding out on me."

"See? I told you," Lara said. "Worth hanging on to him for the root beer alone."

Gil suddenly seemed self-conscious, almost shy. He fiddled with his watch-band while his fiancée and his daughter beamed at him.

"Only the best for my girls," he said. "I know I've made mistakes, but we're family. We're a team. We always stick together."

And just for a moment, her spirits as fizzy as the root beer in her glass, Lara let herself believe him.

Chapter 7

Lara took Linus with her to the TV studio on the morning of her interview with Claudia Brightling. Given Rufus's tendency to bolt, Maverick's contrary streak, and Zsa Zsa's propensity to whine in unfamiliar environments, the placid red mutt seemed like her best bet. She wouldn't have to worry about him barking, escaping, or nosing the interviewer in the crotch while on the air.

As soon as they entered the green room, the production assistants started fawning over Linus as though he were a four-pawed rock star, offering him treats and belly rubs. Then Claudia ducked in to say hi, and as she reintroduced herself, Lara had, as Kerry would've called it, one of her "Miss Cleo" hunches.

She unscrewed the cap of her water bottle and asked casually, "Do you have a dog right now?"

"No." Claudia's bright smile flickered for a moment. "I lost my beagle to cancer a few months ago."

"I completely understand. My Chihuahua was with me for thirteen years. It's like losing a family member." The psychic tingling intensified. "Have you ever had a spaniel? Because my friend Kerry just rescued a gorgeous black cocker named Lola—she might be purebred—and I'd love for you to meet her."

Claudia shook her head. "Stop."

Lara backed up, stumbling over Linus's leash. "Too soon for another dog? I'm sorry. I didn't mean to be insensitive."

"No, no, it's fine." Claudia's hazel eyes gleamed. "I actually love spaniels. But I want you to save this for when the cameras are rolling."

"Oh."

"You can walk me through the match-making process on-air and suggest a new dog for me at the end of the segment." Claudia turned to her producer, who was standing by with a sheaf of papers and a headset. "Great material, right?"

And so, thirty minutes later, Lara found herself perched on a green love seat with Linus curled up at her feet and Claudia seated across from her. Despite the bright lights and the hustle of production, Linus fell asleep as soon as they sat down.

"Our guest this morning is Lara Madigan, cofounder of local dog rescue group Lucky Dog," Claudia said into the camera. "Lara is more than just a rescuer—she's a canine matchmaker who will handpick the perfect dog for your family." She consulted her note cards and turned to Lara. "What are some of the things you look for when considering which dog should go with a new client?"

Lara took a deep breath and tried to speak slowly and clearly. "Oh, lots of things. I consider a family's schedule, discipline style, and activity level. I would never recommend a low-energy dog like Linus here to a marathoner, or an emotionally sensitive breed like a Doberman to a household where there's a lot of chaos and yelling."

Right on cue, Linus started snoring.

"So you have a set list of criteria," Claudia said.

"Yes, but in the end I usually go with my gut." Lara tilted her head and tried to explain. "Pairing a dog with an owner is sort of like pairing a wine and an appetizer—sometimes the most unexpected combinations turn out to be the best. When I first started the rescue group with my friend Kerry—hi, Kerry!— I tried to quantify everything with surveys and checklists and interviews. But eventually I realized that people aren't always good at predicting what they want in a dog. Honestly, it just comes down to chemistry."

Claudia leaned down to give Linus a little pat. "So are you equally skilled at human matchmaking? Did you help all your girlfriends meet their husbands?"

Lara laughed. "No, my skills are strictly limited to finding canine soul mates."

"You're a trainer as well as a rescue worker—correct?"

Linus's warm, solid body draped across her feet felt very comforting, and Lara started to calm down and enjoy her moment in the spotlight. "I'm not a certified behaviorist, but I do have several years of dog training experience. Most behavior problems aren't difficult to address. But you have to know what results you want, and you and the dog have to work together. Discipline is always a team effort."

Claudia addressed the camera directly. "We're going to do something extra special today. I've asked Lara to work her magic and find a dog for me, right here on the show."

Lara forgot about the lights and the crew and the commercial break coming up in exactly sixty seconds. She squinted slightly and tried to see past Claudia's stylish silk blouse and dazzling white smile and poised public persona. None of that mattered to a dog.

She was waiting to catch a glimpse of the soul underneath.

"So, Claudia." Lara crossed her ankles and settled back against the cushions. "Tell me about your childhood. Did you have a dog growing up, and if so, what kind?"

"Thank you so much." Claudia gave Lara a quick little hug when they wrapped the segment. "You did great. And I can't wait to meet Lola."

"You two are going to hit it off," Lara predicted. "I can feel it."

The producer strode over, giving them a thumbs-up. "We're already starting to get calls from potential adopters for Linus."

"Already?" Lara tugged the sleepy pooch to his feet and scratched him behind the ears. "Well, they'll have to fight for him. He's a good boy. Who's my good boy?"

Linus thumped his tail, his jowls quivering.

"By the way, how's it going with Peter?" she asked Claudia.

"So far, so good." Claudia held up crossed fingers. "You know, he's not really my type, but it's very refreshing. He's sensitive and stable. And of course Murphy is adorable. Do you think he and Lola will get along?"

"I know they will. Up until two weeks ago, they were housemates."

After exchanging air kisses with Claudia, Lara headed out to the parking lot. As she helped Linus into the back of the station wagon, her phone rang. "Hello?"

"Why didn't you tell me you were going to be on TV? Your eyebrows look like caterpillars and your cuticles look like you've been buried alive and were trying to dig yourself out."

"Hi, Mom." Lara opened the driver's-side door and braced herself for the worst. Justine called her exactly once a week, at precisely eight p.m. every Sunday evening. This never deviated, no matter what her mother was doing, or in which time zone she was doing it. Only a crisis—or, in this case, a code red fashion emergency—would warrant a weekday check-in.

"And what on earth were you *wearing*?" Her mother sounded personally offended. "Don't you have access to an iron?"

Lara kept her tone upbeat and tried to change the subject as quickly as possible. "How's everything going with the build-out of the new salon?"

"Listen to me." Justine adopted the cajoling tone of a police negotiator trying to talk a jumper off a bridge. "I know you like to think of yourself as a tomboy, but at a certain age you have to put together a maintenance routine or you'll simply *decay*."

Lara grabbed a tissue from the glove compartment and started swiping at the layer of dog hair on the dashboard. "No one was looking at me, Mom. They were looking at the dog."

"Don't kid yourself. If you're on TV, people are looking at you." There was a faint sound of clacking computer keys on Justine's end of the line. Clearly, her mother was multitasking. "But we'll get through this. I've asked Jessica to come in early tomorrow and I've booked you

for the works: brow wax, highlights, facial, manicure . . ."

Lara grimaced. "I have to work tomorrow morning."

The keyboard clacking stopped. "You
cannot possibly meet with potential clients looking like that."

"The dog world isn't like the salon
world. Most of the vet techs and clinic
managers I meet with are even more
low maintenance than I am."

"Your client can look as schlumpy as
she wants. That's her prerogative. *You're*
the one providing a service. *You're* the
one trying to sell something. So *you're*
the one who has to look polished and
professional."

Lara had reached her limit. "Well, it's
been great catching up, but my other
line's beeping."

"Don't you take another call when
you're on the phone with me," Justine
commanded. "That's rude. Now. When's
the last time you had your upper lip
waxed?"

Lara lapsed into sullen adolescent
monosyllables. "Don't know."

"Your cuticles trimmed?"

"Beats me."

"Your eyebrows shaped?"

"Two days ago!" Lara lifted her head in triumph. "I tweezed them myself."

"Yourself?" Justine sighed. "Where have I gone wrong? I'd better ask Jessica *and* Diane to come in early."

With the way this conversation was going, Lara was going to tear out her hair before Justine's staff had a chance to style it. "Mom, relax. It was just the local morning news. I'm not going on *Good Morning America*."

"And you never will, with that attitude. How many times do I have to tell you? *Appearances matter.* Even if you don't care what you look like, other people do."

Lara refused to break the silence that followed. These long, loaded pauses were one of her mother's most effective power plays, but she was not going to cave. Not this time.

Finally Justine softened her tone. "Who would you rather contact about adopting a dog: a well-groomed young lady with a flattering haircut and a lovely outfit or a bushy-browed fashion victim with unfortunate pores?"

Lara rolled her eyes. "I have to go to the salon for the rescue dogs is what you're saying."

"Exactly. It's a noble sacrifice for the greater good."

Her mother always had been a master of strategy. "Well, then . . . I guess I'll see you tomorrow morning."

"Oh, I won't be there—I have to fly to Los Angeles to meet with a team of potential investors. We're talking about expanding into the Southern California market."

"Wait—then why am I doing this?" Lara asked. "I only agreed to make you happy."

"Believe me, the knowledge that Jessica is waxing and buffing and dermaplaning you will make me ecstatic, even across state lines."

"What's dermaplaning?"

"I'll speak to you on Sunday evening." And with that, Justine clicked off the line.

*   *   *

"Dermaplaning, as it turns out, is when the aesthetician takes a tiny little razor blade, douses your face with acetone— a.k.a. *nail polish remover*—and scrapes off the entire first layer of skin, along with every single hair on your face," Lara informed Kerry over lunch the next day.

"Is that why your cheeks are so splotchy?" Kerry asked.

Lara nodded, gingerly patting her face. "Yep."

"Does it sting? It looks like it stings."

"Yep."

Kerry forked up a bite of omelet. "But on the upside, your nails look great."

"Thanks. Before I left, the stylist gave me an at-home manicure kit, complete with top coat, emery board, and an orange stick that's allegedly going to keep my cuticles at bay." Lara glanced down at her newly shaped and gleaming talons. "I ask you: When did we, as a society, decide that a tiny rim of flesh at the bottom of your nail was the root of all that is evil and slovenly? What's so horrible about a cuticle? It's just a few molecules of skin."

Kerry grabbed the dessert menu. "I think you need a piece of pie, stat."

"And you know what the worst part is?" Lara gnawed her lower lip. "Even though she wasn't there this morning, and even though I probably won't see her face-to-face until next month, I still feel guilty because I disappointed my mother. I embarrass her."

Kerry stopped waving at the waiter and gave Lara her full attention. "That's not true."

"Yeah, it is. I've always embarrassed her." Lara shredded her paper napkin into long, thin strips.

Because Justine had made her name in the beauty industry, it was easy for people to dismiss her as superficial. But beneath her flawless complexion and shiny black hair, Justine was shrewd, stubborn, and uncompromising. She had been a receptionist before Lara was born, booking appointments and greeting clients at a chichi Scottsdale salon. After she had Lara and divorced Gil, she enrolled in business classes at the local community college and worked her way up from receptionist to stylist to salon owner, never complaining, tiring, or backing down from a fight.

Even when she and Lara lived in a dumpy studio apartment by the freeway and ate dinners of Kraft Singles and Wonder Bread, Justine portrayed an image of success, fueled by sheer force of will. Lara always had the "right" clothes, attended the "right" schools. No one would ever guess that their family teetered on the edge of deprivation.

Though she could bend everyone else to her will, Justine's influence didn't extend to her only child. Even in elementary school, Lara's French braids would unravel and her outfits would get rumpled and stained.

"I will never be the kind of woman my mother is," Lara told Kerry. "Or the kind of woman she wants me to be."

"Well, why would you want to?" Kerry countered. "She has all this power and money, but she doesn't enjoy any of it."

"Yeah, but she doesn't ask for much. The least I could do is take care of my cuticles for her." Lara fanned out her fingers, inspecting Jessica's work. Her hand looked like it belonged to someone else. Someone who spent her days toting around eighteen-hundred-dollar handbags. "And my highlights and my eyebrows and my pores."

"But that would cut into our dog grooming time," Kerry pointed out.

"True." Lara blew a strand of hair off her face. "See, this is why my standards are so low. I figure as long as I don't have ticks or mange or visible open sores, I'm presentable. Compared to Mullet, I'm a supermodel." Lara brightened as their server approached. "We'd like two slices of pie, please. Lemon meringue for her and French silk for me."

"It's like you read my mind." Kerry had been on a major lemon kick all through her third trimester. "Speaking of Mullet, I got a new inquiry for her."

"Through the Web site?"

"Yeah. An older lady who wanted a companion, but the meet and greet was a disaster. Mullet wouldn't even come out and say hi. This poor woman drove all the way over from Sun City, and Mullet just sat under the kitchen table, glared at her, and peed on the floor."

Lara shook her head. "Subtle." Her cell phone chimed, but she didn't want to answer while she was eating.

"Pick up," Kerry urged. "It's probably Oprah, offering to give you your own talk show now that your cuticles are under control."

Lara was laughing when she answered the call. "This is Lara Madigan."

"Hel-lo," trilled a melodic, cultured female voice. "This is Cherie Chadwick. I watched your news interview yesterday, and I'd like to hire you."

Lara took a sip of water and tried to sound professional.

"Hi, Cherie. I'm so glad you've decided to adopt a rescue dog, and I'll do everything I can to find a great match for you. But you don't really 'hire' me. The only fee you'll have to pay is a donation to the rescue group once you've completed the adoption application and home interview."

"You misunderstand; I already have a dog. A purebred Bernese mountain dog."

Lara shot Kerry a puzzled glance. "Oh."

"I'd like to start showing her," Cherie continued, "and I want you to be my handler."

"What you're describing is conformation competitions, and I don't have any experience with that sort of thing." Lara tried to explain the difference between conformation shows, which were the canine equivalent of a beauty pageant, and competitive obedience trials. "I do basic training and behavior modification, not dog shows."

"That's immaterial to me." Cherie sounded relentlessly upbeat. "I want someone who understands dogs and has stage presence. That's you. I live in Mayfair Estates. Are you familiar with the neighborhood?"

Mayfair Estates was a posh gated community in North Scottsdale, tucked away in the hills and bordered by a vast nature preserve. Home values started at two million dollars and shot up exponentially from there; country club membership fees alone were more than Lara's take-home salary. Lots of pro athletes lived there, along with CEOs, trust fund babies . . . and Justine.

"Oh yes," Lara said. "My mother lives there."

"Your mother?" There was a pause on the other end of the line. "Are you Justine Madigan's daughter?"

"Yes, ma'am."

"Really." Cherie's cheeriness gave way to incredulity. "I never would have guessed."

"I get that a lot."

"Fascinating." Cherie shook off her surprise and barreled straight on to her point. "Well, I'd love to have you over for coffee tomorrow and introduce you to Eskie."

Lara slipped in a tiny, fortifying bite of pie, then tried to regain control of the conversation. "I'd help you if I could, but really, I wouldn't even know where to start with conformation work. If you'd like, I can ask around and get you the names of some experienced show handlers."

It was as though she'd never even spoken. Cherie countered with, "I have an unlimited budget, and I'm willing to pay you accordingly."

Lara thought about the mountain of

vet bills that Lucky Dog rescue had in-curred over the last few months and re-plied, "I'll see you tomorrow morning. Is nine too early?"

"Nine o'clock is perfect."

"Great. And, um, Ms. Chadwick?"

"Call me Cherie."

"Did the TV station give out my cell phone number?"

"Of course not."

"Then how . . . ?"

There was that soft musical laugh again. "Oh, I always get what I want. You'll see."

Chapter 8

"We have problems," Evan informed Lara as soon as she walked in the door. "Dog problems."

"Is this about paying for Linus's surgery? Because all his blood work came back negative and Jason said—"

Evan shook his head. "The phone's been ringing off the hook with people asking about 'the dog matchmaker.' When I got home from work, we had six voice mails."

"What the hell?" Lara really started to get annoyed. "The TV station gave out the Web site for the rescue group. How is everyone tracking down my personal contact information?"

"There's no such thing as privacy in the digital age."

Lara kicked off her flip-flops and tried to look on the bright side. "Well, it's pretty pushy to call me at home, but I'm glad people are interested in adopting the dogs."

Evan's laugh was hollow. "No, no, they don't want to adopt—they want to dump the dogs they already have. I got home half an hour ago, and I've already fielded requests from random strangers wanting to unload a neurotic Anatolian shepherd, a dog-aggressive Pembroke Welsh corgi, and a litter of pit bull puppies. They want you to use your matchmaking magic to re-home everyone."

"Did you tell them we can't take any more in right now?"

"Yeah, and then they started with the guilt trips: 'Well, if you can't take them, then I'll have no choice but to take them to the shelter.'"

"So what did you say to that?"

Evan shrugged. "I said that there was a good chance their dogs would get euthanized at the pound, but they have to do what they have to do."

"Evan!"

"What?" He crossed his arms. *They called me.* I'm under no obligation to make them feel good about their crappy choices. Someone has to be the hard-ass."

Lara sighed. "Better you than me."

"Exactly. That's why you're not allowed to answer the phone for the next few days."

"Probably for the best." She put down her work bag and opened the refrigerator to forage for dinner ideas.

The phone rang.

Evan and Lara exchanged a look of mock horror, clutching each other's forearms as the dogs ran in figure eights around their knees.

"It's *them,*" Evan whispered. "We're under siege."

Lara laughed, but as the phone rang a second time, and a third, her resolve wavered.

He sensed her uncertainty and gave her a squeeze. "Don't do it." He reached over and switched off the ringer.

She knew he was right—there was no way they could take in every owner surrender in Phoenix, and in a few days the publicity would blow over—but she still felt bad about it. The dogs didn't have the luxury of turning off a phone and ignoring everything. The dogs would end up . . . where?

"Don't think about it," Evan commanded. "We're going to go get pizza at the place you love on Greenway. And when we get home, we'll take everyone for a nice long walk by the lake."

"You'll come, too?" Lara pressed. Evan usually preferred to stay home and sack out on the sofa while she exercised the dogs.

"I'll come, too," he promised. "And tomorrow morning I'll call the phone company and change our number."

Early the next morning, Lara awoke to the sound of Raggs and Zsa Zsa whining as they ran laps between the bedroom door and the window next to the bed. They usually did this when the garbage truck rumbled down the alley, but today wasn't trash day.

She raised her head, squinted at the clock, and gave Raggs a reassuring pat on the head. "What's up, buddy?"

The little spotted spaniel whined louder, placed his front paws up on the windowsill, and rattled the white wooden blinds with his nose.

"This better be good." Lara rolled out of bed, opened the blinds, and peered out into the backyard. A little squeak of dismay escaped her lips. "Oh no."

Evan sat up. "What's wrong?"

"There's a litter of pit bull puppies in our backyard."

"They look like they're about eight weeks old." Lara inspected the trio of wriggly black-and-white puppies on the kitchen floor while Evan scarfed down frozen waffles and skimmed the *Wall Street Journal* headlines. She lifted one of the pups up to check for evidence of worms or other parasites, and Maverick nosed her elbow aside so he could get a good look at the new arrivals. "And reasonably healthy. I'll pick up some vaccines on the way home and get them started on their shot schedules."

"Mmm," was Evan's response as he pored over a market analysis.

"The good news is they're tiny and adorable, so we should be able to re-home them quickly." Lara winced as the puppy sank his razor-sharp baby teeth into her knuckle. In the fifteen minutes they'd been inside, the roly-poly hellions had already managed to pee on the tile twice and start gnawing a chair leg. "But you know how much work new puppies are."

"I don't, actually."

"I can run home between appointments to check on them and let them out," Lara said. "But then I've got a client dinner at six. So if you come home right after work to feed them—"

"No can do," Evan said.

"Why not?"

"It's Thursday." He finally looked up from the newspaper and took another bite of his multigrain waffle. "Soccer."

"Oh." Lara closed her eyes, put her head next to the rowdy little black guy, and inhaled that sweet, calming new-puppy smell. *Infinitely better than any bong hit,* she thought to herself and smiled. "Is there any way you could skip soccer tonight? Please?"

"Nope." He washed his waffle down with a glass of orange juice.

She paused, taken aback by his curtness. "Why not?"

"Because I don't want to." Evan seemed impervious to the puppy tractor beam. "I told the guys I'd be there tonight, and I'll be there."

"Okay, well, is there any way you could run home, feed them, and then go to soccer? No one will care if you're twenty minutes late."

Evan finished off his OJ and set the glass next to the sink with a clink. "I care."

Lara stared at him, taking in his sullen tone and mulish expression. "Why are you being like this?"

He focused on methodically refolding his newspaper.

She jabbed her finger toward the cocktail napkin contract stuck to the fridge. "You know, according to the terms of our agreement, these are your puppies, too."

He squinted at the napkin for a moment, then shook his head. "I see *slobber* and *shedding* on there. I see nothing about skipping soccer for a bunch of mongrels that are systematically destroying my kitchen furniture."

Lara put the puppies down and slowly got to her feet. "So what are you saying here?"

"I'm saying no." He'd gone from heated defiance to a chilly monotone. "You dog people, you're like a cult. The Cult of Dog. And you pour all your time and money into the cult, but it's never enough, because there's always one more dog. Or three more dogs."

Lara almost laughed. "The Cult of Dog?"

He folded his arms. "I'm not drinking the Kool-Aid."

"Evan, come on! I didn't go looking for these puppies. Someone tossed them over the fence in the dead of night. What am I supposed to do?"

He shrugged and checked his snowy white shirt cuffs for stains. "I'm not telling you what to do. What I am telling you is that I'm going to soccer tonight. On time." His eyes narrowed as he pulled a strand of brown fur off his sleeve. "Enough is enough, Lara. I'm drawing the line."

Her eyebrows shot up. "'Enough is enough'?"

He nodded. "I'm done with dogs."

"What is that supposed to mean?"

He clenched his jaw for a moment, obviously struggling to censor his thoughts. "It means that I lied. I'm not a dog person and I never will be." He snatched the cocktail napkin contract and threw it into the trash.

Lara gasped.

Zsa Zsa stuck her head into the trash bin and started chewing up the contract.

Evan marched into the master bedroom and returned moments later with a tiny black velvet box clenched in his hand. "I've been hanging on to this thing since you moved in, waiting for the right time to give it to you. Planning the perfect proposal."

Lara swallowed hard and then asked,

"Why are there tooth marks on that box?"

"Because one of your dogs was using it for a chew toy."

"Why on earth did you leave it where the dogs could reach it? Honestly, Evan, I've told you a thousand times you need to crate them when you leave the house."

"Here we go again. Blame the victim!"

"You don't love me," Lara accused.

"Don't do that. You know I love you."

"No, you love the person you want me to be," she shot back. "I told you right up front I was a crazy dog lady. Remember our first date? You brought me home from dinner and Maverick had eaten a whole pack of paper towels and gotten an intestinal blockage and you drove us to the emergency vet and stayed there with me for five hours. And still you begged me to move in with you, you bought this ring, and now you come out as . . . what? A cat person?"

Evan shuddered at the very thought. "Cats are even worse than dogs."

"So you're just an all-around animal hater?"

"Not everyone has to be a dog person or a cat person. Maybe I'm a *people* person. Have you ever considered that?"

Lara recoiled as if he had slapped her. "That's just sick."

"You know what kills me? I bought this house for *us*—so we could live here and get married and raise a family." He shook his head in disgust and slapped the ring box down on the kitchen counter. "But I can't take it anymore. I'm sick of the constant shedding and the slobber—God, the slobber is the worst."

Lara's shock vanished in a flare of rage. "No wonder Mullet hates you. Dogs can sense your true intentions."

Evan snorted. "Mullet hates everybody!"

"My dogs are my family." Lara opened her arms to encompass Maverick, Rufus, Raggs, Zsa Zsa, and the pack of pint-size pit bulls dunking one another in the water bowl. "If you love them, a little fur and saliva don't matter!"

"But I don't love them." Evan picked up his briefcase and suit jacket and charged into the family room. "I love *you*, so I thought that meant I had to love them by association." He pointed to the couch like a courtroom prosecutor introducing Exhibit A. "I can't remember the last time I sat down without something squeaking." He shoved one hand between the cushions and yanked out the limp, fuzzy gray corpse that had been a stuffed squirrel before Maverick had ripped open the seams and strewn tufts of white filling all over the house. "Someday I'd like to come home after work, kick back, watch the play-offs, and not have to deal with a drooly, disemboweled squirrel ruining my best work pants."

At the sight of his beloved squirrel, Maverick raced across the room, skidded to a halt, and waited for Evan to start a game of fetch.

"Maverick loves Mr. Squirrel. It's the only thing he brought with him from his previous owner's house. It's like his security blanket." Lara stepped up to the dog's side in a show of solidarity. The barrel-chested Rottweiler didn't even acknowledge her. His gaze was locked on the squirrel.

"This thing is disgusting, and I don't want it in my house."

"It's *our* house!" Lara yelled. The spaniels ran for cover.

Evan raised the sodden, smelly pelt and waved it like a battle flag. "No more Mr. Squirrel!"

The Rottie lunged, planting his hind feet on the ground and his front paws on Evan's chest. Evan toppled back onto the couch. The stack of books on the coffee table went flying.

"Maverick, down," Lara commanded.

The puppies raced in from the kitchen, pounced on the paperbacks, and started shredding the pages in a rousing game of tug-of-war.

"What are you doing?" Lara asked as Evan struggled to his feet and stalked past her.

"I'm putting this festering, bacteria-ridden piece of filth where it belongs." He went into the guest bathroom and threw Mr. Squirrel into the toilet.

"Don't you dare! You're mad at me, not Maverick."

"I'm mad at both of you."

"No!" Lara cried, but it was too late.

Evan flushed. Maverick whined.

And then . . . an ominous gurgling noise bubbled up from the depths of the plumbing.

"I can't believe you did that," Lara said. "I'll never marry you now."

He shrugged, but she could see a flicker of shame and doubt in his eyes. Then he drew himself up and said, "Well, if a disemboweled dog toy means more to you than I do, you might as well flush the ring down, too."

Lara dashed back to the kitchen, snatched up the jewelry box, and returned to the bathroom.

Evan blanched. "Hang on. Let's just calm down here."

For a second, Lara hesitated. She plucked the ring out of the little velvet cushion and dangled it with shaking fingers over the toilet bowl. The diamond's facets caught the light and sparkled with promise and possibility.

Maverick skidded up to the porcelain bowl, peered over the rim, and let out a howl of pure anguish.

Lara dropped the ring and flushed.

Chapter 9

Cherie Chadwick's house—well, *house* was really an understatement; *estate* was probably a better term—was a sprawling, modern, Frank Lloyd Wright–inspired compound constructed with lots of angled glass and concrete. The home was perched atop a hill, situated to offer views of the twinkling city lights on one side and the vast, cactus-dotted nature preserve on the other. Lara had been to this neighborhood many times over the years—her mother had moved to Mayfair Estates when Lara was a sophomore in college—but she had never really explored the quiet, winding streets. Apparently, the community had a strict social hierarchy, and Cherie Chadwick was at the very top. Compared to this place, Justine's custom-built, four-thousand-square-foot spread looked like a falling-down crack den.

When Lara pulled up in her battered old station wagon, she had to announce her arrival at an intercom by the ornate wrought-iron gates, which seemed like overkill, given that Mayfair Estates already had a twenty-four-hour security guard stationed down at the entrance to the community.

But she cleared the gate-within-a-gate, parked her car on the paving stones encircling a fountain in the center of the driveway, and took a moment to get focused. Okay, so she had just flushed her love life down the toilet—literally. So Evan had left the house that morning without a word or a single glance back. There was nothing she could do about any of that now. The die had been cast. The ring had been flushed.

And she had the feeling she was going to be apartment hunting in the immediate future, so a little extra cash would really come in handy.

She approached the massive front door and rang the bell with the wide-eyed hesitancy of Little Orphan Annie arriving at Daddy Warbucks's mansion.

Given the grandeur of the grounds, Lara was expecting a liveried, British-accented butler to greet her, but instead she found herself face-to-face with the lady of the house, an apple-cheeked, middle-aged woman wearing a violet and lavender tweed blazer, perfectly tailored gray pants, and a whimsical bee pendant fashioned out of yellow and white diamonds. With her silvery white hair styled in a flattering bob and her makeup artfully applied, she seemed warm and welcoming.

"You must be Lara." Cherie took Lara's hand in both of hers. "Thank you so much for dropping by. I need to find a handler immediately, and I have a feeling you're the one."

Lara glanced around the sun-drenched foyer and sitting room, both of which were done up in subtly contrasting shades of white and ivory. Even though she was wearing her nicest work outfit and had showered not twenty minutes ago, she stood perfectly still, afraid to sit down or touch anything. Every item in this house looked expensive, pristine, and breakable. She didn't see a single errant strand of pet hair. "You said you have a Bernese mountain dog?"

"A Bernese mountain dog and a housekeeper who vacuums twice a day," Cherie confirmed with a wink. "Eskie's in the den. Come along, and I'll make the introductions."

Lara followed Cherie down a long hallway. Her voice echoed off the high, vaulted ceiling and she marveled at the collection of abstract oil paintings displayed in recessed niches.

"What can I get you?" Cherie asked as they passed through a kitchen that looked like a set from the Food Network. "Coffee? Tea? Mimosa?"

"Oh, I'm fine, thank you." Lara caught a glimpse of a shimmering pool, complete with rock-lined waterfall, through the patio door. "As I said, I've never worked as a conformation handler—I've only been to conformation shows once or twice—but I'm happy to answer your questions."

"No questions." Cherie glanced back over her shoulder with a smile. "This really isn't up to me. Eskie will decide if she likes you or not."

And with that, she opened a pair of varnished pocket doors, revealing a cozy family room and a huge, fluffy black-and-white dog with expressive chestnut-colored "eyebrows," dainty white-tipped paws, and soft brown eyes.

"Meet Swiss Star's Evening Escapade." Cherie clapped her hand to her heart. "The love of my life."

Eskie greeted Lara with ladylike canine manners—no jumping, no barking, no overly enthusiastic sniffing. The dog seemed friendly and curious, but not hyper or insecure. Clearly she was waiting for Lara to make the first move.

Lara held her ground and used her most authoritative tone. "Eskie, sit."

Eskie's haunches hit the floor.

Only then did Lara offer her palm for sniffs and licks. "Good girl."

Eskie opened her mouth, eyes dancing, in the canine version of a giggle. Lara continued to pet her and Eskie continued to sit, soaking up the affection and offering a paw for a shake.

"She adores you," Cherie murmured. "I knew it."

"She's gorgeous," Lara said. Though Lara had a weakness for unconventional-looking mutts, this Berner was a classic beauty, a real showstopper. "Has she had any obedience training?"

"I took her to a puppy class when I first brought her home from the breeder last year. She can sit, shake, fetch, and lie down."

"Any issues with socialization?" Lara asked. "Is she anxious around other dogs?"

"No, my little Eskie's a social butterfly, aren't you?" Cherie cooed.

Eskie's tail thumped against the priceless Oriental rug, sending flurries of black fur through the air. In the next few minutes, Lara continued to dole out affection and Eskie gave up any semblance of dignity, collapsing on the floor and rolling over for a belly rub.

Cherie clapped her hands together. "Well, it's settled. She has to have you. How much?"

Lara glanced up from her tummy-scratching ministrations. "Sorry?"

"How much to put you on retainer?" Cherie asked. "I want you to handle Eskie exclusively."

Lara planted her palms on her thighs and pushed herself up. "Oh, I can't commit to only one dog. I already have five fosters at home—eight, actually, as of this morning—and several clients I work with on rally and obedience training."

Cherie waved this away. "Yes, of course, your charity efforts."

"I also have a full-time job," Lara said. "I'm a veterinary drug rep, and I don't have a typical nine-to-five schedule, but I still put in at least forty hours per week."

"Fine, fine." This seemed to be the upper-crust-rich-lady version of "whatever." "But I don't want you to handle any other dog on the conformation circuit."

Lara thought of Mullet and Linus and

had to smile. "Don't worry. The dogs I normally work with aren't really the beauty pageant type."

"Perfect. Then let's get started as soon as possible."

Something about Cherie's purpose and pluck seemed forced, and Lara stepped back to examine what was going on underneath all that cheeriness.

She let the room go quiet for a moment, then asked, "You've never entered one of these shows before?"

Cherie toyed with her diamond earring. "No."

Lara nodded. "May I ask why you've decided to take the plunge now?"

"Well, just look at my darling girl! Her markings are perfect. Her personality is delightful. And she's bred from championship lines, you know. Her grandfather placed at Westminster. It would be a waste for her to just sit around at home." At this, Cherie's smile faltered just a bit.

Lara waited.

The older woman sighed. "My husband spent his whole life traveling for work. We had always talked about the trips we would take, the things we'd do together after he retired." She cleared her throat and placed her palm on Eskie's head. "Well, now that he's finally retired, he's taking all those trips we talked about . . . with a twenty-eight-year-old flight attendant."

Lara reached out and touched Cherie's sleeve. "I'm so sorry."

"And you know, I want something young and beautiful, too. I'm not ready to give up on having goals and projects and surprises."

"If that's what you want, then that's what we'll do," Lara promised. "The three of us will be a team. But since we're brand-new at this, I'm not sure all the surprises will be good ones."

"I'll think of it as an adventure." Cherie slipped a check out of her jacket pocket and handed it to Lara. "Are you available to come by tomorrow morning, same time?"

Lara glanced down at the figure written on the check and almost collapsed. "I'll be here at nine."

*   *   *

Lara came home from work as early as she could that night, hoping that she would be able to pick up the dogs, pack her bags, and leave the scene before Evan returned from soccer practice.

No such luck.

When she opened the garage door, his Audi was parked in the usual spot and she could hear the dogs on the other side of the door, waiting to welcome her with the usual fur-and-drool-drenched festivities. Evan must have let them out of their crates.

She greeted Maverick, Zsa Zsa, Rufus, Raggs, and Linus in turn, then looked down the hall for any sign of Evan. The lights were off and the house was silent. Maybe he wasn't home after all—maybe he'd dropped off his car and gone to soccer with a buddy so he could drink microbrews with wild abandon between scrimmages.

She let out a sigh of relief and led the pack into the kitchen to check on the puppies and take an ibuprofen. Her headache had started on the drive to Cheri's this morning and had snowballed into a killer migraine. She needed about a gallon of water, a cold compress, and twelve hours of sleep, in that order. But first she had to relocate five dogs and three puppies to Kerry's house for the night. The apartment hunt would start tomorrow. Although she'd hated to ask Kerry for a place to crash, especially since Richard had come home from his latest trip, she really didn't have anywhere else to go on such short notice.

She'd spent her afternoon considering her options, and had been dismayed to realize that Kerry was pretty much it. Kerry's house, or an extended stay at a hotel for her and a kennel for the dogs. Her phone was full of contact names, and she'd lived in Phoenix for almost her entire life, but somehow she didn't have a lot of close friends left. Not the kind she could call up and ask for lodging at a moment's notice. The realization had brought her up short—how had so many people in her life drifted away? Had they drifted, or had she been too consumed with the Cult of Dog to hang on to them?

"Hey."

Lara startled at the sound of Evan's voice. She whirled around and hid the bottle of Advil behind her back as if caught committing a crime.

He sat at the kitchen table, his face obscured by the long afternoon shadows. A pair of plastic freezer bags rested next to the napkin holder in front of him. One bag held the waterlogged remains of Mr. Squirrel. The other contained the diamond ring.

"God, you scared me." She searched his eyes for a clue about what he was feeling, but came up empty. "I thought you were going to soccer tonight."

"Wasn't in the mood. Came home early."

She noticed the empty food bowls, unstacked and lined up across the wall. "You fed the puppies."

He admitted this with a grudging, almost imperceptible incline of his head. "But that's not why I skipped soccer," he informed her. "I skipped soccer to meet the plumber."

She sat down across the table from him. "Well, it looks like he managed to salvage everything. So that's good, right?"

"Yeah, the squirrel clogged up the pipe so the ring got stuck, too." He jerked his chin in the direction of the engagement ring. "I doubt the jeweler's gonna take it back."

The dogs went quiet and trooped out to the family room as bitterness and regret enveloped the kitchen.

"Are you okay?" Lara asked softly.

"Not really," he replied.

She drew a breath, hoping something poignant and insightful would come out. Something that would let him know how much he meant to her, without begging or offering concessions she wasn't willing to make.

"What now?" She kept her face blank, her voice steady, as though they were discussing the mundane details of their workday. Linus, perhaps sensing her distress, crept back into the kitchen and rested his head in her lap. "I guess I'll go stay with Kerry."

"It doesn't have to be like that," he muttered. "You can stay here until you find another place."

She stared directly at the little diamond time bomb ticking away between them. "It does have to be like that."

At this, he disengaged completely. He scraped back his chair, shoved his hands in his pockets, and walked out to the garage.

Lara heard his car engine start and the garage door opening. The ring was still on the kitchen table.

Her right hand reached out of its own accord, but as her fingers brushed against the plastic bag, she felt pressure on her foot and glanced down to see Maverick sitting next to Linus, staring up at her with soulful brown eyes.

She snatched her hand away, walked up the stairs, and wrestled her suitcases out of the closet.

As soon as she unzipped the first overnight bag, Zsa Zsa hopped in and sat down.

"Don't worry," Lara assured her. "You're all coming with me."

She piled luggage and disassembled crates on the front stoop, then loaded the dogs into the back of the station wagon with their bones, leashes, food, and toys. The pit bull puppies went in the front seat in a cardboard box. This left exactly five square inches for all of her worldly belongings.

She took the disemboweled squirrel soaked in toilet water and left the diamond ring behind.

"Oh, honey." Kerry met her at the front door with a long hug and a glass of red wine. "Make yourself at home."

"You're a lifesaver," Lara said. "I've got an appointment to look at apartments at seven a.m. tomorrow. This is for one night only, I swear."

"Don't worry. My house is your house." Kerry and her home had both undergone what Lara thought of as "the Richard Transformation": Kerry had straightened her hair and curled her eyelashes; the dog-friendly bachelorette pad now resembled a Crate and Barrel catalog photo shoot.

A photo shoot that definitely did not include a brokenhearted best friend crashing in the guest room with a bunch of scruffy dogs and cuticles that would make Elizabeth Arden spin in her grave. "Forty-eight hours," Lara swore. "You won't even know I'm here."

"Don't be ridiculous. You're welcome to stay as long as you like. Oh, and if you could feed the dogs in the morning, I'd really appreciate it." Kerry produced a pocket mirror from her handbag and dabbed on another coat of lip gloss.

"Sure. But where are you going?"

"Hospital." Kerry grinned and reached back to clutch her husband's hand as Richard strode out of the bedroom with an overnight bag. "My water just broke. I think I'm in labor for real."

Chapter 10

"This looks fine." Lara took in the beige-on-beige two-bedroom apartment with bleary eyes. "Can I move in immediately?" She raised her hand to her mouth to cover her yawn, but the real estate agent looked at her sympathetically.

"Late night?"

"My best friend had a baby." Just before dawn Kerry had delivered Cynthia Grace, a chubby-cheeked, seven-pound set of lungs.

"I think we've got a future opera singer on our hands," the doctor said as Cynthia wailed with displeasure during her weigh-in.

The nurses had seemed equally impressed. "You're not going to need a baby monitor, that's for sure."

Kerry had insisted that Lara stay by her side through the contractions, the crowning, and the sweaty-browed pushing. But as soon as little Cynthia was swaddled and placed on her mother's chest, Lara slipped away to give the new family their bonding time.

Then she had returned to Kerry's house, taken care of the dogs, and cleaned the already immaculate house from top to bottom. The doctors had said Kerry might be discharged as early as tomorrow morning, and she had every intention of moving out by then.

"Oh, how exciting." The real estate agent beamed. "Boy or girl?"

"Girl." Lara skimmed the listing information the agent had given her. The rent and utilities looked doable, and there was a big grassy park right around the corner. "So can they run the credit check today and let me sign the lease before the end of business hours?"

"I assume so." The agent looked taken aback. "But I have five other properties I planned to show you. Are you sure—"

"I'm sure." Lara checked the time on her cell phone. Maybe she could squeeze in a catnap before she reported for duty at Cherie Chadwick's house. "Let's start with a six-month lease, if possible." She tried to sound casual. "Oh, and you said the landlord is pet-friendly, right?"

The agent nodded and checked her paperwork again. "Let's see. . . . Yes, it says right here that dogs and cats are welcome."

"Fantastic."

"Up to two animals under thirty pounds each." The agent looked up with a smile, which faded when she saw Lara's expression. "Uh-oh. That presents a problem?"

"I have five foster dogs," Lara said. "And the biggest is over a hundred pounds. I explained this to the receptionist at your office when I called yesterday."

The agent blinked a few times. "Five?"

"Well, eight, technically, but I'm going to an adoption fair this weekend, and I'm sure at least three of them will find new homes after that."

"Eight dogs," the agent repeated.

"Five," Lara corrected. "The other three are practically nonexistent."

"That changes things." The agent put on her glasses and started scanning every listing in her folder. "Are you in any position to buy? Because, given your lifestyle, that's your best option."

Lara rubbed her forehead with the heel of her hand and summed up her current living situation. "I might be in a position to buy in a few months or a year, but I need somewhere to live right now. Like, today."

The real estate agent spent the next hour pleading their case with various landlords while Lara started calling about rental listings on craigslist. The responses were always the same:

"You have *how* many dogs?"

"A Rottweiler? No."

"Pit bulls? No."

"But they're sweet as pie," Lara argued. "I can give you excellent references. I'll put down a big security deposit."

"Lady, you could buy your own apartment building with the security deposit I'd charge. Call back when you have a kitten or a Chihuahua."

Click.

When Cherie opened the door at the Daddy Warbucks mansion, she peered over Lara's shoulder at the suitcase-filled station wagon. "Are you moving, dear?"

"Trying to. So! Where's Eskie?"

Cherie's forehead creased with concern. "You're staying on this side of town, I hope. The closer to Mayfair Estates, the better."

Lara tried to keep her tone light and dismissive. "I'm not really sure yet. Still checking out apartments. Anyway, I made some calls and did some research on the desired behavior for conformation dogs, and I thought Eskie and I could—"

"Why didn't you tell me you were looking for a place to live?" Cherie was practically rubbing her palms together in glee. "Our guesthouse is vacant. You're welcome to stay there as long as you're working with Eskie."

Lara's eyes widened. "That's really generous of you, but I couldn't possibly."

"Why not?"

"Well . . ." Other than the fact that Cherie had serious boundary issues and Lara would basically be her indentured servant? What could possibly go wrong?

"It would be ideal. You and Eskie could bond." Cherie ushered Lara inside. "We just had the whole casita remodeled. You can move in as soon as you like." Eskie joined them in the foyer and gave Lara's feet a thorough sniffing.

"I have, um, several dogs," Lara said. "Would that be a problem?"

"You're a trainer; I assume they're well behaved."

Lara's mind flashed to the pit bull pups gnawing the chair leg and Maverick tackling Evan. "That would seem like a reasonable assumption."

"Then it's settled. I'll give you the key and the code to the gate before you leave."

Danger, Will Robinson! Abort! Abort! "Well, if you're sure . . ."

"I insist."

"It would only be for a few weeks," Lara said, as much to reassure herself as her new employer.

"Splendid, splendid. I'll have my lawyers draw up a rental agreement. Now make yourself comfortable and let's talk dog shows." Cherie indicated a silk settee in the sumptuous ivory living room.

Lara sat. Eskie followed suit.

Cherie bustled off to the kitchen and returned with mugs of coffee and a tall stack of glossy magazines, which she handed to Lara. "We need to discuss our campaign strategy."

"I'm sorry, I'm not following. Campaign?"

"Take a look at these journals. They're mailed out to everyone who's anyone in the dog show world."

Lara glanced at the periodicals: *Dogs in Review,* the *Canine Chronicle, Dog News.* The covers consisted of glamour shots of a Pharaoh hound, a Tibetan mastiff, and a Norwich terrier. Upon closer inspection, she noticed that each dog's owner, breeder, and handler were listed along with the dog's name and kennel.

"Look at this photography." Lara thumbed through the journals. The styles ranged from minimalist black-and-white portraits to vibrant action shots. Every dog was shot to play up the best attributes of its breed: hunting dogs working the field, toy poodles dolled up in rhinestones and beribboned topknots, Portuguese water dogs splashing in a lake. "It's like *Glamour* for Great Danes."

"*Bazaar* for Berners," Cherie threw in with a smile. "Can't you just picture my Eskie on the front? She's definitely cover girl material."

"So you have to campaign to get a cover?" Lara asked.

"No, no—you place an order and write a check. To secure a cover, even a back cover, you have to spend at least three thousand dollars."

Lara's eyebrows flew up.

Cherie smiled. "If you want to win, you have to play the game. A good media campaign translates into blue ribbons: Best of Breed, Best in Show."

Lara pored over the ads and announcements crammed in between articles. She kept glancing up at Cherie to make sure that this was real, that it was not an elaborate practical joke. "Holy cow. These dogs have their own Facebook pages?"

"Promotion can make or break a dog."

Lara set aside the magazines and shook her head. "So you're telling me that as long as you have the right PR, your dog can be a champion? Beauty doesn't matter at the beauty contest?"

"Well, of course it's important to have a fine example of the breed. But a little extra hype never hurts. You'll notice that every one of the Best in Show announcements thanks the judges by name."

Lara started to realize she was in way over her head. "I have to tell you, there's none of this campaign stuff at rally or agility events. We just run the dog and hope he doesn't get disqualified for goofing off during a sit-stay. If you're serious about pursuing the conformation titles"—Lara glanced at the towering pile of journals—"and it seems like you are, you might be better off hiring a handler with a lot more experience. Or *any* experience."

"You'll do fine." Cherie scratched Eskie's ears and smiled indulgently as the dog drooled on her pristine white sofa. "You have the right look for a dog handler—attractive, but not distractingly so. No matter how spectacular my Eskie is, the fact is that from a distance, it's hard to tell one Berner from another. Judges are much more likely to remember a handler than a specific dog. You're tall, which is always helpful, and your bone structure is lovely." Cherie tilted her head, assessing Lara as if she were a terrier in the show ring. "I'd like to arrange a photo shoot for you and Eskie as soon as possible. Does Monday work for you?"

Lara pulled out her phone and scrolled through her work schedule. "I'm available between ten and eleven thirty."

Cherie made a note of this. "You'll have to dress appropriately for photos and competitions, of course."

Lara flushed. Her work clothes might not be Armani, but they weren't *that* shabby. "No problem. I have a basic black suit."

"I don't think black's the right way to go." Cherie flipped through the magazine pages, pointing out the handlers' outfits. "You don't want to take the focus off the dog, but you need to be distinctive in your own right. Maybe a plum velvet blazer or a smart brown tweed. I'll make an appointment for you with my shopper at Neiman Marcus this weekend. What's your skirt and jacket size?"

"European or American sizing?" Lara replied automatically. Years of shopping with Justine had trained her well.

Cherie seemed pleased by this response. "Give me both and we'll let the shopper take it from there. And, of course, in addition to your training fees, you'll keep any prize money Eskie wins at competition. That's standard."

Lara called for a time-out. "Hang on.

So you're saying that there's essentially no money to be made in dog shows?"

"Well, not unless you're winning Westminster or the Eukanuba National Championship." Cherie cupped Eskie's face in both hands and bestowed a loud kiss on the dog's nose.

"But all of this advertising and training and grooming is going to cost a fortune! Even if you breed Eskie and charge an arm and a leg for her puppies, you're never going to recoup what you've spent."

Cherie rested her cheek on the top of Eskie's broad, furry head. "This isn't about money. It's about my darling girl, who would still love me if all of this were gone."

Lara took another look around the palatial, professionally decorated house and realized that were it not for the sound of Eskie's steady panting, it would be absolutely silent.

"I'm sure we have great things ahead," Lara said. "Plus lots and lots of work. So let's get started. I'd like to take Eskie for a walk now. The two of us need to start bonding and working as a team."

She followed Cherie back to the front entryway. "We'll be back in twenty minutes or so."

As Lara and Eskie started down the driveway, Cherie waved to them as if seeing her child off on the first day of kindergarten. "Have fun, you two. Oh, and say hello to Ivory for me."

"Who's Ivory?" Lara called back.

"She's our neighborhood greeter." Cherie laughed at Lara's confusion. "You'll know her when you see her."

That afternoon, Lara got another phone call from her mother, the second in a week before the appointed hour of eight p.m. on Sunday. Either the apocalypse was nigh or she had *really* screwed up.

She couldn't help cringing as she answered the phone. Before she could even get out a "hello," Justine launched into her interrogation.

"Is it true that you're homeless and casting about for a place to live?"

"Hi, Mom. Still the master of understatement, I see."

"Answer my question."

"I'm not homeless. I—" *I broke up with Evan,* she started to say, but she couldn't force the words out of her mouth. She wasn't ready to talk about that. She definitely wasn't ready to hear her mother's *I told you so.* "I'm staying at Kerry's for a few days and trying to find an apartment that will take a renter with five dogs. But Kerry finally had her baby last night—"

"And why do I have to hear about all this from Cherie Chadwick?" Justine demanded.

"I wasn't aware that you knew Cherie Chadwick."

"I know everybody," Justine said. "And Cherie has friends that have standing appointments at Coterie. If you need a place to stay, you'll stay with me."

"Um . . ." Lara tried to stall. "That's really nice of you. I appreciate it. I do. But the thing is, I'm not sure—"

"When can I expect you?"

Lara took a deep breath. "Mom, I'm twenty-nine years old. I don't want to be moving back in with a parent at this stage of my life."

"I don't particularly want you to, either, but here we are." Her mother's tone left no room for argument. "Be practical, Lara. You said it yourself: Where are you going to find another landlord that will let you have five dogs?"

"It's eight right now, actually." Lara explained about the midnight puppy drop-off, and Justine made a noise that was equal parts frustration and impatience. "See? I haven't even darkened your doorstep, and already you're annoyed with the dogs."

"This has nothing to do with the dogs. This is about you." Justine's voice was cold and clipped. "Frankly, I can't believe you let yourself get into this situation in the first place. I raised you to be self-reliant. You can't depend on a man to take care of you."

Lara took a moment to calm down and choose her words. "I wasn't depending on anyone to take care of me. Evan and I were a team. He paid the mortgage; I paid the utilities."

"A team." Justin scoffed. "Right. And now that things have gone south, he's still snug and secure in his house and you're out on the street. How many times did I tell you? Men will always let you down. No matter how much you think you love them or they love you."

Lara closed her eyes and dug her fingernails into her palms. "If you're going to start this conversation again, I'm hanging up."

"First of all, you will not hang up on me, and secondly, you will not move into Cherie Chadwick's guesthouse. I'm a respected member of the Mayfair Estates community. I have clients here, and social contacts. How will it look if my daughter is living in one of my neighbors' guesthouses, like an employee?"

Lara opened her eyes again. "What do you care how it looks? It's my life."

"Appearances matter."

"I hate when you say that."

"That doesn't mean it's not true. If you're living at Cherie's house instead of mine, people will talk." Lara's first impulse was to retort that Justine couldn't force her to do anything, that she didn't owe her mother blind obedience.

Then she thought about everything her mother had done for her. All the sacrifices Justine had made when they had no money so that Lara could have little treats. All the prep school and college tuition checks she'd signed once the salon started making a profit.

Lara owed her mother a lot, and so far she'd done nothing but disappoint her.

"Fine." She relented. "I'll stay with you until I find my own place. But it's extremely temporary, and I'm paying rent."

"If that's the way you want it, then I'm also collecting a security deposit due to the unpredictable and destructive nature of your animals." From the way she said this, Lara suspected Justine had somehow heard about the shredded Prada hobo. "When can I expect your arrival?"

"Let's discuss this over dinner," Lara said, hedging. "Are you free tonight?"

Justine exhaled loudly. "You know I'm busy. I'm happy to let you stay at my home, but you can't expect me to drop everything to coddle you."

Lara tried to soften the sting of this remark with a halfhearted attempt at humor. "Mother, you wound me. I did your bidding and got my eyebrows landscaped and you're *still* embarrassed to be seen with me in public?"

There was a silence. Then Justine said, "Not everything is about you."

"I know that, Mom. I'm sorry." Lara's voice broke, and she forced herself to regain control of her emotions. Her mother hated tears even more than scraggly cuticles and downy upper lips. "I didn't mean—"

"I have to go," Justine said crisply.

"Wait, will you just let me—"

"I haven't got time for this, Lara. We'll talk when you come to the house. Good-bye."

Chapter 11

"Hi, sweetie." Shelly, her mother's housekeeper, greeted Lara with a warm smile. "I'm so glad to see you. It's been too long. How're you doing?"

Justine had hired Shelly fifteen years ago to manage the day-to-day details of her personal life. A pathologically organized divorcée with grown children, Shelly attended to all the things Justine didn't have time for: buying groceries, cooking dinner, doing the laundry, and keeping up with the car, yard, and pool maintenance. When Lara was in high school, Shelly had scheduled her dental appointments and driven her to and from swim meets and band practices.

"I'm your mother's stay-at-home wife," Shelly used to say with a laugh.

"But with paid days off and benefits, which is more than most wives get," Justine would add wryly.

"Hi." Lara hugged the kindly older woman, drinking in the smell of lavender fabric softener and freshly baked bread.

"She's not here," Shelly said, anticipating Lara's question. "Still at work."

"But it's almost ten."

Shelly raised her palm in a *don't get me started* gesture. "She's been holed up in her office for the last few weeks. I haven't seen her in at least a month—we've been communicating by e-mail. She works too hard. You should tell her to take it easy."

"Yes, because she values my opinion so much." Lara rolled her eyes and stepped into the foyer.

Her mother had redone the floors again. That was the first thing Lara noticed. Justine's home was in a state of constant renovation—new paint, new furniture, new patio flagstones—but she hadn't mentioned she had ripped out the marble tiles in the entryway and replaced them with rich, gleaming hardwood.

"Wow." She leaned over, peering at the planks of cherry, which were interwoven with strips of dark, smooth material. "Is that *leather*?"

Shelly nodded. "Incredible, right? The contractor said it was the latest trend in high-end flooring design."

"It's gorgeous." Lara regarded the sleek, glossy surface with equal parts awe and dread. The thought of the scrabble of canine claws against this leather sent a shiver down her spine. "Would you mind opening the garage door? I think I'm going to bring the dogs in through the side."

"Sure thing, sweetie." Shelly led the way to the kitchen. Every surface in this room was hard and shiny—polished granite, stainless steel, gleaming glass—but Shelly somehow managed to make it seem homey with strategically placed bowls of fresh fruit and flowers. "It's good that you're here. I was actually supposed to leave for vacation this morning, but I decided to stay until you got here. I worry about her."

Lara snagged an apple as they passed a fruit bowl. "My mom can take care of herself."

"I know, but . . ." Shelly shrugged one shoulder. "She misses you. She'd never come right out and say that, but she does."

"I'm standing in her kitchen, and she's not here to see me," Lara pointed out.

"Well"—Shelly half smiled—"she likes to give you your space." Her expression sobered. "I heard you and Evan broke up."

Lara twisted the stem of her apple. "Yeah."

"If you need to talk—"

"I don't." She hadn't meant to sound snippy. "Not quite yet. But thank you."

Shelly gave her a sympathetic look, then pulled her in for another hug. "You'll get through this," she promised. "You'll get through it and come out even better on the other side. Now, since you're going to be staying a while, and the dogs need access to the outdoors, I decided not to put you in your old bedroom. Instead, I got the east wing all ready for you."

"The east wing. Sounds like I'm touring the White House."

"Well, the guest quarters there are almost as big as the master suite, and we put in those French doors last year. I even asked the landscaper to fence off part of the yard so your dogs can go outside and play without tearing up the oleander bushes." Shelly waited a beat. "By the way, how many dogs are currently in your possession?"

Lara shook her hair back over her shoulder. "Uh, not that many."

"Define 'not that many.'"

"Five real dogs and three puppies." She laughed at the look Shelly gave her. "The puppies will probably find homes by the end of the week." Lara perked up as a thought occurred. "In fact—"

"No." Shelly cut her off before she could finish the sentence.

"Don't say that until you meet them. The little boy is a sweetheart and a half. And he's so cute, with big pink splotches on his nose."

"My cat would have a conniption," Shelly said firmly. "That puppy wouldn't last a day." She showed Lara to the bedroom at the back of the house—a large, sunny suite that Justine rarely used for guests because the pool filter was on the other side of the exterior wall.

The bed was blanketed with white-on-white linens. A stack of spa-quality towels rested on the bathroom counter. Lara immediately started stripping off sheets and duvets.

"What are you doing?" Shelly exclaimed. "Those are brand-new!"

"Which is why you don't want a bunch of dogs trying to make a cozy nest out of them. I have my own blankets in the car."

Shelly accepted the armful of Egyptian cotton with a disapproving frown. "Justine's not going to like this. She's got very specific ideas about how each room should look."

"'Appearances matter,'" Lara sing-songed. "Don't worry. I'll tell her you tried to stop me."

Shelly started toward the garage, but

Lara waved he off. "I'll get the boxes and the dogs. It's getting late. You don't have to stay up on my behalf—go start your vacation."

"I'm staying up on *my* behalf, not yours," Shelly assured her. "And I'm out of here first thing tomorrow morning. Tell you what— while you bring in the dogs and get settled, I'll go heat up some dinner. I have some of my home-made chicken soup in the refrigerator." She gave Lara a critical once-over. "You'd better have two bowls. You look like you're wasting away. Heartbreak'll do that every time. Now make yourself comfortable, and let me know if you need anything."

Lara started salivating at the thought of Shelly's fresh, noodly soup. "Thanks, Mom."

Shelly shot a warning look over her shoulder. "Don't even joke about that."

Lara instinctively corrected her posture like a slouchy teen chastised. "Sorry, sorry."

"You and Justine will do just fine. A little time together will do you both good." Shelly headed back toward the kitchen. "I'm going to watch *True Blood* later. Want to join me?"

An hour later, after Lara and Shelly had ogled hot Southern vampires and shared scraps of chicken with the dogs, they defrosted a chocolate marble cheesecake Justine had stashed in the freezer for unexpected guests and caught up on each other's lives. For the first time since she'd flushed Evan's engagement ring, Lara could envision what life would be like when all her raw pain scabbed over. She started to believe that she would heal, that she hadn't thrown away her last chance for happiness.

"It's good to be home," she mumbled through a crumbly bite of cheesecake.

But when she fell asleep at midnight, sandwiched between Linus and Maverick on the California king pillowtop mattress, she realized she still hadn't seen or spoken to her mother.

"Eskie, stack."
Wag, wag, wag.
"Stack."

Bounce, bounce, bounce.

"Eskie—" Lara broke off as the exuberant black-and-white dog pranced in place to get the attention of two passing joggers. Laughing, and well aware that she was breaking all her own training rules, Lara looked into the dog's sparkling brown eyes and repeated the command once more. "Stack."

Eskie licked her right on the lips.

"And we're officially bonded." Lara wiped her mouth on the back of her sleeve. "Listen, missy, don't think a few sloppy kisses are going to get you out of this." She tugged Eskie's leash and resumed walking to the end of the cul-de-sac. To refocus the dog, she pivoted quickly. Eskie stayed right by her side.

Twenty minutes into their morning walk, Lara had introduced a few new training terms and it was obvious that Eskie would be a star pupil . . . when she wanted to be. But she was really still a puppy, and trying to teach her to "stack"—stand motionless with her muzzle slightly lifted while Lara held her neck and guided her legs into a proper show dog pose—was proving a bigger challenge than Lara had anticipated.

Even though she no longer had to fight her way across town in rush-hour traffic to get to Cherie's house, Lara had gotten up extra early this morning to try to catch Justine. But her mother must have come home after midnight and then left again at the crack of dawn; the only evidence that she had been there at all was the fading aroma of coffee in the kitchen.

Lara tried not to take it personally that her own mother was avoiding her.

"Okay, one more time and then we can run for a bit." She stopped, brought Eskie around in front of her, and produced a treat to get her attention.

"Stack."

And Eskie did. Instantly and perfectly, the dog struck a pose worthy of a *Canine Chronicle* photo shoot.

"Good girl!" Lara hit the little clicker with her thumb to let Eskie know she'd gotten it right, but before she could follow up with a treat, they were interrupted by a high-pitched yip.

Eskie broke her pose and strained forward in excitement.

A tiny white Maltese trotted toward them. Though the dog had no leash and no owner in sight, she strode forward with great purpose until she reached Lara's feet. Then she stared up and waited for lavish affection to come her way.

Lara obliged with an ear scratch, but she didn't see any tags or identification on the little dog.

"Are you lost?" she asked.

The Maltese certainly didn't seem lost; in fact, she and Eskie seemed delighted to see each other. They greeted each other with quick sniffs, then launched right into a vigorous game of chase. Though the tiny white dog was dwarfed by the Bernese mountain dog, she showed no fear as she darted between Eskie's legs and dropped her front paws in a play bow.

"Oh, *there* you are! You're late today." A bronzed, buxom woman in her late twenties waved from the driveway across the street, then hurried toward the street, holding a copper watering can in one hand and a baggie of treats in the other. With her wedge-heeled espadrilles, flirty pink dress, and long platinum extensions, this lady was a shoo-in if Bravo ever decided to film *Real Housewives of Scottsdale*.

"Hi there, pookie." She leaned down and made kissy faces at the Maltese, who wagged her tail and twirled in circles. "I've got your favorite today: chicken flavor." She opened the bag and started doling out treats. Eskie immediately stacked in an attempt to score some chicken for herself.

Lara hit the clicker for Eskie and asked the woman, "Is this your dog?"

"No, this is Ivory. She makes the rounds every morning." The woman scooped up the Maltese and cradled the dog in her arms. "She's kind of the neighborhood busybody. She just loves Eskie."

Lara glanced back down the street. "Where's her owner?"

"I don't really know who she belongs to, but they take very good care of her. She always has the most darling little haircuts."

"Letting her roam the streets is not 'taking good care of her,'" Lara fumed. "She could get snatched by a coyote, hit by a car. . . ."

"Hi, Eskie." The real housewife patted the black-and-white giant on the head and looked up at Lara with renewed interest. "You must be the Dog Doyenne."

Lara blinked. "The what?"

"That's what Cherie called you. She said you have a special gift for working with dogs." The woman tugged down the hem of her skirt as a breeze kicked up. "Are you available for consultation? My friend Kayla could use some help with her dog."

"What's the problem?" Lara asked.

"It's probably better if she explains it. Would you mind giving me your name and number?"

Lara obliged, and by the time she'd handed a business card to the neighbor, the Maltese had started down the other side of the street with her fluffy white tail wagging good-bye.

"Bye-bye, Ivory! See you tomorrow!" the blonde called after her.

"Rich people are weird," Lara told Eskie as they hiked back up the steep hill to the Chadwick estate. "Free-range Malteses, hundred-thousand-dollar dog show campaigns, calling me the Dog Doyenne. But their checks always clear, so I guess I can't talk too much smack."

At the word *smack*, Eskie stopped heeling and jerked herself into a regal stack that would have blown away the competition at the Westminster Kennel Club.

Lara laughed and hit the clicker. "Good girl."

Chapter 12

"So, how's motherhood?" Lara asked as she surveyed the chaos in Kerry's living room. She'd swung by after work to drop off a take-out dinner and pick up a report from the front lines.

"Well, except for her constant scream-ing, my constant crying, the sleep de-privation, the hormonal whiplash, the bloating from the saline IV at the hospi-tal, the conflicting advice from every random jackass I meet on the street, and the cracked nipples, it's awesome. Totally fulfilling." Kerry dug another Oreo out of the bag on her coffee table. Her sofa had become baby care command central, with wipes, pacifiers, cloth bibs, discarded onesies, and breast pump accessories scattered across the carpet. Despite the lure of processed snack food and chewy cloth goods, the dogs were nowhere to be seen. They'd retreated to the bedroom after Cynthia unleashed the full power of her tiny lungs. "And these cookies are really helping me lose the baby weight. Oh, and Richard has another business trip on Tuesday."

Lara was appalled. "He's leaving you all alone?"

"No, no. His mom is coming for a week. And so is my mom. Together. In the same house. Hold me—I'm scared." Kerry winced as she shifted positions. "Ow. I'm such an idiot—my doctor offered me Percocet but I said no, I'd stick to Advil. *What to Expect When You're Expecting* brainwashed me."

"How can I help? Do you want me to take her for a few hours? You could go grab a nap and a shower." Lara felt a bit panicky as she held out her arms to accept the squalling pink newborn.

"Thank you for offering, but no." Kerry's head fell back against the cushions. "I'm completely fried from feeding her and holding her twenty-four-seven, yet I start to hyperventilate at the thought of being separated from her. This will get easier, right? Tell me this will get easier."

Lara's eyes widened with every syllable. "It . . . will get easier."

"Oh my God, I'm never going to sleep again."

"Yes, you are. Now, seriously, let me know what I can do to help. If you want me to take the dogs for a while—"

"No, no, no. I promised myself I wouldn't dump the dogs for the baby. I hate people who do that. I made a commitment to them, and I intend to keep it. In fact, I'll see you at the adoption fair on Sunday."

Lara shook her head. "You're not going to that."

"Oh yes, I am."

"But you . . ."

"I know, I know. But Richard says I need to take a break from the baby and get out in the fresh air. Well, actually, his mother said that, so of course he agreed." Kerry glowered. "So I'll be pumping my first bottle and heading back out into the trenches." She grimaced, looking down at her holey sweatpants and baggy, milk-stained shirt. "Who wouldn't want to adopt a dog from me, right?"

"You look great." Lara always defended her friends, even from themselves.

"Yeah, right. Lie to yourself; don't lie to me. Hey, after the adoption fair, maybe we can hit the back alleys and try to score some Percocet." Kerry patted the baby's back until Cynthia burped, then fell asleep. "Now, please, I beg you, let's talk about something other than sleep schedules and breastfeeding and spit-up. What's new with you? Have you talked to Evan since you moved out?"

"Not a word." Lara settled down next to her friend and nibbled an Oreo. "No calls, no texts, no e-mails, nada. The man is done with me."

Kerry raised an eyebrow. "Have you called or texted him?"

"No. What am I going to say?"

"'Sorry I flushed your ring down the toilet. Let's get a gallon of disinfectant and try again'?"

Lara crossed her arms. "He's the one who started flushing things down the toilet, not me. He's the one who Power-Pointed me into moving in and then decided he doesn't like dogs and never will."

"That is pretty bad," Kerry admitted.

"The man said, and I quote, 'I'm not a dog person. I'm a people person.'"

Her friend's jaw dropped. "Wow. You think you know someone. . . ."

Lara shoved another cookie into her mouth and waved her fist. "If I want someone to criticize my life choices, I can just call my mom. I don't need my boyfriend trying to play Extreme Personality Makeover, too."

"Speaking of which, how's life over at Chez Justine?"

"Solitary. I'm not even sure my mom actually lives there. She comes home every night after I go to bed and leaves every morning before I get up."

"You haven't seen her at all?"

"Nope. She comes and goes like a phantom. Even the dogs don't hear her."

"Is she avoiding you?"

"I called her yesterday and asked her that, and she got all huffy and told me to get over myself. She's all, 'Everything isn't about you.'"

"Your mom scares me." Kerry gazed down at her wrinkled little infant. "I can't imagine treating my own kid like that."

"My mom scares *me*," Lara said. "But I can't blame her too much—I drove her to this. She spent her whole life trying to help me become a confident, sophisticated businesswoman who could take over her empire, and instead she got stuck with the Dog Doyenne. Oh yes, that's what they're calling me in Mayfair Estates."

"Rich people are *so* weird," Kerry said. "And I don't care what she wanted you to be. You're a great daughter and she should love you unconditionally."

"She loves me. She just doesn't *like* me very much. But that's how she is— she doesn't like anyone. Something's up, but since she obviously doesn't want to tell me, it gives me extra motivation to find my own place ASAP. Want to come house hunting with me next week?"

"Sure. You won't mind if I have to stop every forty minutes to nurse a screaming newborn, right?" Kerry reached for another Oreo.

Lara got up, poured a glass of milk, and handed it to her friend. "You need the protein. The vitamin D. Whatever."

Kerry rolled her eyes but took a sip. "So, got any big plans tonight? Hot date with a hunky vet?"

Lara picked up a rose-printed onesie and examined it. "I'm stopping by Evan's, actually."

"Really."

"Yeah, I left the dogs' Frontline in the cabinet there, and they're due for their dosage."

Kerry threw back her head and yawned. "Uh-huh."

"It's been a month since their last treatment. It's not like I'm making up some excuse to see him. I mean, I'm hoping he won't even be home."

"Lara. Take a good look at me. Do I look like I give a single, solitary rat's ass about your ulterior motives to go to your ex-boyfriend's house?"

Lara took in the bleary eyes, the un-hooked nursing bra, the Oreo crumbs on Kerry's chin. "No, you do not."

"All right, then. Let's move along."

"But just so we're clear, I don't have ulterior motives."

"Mm-hmm. Whatever you say." Kerry walked Lara out to the driveway, then waited until Lara was closing the car door before yelling, "Happy stalking!"

And Lara couldn't even pretend to be annoyed because it was the first time all afternoon she'd seen Kerry genuinely laugh.

Evan's house hadn't changed in the week since Lara had vacated the prem-ises.

The cute little white Jetta in the drive-way, though? With the sparkly pink heart sticker in the rear window? That was new.

For a moment Lara just sat and stared, too astonished to feel anything.

I should have known. He never

wanted my old, rusty, fur-coated station wagon. The second I gave up my spot in the garage, he filled the void with some sleek little sedan. Mr. People Person.

But wait. There was no reason to jump to conclusions. She could think of a million innocent explanations. Like . . . the VW probably belonged to Evan's . . . um . . . cleaning lady. Whom he had hired right after she moved out. And who came by to clean at seven o'clock on Friday evening. Or his sister. Who worked as an independent film producer in New York, and who would sooner shave her head than adorn any of her worldly belongings with a sparkly pink decal.

Lara pulled away from the curb as quickly as possible.

Her heart was still hammering as she rounded the corner, so she startled a bit when her cell phone rang. When she glanced at caller ID and saw the name of a local hospital, her pulse kicked up again.

"Is this Lara Madigan?" asked a very calm female voice.

"Yes, it is."

"You're Justine Madigan's daughter?"

Lara confirmed this and asked, "What's going on? Is she okay?"

"This is Jeannette Viteri. I'm on staff here at McDowell Medical Center. Your mother checked into the emergency room complaining of chest pains. She's undergoing a few tests right now, but I thought I should call and—"

"I'll be right there."

Chapter 13

"I'm *fine*." Justine barely glanced up from her BlackBerry when Lara appeared in her curtained-off portion of the bustling ER. "Go back to work."

Lara took one look at her mother's face and gasped, then clapped her hands over her mouth in a belated attempt to hide her shock. Justine always looked flawless. Her olive complexion was smooth and clear, her thick black hair was artfully layered, and her body was lithe and toned. Lara hadn't glimpsed her without lipstick in at least a decade.

So to see her mother like this—scowling and clad in an oversize, wrinkled blue hospital gown—was jarring. But even more alarming was her mother's face. Justine's cheeks and forehead were splotched with large, uneven patches of dark and light pigment. And this wasn't subtle discoloration; it was impossible to ignore.

"Oh my God," Lara finally forced out. "Mom, what happened?"

Justine heaved a weary sigh and put aside her phone. She looked Lara straight in the eye, defying her to glance away. "I'll tell you what happened. These so-called medical professionals have wasted an inordinate amount of time and resources and panicked you for no good reason. That's what happened."

"The good news is your mother's heart is fine." A nurse strode in and addressed them both with determined good cheer.

"I have costochondritis," Justine told Lara. "A simple inflammation of the cartilage over the rib cage. I had a few chest pains, but it wasn't a cardiac issue."

"We did an EKG and a chest X-ray just to make sure," the nurse added.

Justine picked up her phone and resumed clicking like a ten-year-old with a Game Boy. "May I go now, please?"

The nurse kept right on smiling. "Just as soon as we get the results of your blood work."

"So you're sure your heart's okay?" Lara sank onto the sheet next to Justine's feet.

"Couldn't be better. I have the blood pressure of a teenager," Justine boasted.

"That is not what the doctor said," the nurse corrected. "He said you're under way too much stress and you need to take a break, or you will have a true cardiac event. This is your body's way of warning you."

This was the part where a normal mother and daughter would hug, maybe even cry a little with relief. But Lara couldn't even get Justine's attention right now, let alone a tearful embrace. So she stayed at her post at the foot of the bed.

"What happened to your face?" As she asked this, she noticed that Justine's hair looked different, too, shinier and coarser than normal. "What's going on?"

Justine turned her head to one side, hunching her shoulder to shield her face from Lara's gaze. "I told you: I'm fine."

Lara couldn't stop staring at the discoloration on her mother's cheek. "But what causes costochon—whatever?"

"Nothing," Justine said firmly. "It's just a fluke."

"It's often stress-related," the nurse said.

"Mom." Lara hesitated, then reached across the starched white sheets and squeezed Justine's hand. Her mother's fingers felt cool and limp. "You have to cut back. You're literally working yourself to death."

Her mother snatched her hand away. "Don't tell me what to do."

"I'm not—"

"Her doctors have already told her what to do," the nurse said to Lara. "She's taking a leave of absence from her job, effective immediately."

"An extremely short leave of absence." Justine smoothed her hair, and the part line in the center shifted slightly. Was she wearing a *wig*? "Against my will. There's nothing wrong with me."

Guilt flooded through Lara. If she had just followed Justine's master plan, her mother wouldn't be lying here, suffering stress-related chest pains and worrying about how the salons would survive without her. Lara was supposed to be helping by now. Lara was supposed to be taking over.

Justine closed her eyes in a bid for patience. "I just want to get out of here."

"Your face," Lara whispered. "Tell me the truth. What's wrong?"

Justine's icy veneer shattered, and for a moment she looked lost and vulnerable. Then she turned away again, covering her cheeks with her hands. "Stop looking at me."

But Lara couldn't. She didn't recognize this woman at all.

All around them, Lara heard beeping and the squeak of rubber shoe soles against linoleum tile and the murmurings of other families getting on with their lives. Their little pocket of space was totally silent.

"Vitiligo," Justine said at last. "That's the official diagnosis. I've been to three dermatologists and an autoimmune disease specialist, and they all said the same thing."

Due to Justine's work schedule and their strained relationship, Lara didn't spend much face time with her mother. But it had been only three months since their last family dinner. "Was this going on the last time I saw you?"

"It was starting, yes. I was still able to cover it with makeup at that point."

"Why didn't you tell me you were having health problems?"

"It's a skin condition that means I have to spend the rest of my life getting stared at," Justine said sharply. "It doesn't affect my health in any other way. Allegedly."

Lara frowned. "Allegedly?"

"Vitiligo explains why my face looks like hell. It does not explain, however, why my hair started falling out."

"What did the doctors say about that?"

"They said it could be stress. Or it could be hormones. Or environmental factors. In other words, they have no idea, but they're exiling me from my own salons."

Lara took a moment to digest this. She couldn't imagine her mother outside the confines of Coterie. Justine's whole life was defined by her career. "So what happens now? Are you going to travel?"

Justine seemed disgusted by the mere suggestion. "No." She tugged up the shoulder of her hospital gown. "I'm going to go home and be ugly."

"Mom."

"Stop looking at me."

Lara did as she was told.

"Don't look at me, don't judge me, and don't pretend you have the vaguest idea what I'm going through. Now, I have important calls to make. Good-bye, Lara." Justine dismissed her with a tilt of her head.

"I'm not leaving."

"Yes, you are. I'll see you at home."

But Lara didn't see her mother at home. She heard Justine's car pull into the garage at midnight, but by the time she made her way down the long, echoing hallways, Justine had already barricaded herself in the master suite. So she rose with the sun on Saturday morning, hoping to coax her mother out with pancakes and fresh-squeezed mimosas, but Justine ignored all the knocks on the door.

Lara ate by herself, standing over the kitchen counter and tossing scraps to the dogs. Maverick, who had been fanatical about keeping Mr. Squirrel clamped in his jaws at all times since the big breakup, let go of the stuffed animal long enough to scarf down a few crumbs.

"It's okay, buddy," Lara assured him. "No one's ever gonna flush him again. Not on my watch." She had put Mr. Squirrel through several cycles in the washing machine and dryer, which had done nothing to improve his bedraggled appearance.

Since the morning was sunny and cool, she put on her sneakers, jeans, and a fleece hoodie and walked the mile or so up to Cherie Chadwick's house. After her training session with Eskie, she headed back down the hill a few blocks to meet with Kayla, the referral from the Real Housewife who had christened Lara the Dog Doyenne.

As she rounded the corner to Kensington Court, Lara spotted Ivory the Maltese tagging along next to an elderly woman walking her Scottie. Still no sign of the tiny white dog's owner, but Lara didn't have time to investigate; she was running a few minutes late as it was.

She double-checked the address as she arrived at her new client's home: another Spanish-style mansion, another lushly landscaped front lawn.

And another stunningly beautiful homeowner. A tall, lithe brunette opened the door when Lara rang the bell. Her shiny hair was pulled back in a low ponytail, and her makeup, manicure, and eyebrows were impeccable, even at this hour on a Saturday morning. Her tight pink tank top and gray yoga pants showcased a lean, muscular physique that was probably the product of years of dance or Pilates.

This is the kind of woman my mother wishes I could be, Lara thought.

"Are you Lara?" Her expression was simultaneously relieved and guilty. "Thank you so much for coming. I'm desperate."

Lara smiled. "I get that a lot."

"I'm Kayla Ramirez. And this"—she glanced back toward a snoring yellow lump on the stair landing—"is Roo." Kayla clapped her hands. "Roo! Wake up, Roo. Come here, buddy!"

Roo opened one eye, which Kayla rewarded with a display of enthusiasm worthy of a varsity cheerleader.

The house looked professionally decorated and white-glove clean. Every surface was gleaming, every vase and plant and framed wedding portrait expertly placed. Even the smells were inviting—a subtle blend of vanilla and cinnamon that made Lara think of sweet rolls fresh out of the oven.

At Kayla's urging, Roo finally got to his feet and lumbered down the stairs. He gave Lara's hand a desultory sniff, then collapsed back on the floor with a snort.

"I know he's overweight. I know." Kayla stared down at the tile floor. "We call him our yellow flabrador. But he's such a good dog, and he always seems so hungry."

"That's Labs for you." Lara crouched down to get a better look at the dog. "How old is he now?"

"Almost six."

"And how long has he been obese?"

Kayla flinched at the word, but there was no denying it. "About two years now, I guess. He was roly-poly even as a puppy, but really energetic. We used to send him to doggie day care to tire him out. As he got older and mellower, he wanted to lounge around on his bed all day, and we let him. It was such a relief after all the chewing and digging and barking and jumping. And now . . ." Kayla trailed off. "Please don't yell at me."

Lara looked up in surprise. "I'm not here to yell at you. I'm here to help you and Roo make some changes."

"I know it's unhealthy." Kayla hung her head in disgrace. "And I know it's my fault. But he just . . . I just . . ."

"Don't waste time and energy playing the blame game," Lara said firmly. "We're going to make a fresh start. You and I are going to come up with a plan of action together, but in the end, you're the one who will need to follow through."

"Absolutely." Kayla nodded, but Lara sensed a lack of resolve. She was starting to notice this pattern with wealthy clients: They wanted to call Lara in, write a check, and declare the problem solved. But Roo was going to have to lose weight the same way he'd gained it—slowly and steadily, with constant support from his owner.

"When's the last time he had a checkup?" Lara asked.

"Last week." Kayla straightened the hem of her tank top. "The vet gave me a stern talking-to. That's why I called you."

"Did your vet run any blood work?"

"I think they said they were doing a junior blood panel. Why do you ask?"

"The first thing I need to do is rule out thyroid problems or metabolic disorders." Lara stood up and got down to business. "Is he on any medication? Steroids like Prednisone?"

Kayla shook her head. "No, he's fit as a fiddle." She reached down to rub Roo's exposed belly. "My fat little fiddle."

"Okay, good." Lara dug a pen and notepad out of her bag. "Then let's get to work. How much are you feeding him right now?"

"Two cups of kibble. One cup in the morning and one cup at dinnertime." Kayla crossed her heart and hoped to die. "We used to sneak him a lot of treats and table food, but we've really cut back on that. At least, I have."

Lara glanced at Roo's monogrammed food bowl, which looked as though it would hold at least five cups. "May I see the food scoop, please?"

"Sure." Kayla opened the door to the pantry and pulled out a huge plastic cup. Big Gulp size.

"Well, here's your first problem. Your cup is way bigger than a cup." Lara asked Kayla to find a calibrated measuring cup, and they compared it with the oversize food scoop. "Also, he's got to start walking, but take it easy; nothing too strenuous. Keep it slow and short. For the first few weeks, every little bit of exercise will help. But weight loss is seventy percent about diet and only thirty percent about exercise."

"I'm aware." Kayla smiled wryly and spread her hands across her taut stomach. "I could probably teach a nutrition seminar at this point."

"So here's what we're going to do." Lara jotted everything down on the notepad. "I want you to give him a half a cup of kibble at every meal, mixed with pinto beans and brown rice."

"That's all?"

"Yep. You're going to feed him that for a month, supplemented with a daily multivitamin. After thirty days, we'll start adding cooked chicken, green beans, carrots, and peas."

Kayla looked hesitant. "So I shouldn't switch him over to low-cal dog food?"

"I'm not a big fan of low-cal kibble," Lara said. "I'd much rather you feed him whole foods. The key, though, is going to be feeding him the proper amount for his size and activity level."

"Portion control," Kayla murmured.

"Exactly. Labs only need two cups of food per day. Two and a half, max."

Kayla glanced at the measuring cup and wrung her hands. "I feel like you want me to starve him."

"That's why we're going to take this in baby steps," Lara said soothingly. "We aren't depriving him; we're trying to help him."

Kayla took a few steps back, crossing her arms.

"You look upset," Lara said.

"I'm sorry. I just . . ." Kayla knelt down next to Roo, and he rolled over. "When my husband and I started dating, I was a model. He likes me to look a certain way, and so do I. I know what I have to do to stay in shape—the stretching, the cardio, the free weights—and I do it. I go to the gym six days a week. I count calories. I eat clean. I've always been very disciplined, but I just can't bring myself to force all that on my poor boy." She and Roo shared a look of soulful compassion. "I can't ever indulge, and so I indulge the dog. And yes, I know how insane that sounds."

"It's not insane at all," Lara assured her. "If you understand how you two got into this pattern of behavior, it'll be much easier to figure out how you can get out."

Kayla laid one hand flat against Roo's well-padded rib cage. "I get what you're saying, and I'll give it a try. But I know how it feels to want one more bite, to be starving for it, and when he looks up at me with that sad, hopeful expression, well, I can't say no."

Lara mulled this over for a moment. "Here's an idea. Both of you can work on this together. Roo needs more discipline in his diet, and it sounds like you need less. What if you both have a treat every day? A tiny little cheat that no one will ever know about."

"I can't do that." Kayla's eyes widened. "If I have one sip of wine, I'll chug the whole glass. If I eat one bite of brownie, I have to eat the whole thing."

Lara was starting to understand the

psychological significance of the huge plastic kibble scoop.

"Okay," she said in her most calming, reasonable tone. "Then once a week, drink a whole glass of wine. Eat a brownie. Just try it for thirty days. And next month I'll come back and we'll see where we are."

Kayla's bravado gave way to visible fear. "I'll be as fat as Roo."

"From one brownie a week? I doubt that. In fact, I'll bet you that you won't gain a single pound."

Kayla nibbled her lower lip, her eyes worried.

Lara deliberately relaxed her posture and waited for her client to do the same. "All I can ask is that you try. I'm not telling you to start mainlining sugar and alter your lifestyle forever. I'm just asking you, both of you, to follow the program. If a month sounds overwhelming, let's start with a week. How about that? I'll come back next Monday and see how it's going."

"And I'll take him for a walk every day?"

"A *short* walk," Lara emphasized. "Just around the block once or twice."

"I can do that." Kayla took a deep breath. "Maybe I'll try to get my husband to come with me."

"Great idea. You're all in this together."

Kayla brightened. "He's not much of a gourmet cook, but he can probably handle pinto beans and potatoes. And then, next weekend, we can all go to McDonald's and give my baby a Big Mac."

Lara laughed. "I was thinking more like plain nonfat yogurt."

"*I* still get a chocolate croissant, though, right?"

"Absolutely."

Lara felt good about the paycheck she pocketed on her way out the door, but she felt even better about Roo's prospects. The high of a successful consult was addictive. No one was criticizing her or demanding that she turn her whole personality inside out. She had done her job, she had earned the appreciation, and she was a beacon of hope to flabradors everywhere.

On her way back to Justine's house,

she crossed paths yet again with Ivory. The spunky Maltese gave her a friendly little yip as she trotted past.

"That's right." Lara put a little extra spring into her step. "I'm the Dog Doyenne, and don't you forget it."

Chapter 14

"Mom?" Late Sunday morning, Lara rapped softly on the massive double doors that closed off the master suite from the rest of the world. "Are you awake?"

She waited, breath held, ears straining for any sound of life from within. But there was nothing except the steady, murmuring drone from the TV.

"Mom?" She knocked again, louder this time, and tried the doorknob. Locked.

This was getting ridiculous, and also kind of creepy. Knowing that Justine was physically present in the house, but never seeing her, was starting to freak Lara out. Even the dogs picked up their pace when they scuttled past Justine's doorway, as if a scaly, taloned hand might dart out and snatch them.

Plus, Justine had never been the reclusive type. She thrived on energy and chaos. She loved to charge into a crisis and start giving orders and implementing strategies.

So Lara grabbed her cell phone and dialed.

On the fifth ring her mother picked up. "Hello?"

"Hey, Mom. It's Lara. Remember me? Your daughter? I'm right outside your bedroom door."

"What do you want?" Justine's voice sounded thick and throaty, as if she had just woken up and was still getting her bearings.

"Just to chat. May I come in?"

There was a long pause.

"Mom?"

"Yes?"

Lara rested her fingers on the knob. "Let me in."

There was another long pause; then at last the knob twisted and the door swung inward. Her mother stood in the shadows, her arms folded tightly over a pair of wrinkled turquoise silk pajamas. The room was so dark that it took Lara a few moments to determine that Justine's face was devoid of makeup, and her hair, once so thick she'd had to shape it with thinning shears, now appeared unwashed and sparse, exposing pale flashes of scalp. There were dark circles under her eyes and faint creases around her mouth, eyes, and forehead.

Lara couldn't hide her pity and dismay, and Justine bristled in response. She stood up taller and fanned out her fingers to cover the uneven patches of pigment on her face. "See? This is why I can't leave the house. That's exactly how I *don't* want people to look at me."

"It's not your face," Lara said, so quickly that she knew she sounded insincere. "It's just . . . you're wearing pajamas, and it's almost noon."

"So what?" Justine started back toward her king-size bed, which was heaped with fluffy pillows and a blue silk duvet.

At times like this, Lara desperately wished she had a sibling. She didn't know how worried she should be, and it would be so helpful to have someone to check in with. Someone to say, "Oh, you know how she is. She'll bounce back" or "I've never seen her like this before. You're absolutely right to be concerned."

Justine was intensely private about her personal life—or lack thereof—and Lara knew that any attempt to nudge her mother toward therapy or group support would be met with scorn.

The only person who might have a frame of reference for this kind of situation was Gil, but she could never tell her father about this. Justine would consider that the ultimate betrayal. As far as Gil was concerned, Justine was bulletproof. He still spoke about his ex-wife with a combination of awe and intimidation.

"How may I help you?" Justine tucked her feet under the covers and reclined against the pillows.

"I wanted to ask how I may help you, actually." Lara swept out her arms to indicate the cold, dark, stale-smelling suite. "This is not healthy."

"You're here for a pep talk? Spare me. I'm taking a nap."

"You've been napping since Friday. I know you're, um, making some big adjustments right now, but you shouldn't be holed up here in the dark."

"The doctors said UV exposure's not good for my face."

"That means you put on sunscreen and a hat. No one advised to you to spend all day, every day, wasting away watching . . ." Lara squinted at the TV screen. "What are you watching?"

"*Sopranos* marathon. I never got to see this series when it originally aired, you know."

"No wonder you're depressed."

Justine lifted her chin. "I'm not depressed. I don't get depressed."

Lara shot her a sidelong glance. "I just Googled *clinical depression* and you've got every symptom: constant sleepiness, social withdrawal, loss of appetite, irritability. . . ."

"Irritability is my natural state." Justine paused the TV, then dropped the remote control as if the effort of holding it exhausted her. "Did you barge in here just to play armchair psychologist?"

"I'm trying to help. I'm worried about you."

"Worry about yourself. I'm perfectly capable of taking care of myself and I always will be." Justine's voice rose at the end of this statement, as if to imply that Lara's future wasn't nearly so secure.

Lara ignored this barb and regarded her mother with compassion. "When's the last time you ate?"

Justine narrowed her eyes. "Don't you talk to me that way. Don't patronize me. This is my house, I'm a grown woman, and if I feel like sleeping all damn weekend, I will. Mind your own business."

Lara flinched at the hostility in her mother's voice, but she didn't back down. "Well, I'm making lunch, so you can either tell me what you'd like, or you can have a peanut butter sandwich."

"I detest peanut butter, and you know it."

Lara did know it. Justine's taste ran more toward sashimi and scallops.

"Well, my cooking skills are pretty much limited to PB and J, cereal out of the box, pancakes, and pasta. Take your pick."

"Get out and stay out." Justine pointed imperiously at the door. "I'm not one of your charity cases. Save your Mother Teresa complex for your dogs."

"It's not a Mother Teresa complex. It's lunch. So pancakes, pasta, or peanut butter—what'll it be?"

"I haven't touched pasta in ages, but it does sound tempting," Justine admitted. "That's one thing about *The Sopranos*—all the characters are constantly gorging on carbohydrates."

"Perfect. I have an hour before I have to leave for the adoption fair. Let's go make spaghetti."

"Cooking? On the stove?" Justine seemed baffled by this idea. "Call Nick's and order takeout."

"No, Mom. We can cook. You have a

fully stocked kitchen with restaurant-grade appliances."

"Purely for aesthetics and resale value. I don't even know how to turn on the stove."

"Between the two of us, I'm sure we can figure it out."

"I'm comfortable right here."

Lara put her hands on her hips. "You can't stay in bed all day. You need to get out of those pajamas and put on real clothes. And while I'm out in the kitchen, I want you to take a shower." She opened up the plantation shutters to let in some sunlight. "Oh, and change the channel. All these mob whackings can't be good for your mental state."

Justine hit PLAY on the remote and jacked up the volume. "You know, last time I looked, you didn't sign my paychecks. You can't tell me what to do."

"It's for your own good." Lara walked into the huge mirrored bathroom and turned on the shower. "Get cracking."

When she returned twenty minutes later, carrying two servings of salad and marinara-sauced linguine, she found Justine combing out her wet hair. She had swapped her pajamas for a dark green cowl-neck sweater and black drawstring cotton pants that looked suspiciously like sleepwear.

Lara leveled her gaze. "I thought we agreed the pajamas had to go."

"These aren't pajamas," Justine said. "It's loungewear."

"You are so stubborn."

"You mean I'm a good negotiator."

Lara set the tray on the nightstand next to the bed, then handed her mother a white cloth napkin, a fork, and a crystal goblet of ice water.

Her mother wrinkled her nose at the water. "I'd prefer a lovely glass of Cabernet, please."

"Before noon? I don't think so."

Justine took a tiny bite of pasta, then made a face. "Is this *jarred* tomato sauce?"

Lara nodded. "I couldn't find any of Shelly's homemade sauce in the freezer."

"Did you grate the Parmesan yourself, at least?"

"Yes, your majesty."

Justine set aside her lunch and flopped back against the pillows. "I know what you're thinking. I know that to you I seem vain and superficial."

Lara didn't reply. She sat motionless, hoping that her silence would encourage her mother to keep going.

"My entire life, people have depended on me. For their salary, of course, but also for direction. I have the answers. I make the hard decisions. And I'm comfortable with that; it's part of being a business owner. But now . . . My face is who I am. It's my identity. And now it's ruined."

"It is not who you are," Lara argued. "What about all those old sayings: 'Beauty is only skin deep'? 'Beauty is in the eye of the beholder'?"

"All said by people not making their living in the beauty industry. It doesn't bother me if people hate me. I couldn't care less how my employees feel about me as long as they respect me. But the pity, the stares, and the whispers, and the way I was being 'handled' . . ." She shook her head. "I'd almost rather stay locked up in this empty house. My cardiologist gave me an excuse to be weak, and I took it."

"The last word I would ever use to describe you is *weak*. You're so strong, it's scary. And your house isn't empty," Lara pointed out. "You've got your unmarried, underemployed adult daughter crashing with you."

"Yes. That *is* a comfort."

Lara saw her opening and made her move. "And since I'm here—very temporarily, I might add—we should do something together."

Justine nodded at the linguine and the television. "We are doing something together."

"No, I mean really *do* something. Ooh, I know. We could go to a movie."

Justine shuddered. "No. I can't abide movie theaters. The sticky floors, the constant ringing of cell phones . . ."

"Okay, we could go play tennis. We'll wait until the afternoon sun goes down."

Justine glanced down at her legs as if doubting their ability to support her. "I don't have the energy for tennis today."

"Once you get out there, you might surprise yourself."

Justine sipped her water. "I've already

asked you once not to patronize me. If I have to ask again, this lunch is over."

Lara had no choice but to play her trump card. "I'll go shopping with you."

This caught Justine's attention. "Well, well, well. You *are* desperate to bond."

"Yep. This is it—your big chance to make me over. I can't promise I'll buy anything, but I'll try on whatever you pick out."

Justine considered this offer for a fraction of a second, then shook her head. "I cannot go shopping right now. People will recognize me at all the stores that matter: Neiman Marcus, Barneys, Saks."

Lara held up both hands. "Easy, there. I was thinking more along the lines of Old Navy and Target."

Justine stared at her as though she had suddenly started speaking Swahili.

"Fine, I give up. You win. We won't bond." Lara shoved a bite of salad into her mouth and crunched furiously. "But I'll have you know that they have some really cute stuff at Target."

Justine pointed to the drawer of her nightstand. "Open that for me, please."

Lara opened the drawer with some trepidation to find, where other women traditionally stashed celebrity tabloids or naughty bedroom toys, a sleek navy blue laptop computer.

She handed this to Justine, who powered it up and slid on a pair of stylish eyeglasses. "All right," Justine murmured, clicking open the Web browser. "Neiman Marcus it is. Let's start with denim."

"No, no, no." Lara shook her head. "I said I'd go shopping with you—as in leave the house. I never agreed to online shopping."

"You didn't specify method or venue." This semantic victory seemed to energize Justine. "It's time to bring your style into the twenty-first century."

"What are you looking at? Mom, no. I need jeans that I can train dogs in," Lara protested. "I don't want my ass crack hanging out every time I'm leaning over teaching Eskie to stack."

"How about these?" Justine pointed out a pair of dark-wash skinny jeans.

Lara glanced at the price tag. *"A hundred and eighty-five dollars?* If you're going to spend that kind of money, I'd rather you just write the rescue group a check."

"This is exactly why I don't send you money for Christmas or your birthday. You never buy anything for yourself. You'd rather run around in those tragic boot-cut rags like a ranch hand and spend your last penny so some flea-bitten husky off the street can get his teeth cleaned. At some point, all this selflessness stops being noble and crosses the line into stupidity. Most daughters would love it if their mothers offered to buy them a whole new ward-robe. What's wrong with you? Who turns down free designer jeans?"

"I'm sorry." Lara hung her head. She knew that this disconnect between them wasn't just her mother's fault. Both of them had become so defensive that they couldn't share anything. Bonding would somehow be an admission of weakness.

Justine was still staring at her. "If I can't go out and you refuse to shop on-line, then what do you suggest we do?"

Lara glanced at the laptop and said,

"We could play a game. You could download Solitaire or Minesweeper, or even Scrabble."

"Scrabble." Justine's deep freeze thawed a degree or two. "Remember when we played up in Paul's cabin in Sedona?"

During the long, brutally hot Phoenix summers of Lara's childhood, Justine had exploited every social connection she had to escape the heat. She and Lara would spend a week in San Diego at a client's condo, or three days in Tucson at a hair coloring seminar. One of Justine's early mentors at the salon, Paul, had invited them to his summer house in Sedona. The cabin had spotty phone service and no TV at all, just a drawer full of battered old board games. Lara and Justine spent their days hiking and swimming, and in the evenings they played marathon games of Scrabble. Justine had never let Lara win—"The real world won't mollycoddle you, and your mother shouldn't, either." She beat her soundly every time, but Lara always demanded one more rematch.

Lara nodded. "I've gotten a lot better

since then. I can spell words besides *dog* and *it*."

"After all those years of outrageously overpriced private schools, I should hope so."

"Here." Lara commandeered the computer and found the Web site. "We'll sign you up for an account and I'll start a game. We can play on our phones, even. We don't have to be in the same room."

"If you insist. I just hope I don't humiliate you too badly." Justine took off her glasses and set them on the nightstand. "I look forward to our first game. Right after I take another nap."

"But you just got up."

"Good night."

"But you—"

"Close the curtains on your way out, would you? And please keep the dogs quiet." Justine burrowed under the covers.

Lara gave up, closed the curtains, and turned off the lights. For now, she would let sleeping mothers lie. She pressed a few buttons on her phone, studied the Scrabble tiles on her virtual board, and started a game with the only word she could come up with: WELL.

She waited for Justine's countermove. And waited and waited and waited.

Thirty minutes later, as Lara was en route to the adoption fair, her phone buzzed. When she stopped for a red light, she checked her messages and saw that her mother had built a longer, higher-scoring word off of WELL: WAVING.

Game on.

Chapter 15

"We want that one." A middle-aged couple gazed down at Lara, both of them smiling with anticipation.

Lara managed to maintain a straight face, but Kerry broke into a coughing fit. Weekend adoption fairs were always a lot of work, and today had been especially hectic. They'd arrived at the outdoor plaza at noon with all the dogs in tow. By twelve thirty, it was drizzling, and by the time they put up a makeshift awning over the X-pen holding the dogs, the grass was slick and muddy. Lara was damp, cold, and depressed. Kerry, in the throes of a massive maternal anxiety attack, was checking her text messages and dialing her mother for baby updates every two minutes. No matter how many times Lara urged her friend to pack it in and go home, Kerry refused.

"I'm not abandoning you," Kerry insisted. "I refuse to give in to the tidal wave of bonding hormones flooding my brain."

"Cut yourself some slack," Lara said. "You just had a baby a week ago."

"Everyone says I need a break from the baby—my mom, Richard, his mom . . ."

"You're not getting a break; you're having a nervous breakdown. Two hours away from Cynthia is plenty. Skedaddle."

"Never." Kerry got a steely glint in her eye. "I made a commitment to these dogs, and I'm keeping it." She paused. "Unless I get engorged and have to go pump. Then all bets are off."

The pit bull puppies had found homes within the first hour, but since then they hadn't had a single serious potential adopter.

Until now.

"Which one?" Lara prayed that the couple on the other side of the folding table wasn't talking about the dog she thought they were talking about.

The wife let go of her husband's hand and pointed. "That cute little white fluff ball right there."

"Ah." Lara took a breath. "That would be Mullet."

The wife turned to her husband and put her hand on his arm. "Don't worry; we can change his name."

"*Her* name, actually. She's a five-year-old Shih Tzu mix, and she's one of our special-needs dogs."

"She's cute as a button." The wife crouched down and waggled her fingers through the wire X-pen in an attempt to coax Mullet to come over. Mullet, already outraged by the indignity of being jailed with other dogs so clearly inferior to herself, curled up even tighter and ignored this overture from an inconsequential human.

"She's young and relatively healthy,

but she came to our rescue group with a few medical issues," Lara continued. "She's almost blind in one eye, she hates having her paws touched, and those bare patches on her skin may never grow in."

"Blind?" The woman melted. "That's so sad. She must have been abused."

"We don't know her history," Lara said, exchanging a look with Kerry. "And in cases where we don't know for sure, we try not to speculate. It's possible her vision problems were congenital, or due to an unresolved infection. In any case, she gets around just fine, and it's important not to baby her or let her get away with bad behavior."

The woman wasn't even pretending to listen. She was too busy oohing and aahing. "Poor widdle baby. She just needs someone to love her."

Mullet lifted one corner of her mouth in a silent snarl.

Lara gave up trying to reason with the wife and appealed to the husband. "Tell me a bit about your situation. Why have you decided it's time to add a new dog to your family?"

He scratched his neatly trimmed gray beard and inclined his head toward his better half. "Pam's a real animal lover. Cats, rabbits, horses, you name it. And we had a dog for a long time, a little fluffy one like, uh, Mullet here."

"My precious Petty." The woman's eyes went misty. "What a doll. That dog could read my mind, I tell you. She went into kidney failure and we had to put her down, and I swore up and down that I was done with dogs forever."

The husband winked at Lara. "That was two months ago."

Pam waved his comment away. "Cats just aren't the same. And this little cutie, there's something about her that reminds me of Petty."

When Pam leaned over the top of the pen to pet Mullet's ear, Mullet pulled away with a haughty headshake. Then the dog leaned forward, tongue out, but instead of licking Pam . . .

"She spat on me!" Pam snatched her hand away.

"Don't be ridiculous," her husband said. "Dogs can't spit."

Mullet flounced over to the other side of the pen and settled back down.

"Total brat," Kerry muttered.

"Tell me about Petty," Lara urged. "What was special about her?"

Pam hesitated for a moment, her smile turning sad and nostalgic. "Everything. She was so smart and funny. She could do all kinds of tricks. But mostly, you know, she was my snugglebug. She watched TV with me, kept me company while I crocheted, listened to me."

"So you're looking for a cuddly dog that enjoys social stimulation."

The couple nodded in unison.

Lara turned to Kerry for backup, but Kerry was suddenly preoccupied with refilling the portable water bowl. "Here's the deal. Mullet can be a bit . . . aloof. She's very slow to warm up, and she's not much of a cuddler. If you want a true-blue sweetheart, though, you might want to consider Zsa Zsa." Lara clapped her hands and the poodle immediately trotted over, eyes sparkling and tail wagging.

Pam didn't even glance at the larger dog. "Oh, I know what I want. I've had lots of Shih Tzus over the years. They can be temperamental, but I adore the breed. Poodles just can't compare."

Her husband regarded Lara with a steady, open countenance. "We'll give her a good home. I can give you references, if you want. Our vet, our groomer—they'll tell you."

Lara shoved the wet, curling tendrils of hair out of her face and went in search of Kerry.

"This perfectly nice, normal couple is asking to adopt Mullet. What do I do here?"

Kerry shrugged. "Let 'em fill out an application and schedule a home visit."

"But they're not the right match for her. You saw the way she was giving them the stinkeye."

Kerry put down the water dish and stepped back as the dogs swarmed in to drink. "Let me ask you something: Why did you make me drag Mullet out here if you have no intention of letting anyone adopt her?"

Lara floundered. "It's not that I have no intention of letting anyone adopt her, but she needs a *very* special owner. I

honestly don't think these two are prepared for Mullet and her mind games.
They're too nice. Too normal. She'll end
up right back on our doorstep in two
weeks. You know she will."

"Oh, give them a chance." Kerry
rubbed her eyes. "And I'm not just saying that because I'm overwhelmed and
sleep-deprived and Mullet keeps barking right in my ear two minutes after I
finally get to sleep."

"Uh-huh."

"Mullet gets a family; I get peace and
quiet. Win-win, baby."

"Ooh." Lara glanced at her cell phone.
"It's my turn to make a word." She explained about her online game with Justine.

"And that's your idea of mother-
daughter bonding?" Kerry marveled.
"Each of you in your separate corners,
trying to beat each other at Scrabble?"

Lara nodded. "Fun, free, and educa-
tional to boot."

"Good Lord. No wonder you prefer
dogs to people."

"People have their advantages," Lara
allowed, wincing as she saw her moth-

er's latest move: BOXY, with a double-word score. "Dogs aren't very good at spelling. You'll hardly ever see them playing *queenly* for a triple-word score. Well, maybe a Border collie."

"So what's the verdict?" Pam called from the other side of the X-pen. "Can we take her?"

"I'm getting the application forms together right now," Lara replied.

"Oh, thank you. Thank you. I know I'm the one she's been waiting for." Pam knelt down and called to Mullet.

Mullet sauntered across the pen until she was directly in front of Pam. Then she pivoted, showed Pam her backside, and used her hind legs to rake the ground, splattering mud and grass in Pam's face.

Pam gasped and reeled back.

"I'm so sorry." Kerry was right there with a roll of paper towels.

"Don't take it personally." Lara scooped Mullet up in one arm and gave the little hellion a warning look. "As I told you, she's slow to warm up."

Zsa Zsa, sensing Pam's distress,

nosed her hand and gazed up at her with compassionate *talk to me* eyes.

"Zsa Zsa is our nurturer," Lara said. "And she's a perfect lady. She would never kick mud at you."

"Never," Kerry agreed. "In fact, I've caught her cleaning the other dogs' paws."

Pam wiped the dirt off her face while her husband gave Zsa Zsa a little pat. Zsa Zsa pressed her head into his palm and closed her eyes.

"I like her," he declared.

"Well. She's bigger than my other dogs, but she does seem sweet." Pam turned her attention to the poodle while Mullet snorted with discontent in Lara's grasp.

"Don't let the long legs fool you. Zsa Zsa's a lapdog in disguise," Lara assured them. "She'll follow you anywhere. You can even let her off leash, and she won't wander."

Pam hesitated, still shaken from Mullet's callous dismissal.

Zsa Zsa dropped into a sit-stay, nose up and ears forward. She lifted one paw in an offer to shake.

Pam knelt in the wet grass, opened the gate to the pen, and threw her arms around the dog. Zsa Zsa rested her snout on Pam's shoulder.

"Hey, what about me?" demanded the husband. "She's my dog, too!"

Lara felt the unmistakable zing of a match well made. She could practically hear the click of puzzle pieces snapping into place.

She stepped back, dusted off her hands, and let the newfound soul mates have a little alone time. "My work here is done."

As she drove back to Mayfair Estates, still basking in the glow of success, her phone rang. Her warm fuzzies turned ice-cold when she saw the name on caller ID: Evan.

She'd been assuring herself for the past two weeks that she didn't care if she never heard from him again, but her nervous system told a different story— suddenly she was sweaty, short of breath, and surging with adrenaline.

She made herself wait a few rings before answering with a cool "Hello?"

"Lara? This is Evan."

She paused a few beats. "How are you?"

"I'm good." He didn't have to sound *so* chipper and energetic.

"Glad to hear it."

"So listen. I . . ." He cleared his throat. "I packed up the rest of your stuff, and I wanted to know when you could stop by to get it."

The nonchalance with which he delivered this blow stunned her. "You packed everything up?"

"Yeah. I went through the closets and the drawers and boxed up everything of yours I could find. All the dog toys, too."

She struggled to recover her composure. "So you opted not to flush them?" She managed to sound as casual as he did. "I'm impressed at your self-control."

"It wasn't self-control," he shot back. "I'm just too cheap to call the plumber again."

"Ah. My mistake."

"So do you want your stuff or not?" he asked, pressing her.

"Yes, I do. Why don't I just swing by Monday morning and let myself in after you've gone to work? I think that would best for all involved."

"No," he said, a bit defensively. "That's no good. I changed the locks."

"You did? Would you mind telling me why?" Her face burned at the memory of her little drive-by last week. Maybe he really did think she was stalking him.

He ignored her question and said, "What time are you working on Monday? I can leave the boxes on the front porch and you can pick them up on your way home."

"I'll be there at six thirty."

"Great."

"Great. See you . . ." Lara trailed off. "Well, I guess I won't see you."

"Okay." Evan sounded distracted. "Bye."

And with that, she was dismissed. She pressed the phone to her ear, furious at him for being able to detach so quickly and furious at herself for not being able to do the same. As she tried to pull herself together, she realized that Evan hadn't hung up the phone. She could hear rustling and what sounded like splashing in a pool on the other end of the line.

For a moment she thought he might be having second thoughts, too. Second thoughts and regrets and reluctance to let go. She parted her lips to confess, "I miss you."

Then she heard Evan's voice, distant but perfectly clear: "All right, honey, that's taken care of. Let's go get some dinner."

Chapter 16

Lara took the dogs on an extra-long walk, and, after a fitful night of tossing and turning and seething, took Eskie on another challenging climb the next morning.

"I will kill him," she snapped into her cell phone. *"Kill him."*

"Don't kill him." Kerry tried to make her see reason. "I'm in no condition to be a star witness in your homicide trial. Tell you what—you can kill him after I lose the baby weight and Cynthia starts sleeping through the night. Deal?"

"Dumping all my stuff on the front

porch instead of dealing with me face-to-face? And making a big point of telling me he changed the locks? Like I'm stalking him? Ha! He *wishes* I were stalking him." As she headed back toward Cherie's house, Lara stomped right past Ivory without even saying hello. Ivory tossed her head and yipped indignantly. "Forget the engagement ring—I should have flushed his precious Swiss watch. Hit him where it hurts. I should have flushed his *Wrath of Khan* poster signed by William Shatner."

Kerry gasped. "His what?"

"Oh yes. He was a major Trekkie in high school. Used to go to the conventions and everything. And you know what? I loved him anyway! I accepted him for who he is!" Lara stopped to stretch her calf muscles and pour Eskie a drink from her water bottle. "Honestly, I'm gone for two weeks and he's calling somebody else 'honey'?"

"It's just a rebound," Kerry said.

"Whatever. I don't care. In fact, I hope the two of them are very happy together. I hope they get married. I hope he re-gifts the toilet ring to her and she wears it for the next fifty years."

"I'm so glad you're not bitter."

"I'm too busy to be bitter." Lara tipped her head back, inhaled the fresh mountain air, and went over her schedule. "I'm squeezing in a quick training session with Eskie right now, and then I have to drop by to check on Roo—"

"Roo?"

"The flabrador."

"Oh, right. Your personal training client."

"Down half a pound from last week, thank you very much."

"I think you're on to something with this dog diet plan," Kerry said. "You seriously could make millions on a late-night infomercial for canine fitness."

"Then I have to meet a new potential client, and then I have lunch with a vet clinic manager from my real job. But I'll drop by your place with dinner, if you want. Shall we say seven?"

"No, no. I'm good. Richard's back in town today and all the mothers are departing."

"Thank God. So you guys finally get to settle into a normal family routine?"

"Yeah, for about forty-eight hours. Richard's leaving for Atlanta on Wednesday." Lara could hear the strain in Kerry's voice.

"Well, don't worry. Auntie Lara will come by to babysit so you can get a shower and a dog walk."

"You're terrified of this baby," Kerry pointed out.

"So are you."

"Good point," Kerry agreed. "See you Wednesday."

For the rest of the morning, in between working with Eskie, congratulating Kayla on Roo's progress, and driving the five blocks to the home of her potential client, Lara exchanged a flurry of Scrabble moves with her mother.

CARMINES

FEZ

ZING

QI

The speed of Justine's responses confirmed Lara's suspicions that her mother was still holed up in her bedroom, probably with the shades drawn. After thirty years of racing ahead at top speed, Justine had finally hit the wall. Lara knew that this behavior was unhealthy, that it was the tipping point for a long, dark slide into deeper depression. But she also knew that Justine wouldn't come out until she was good and ready, and no amount of coaxing, guilt, or "tough love" could change that. No matter how tough Lara might be, Justine would always be tougher.

Depressed or not, Justine was currently dominating the Scrabble game. Lara trailed by almost seventy-five points.

She rearranged her letter tiles on the little screen of her smartphone and tried to rally with the highest-scoring word she could muster: GRIFTER.

At first glance, the house on Collingsworth Circle seemed to blend in with all the other spacious Spanish-style mansions. The front lawn was well maintained, the stucco and paving stones spotless. But Lara sensed something unusual—she couldn't put her finger on it until she noticed the ornate brass door knocker in the shape of a Sphinx head.

When she rang the bell, a chorus of unearthly howls emanated from within. It sounded like a pack of werewolves were having an ultimate fighting competition in there.

The howling stopped as suddenly as it had started, and the door swung inward to reveal a middle-aged matron with unruly brown curls and kind hazel eyes.

Lara offered up a handshake as she introduced herself.

"The Dog Doyenne. We've heard so much about you." The woman beckoned her inside. "Welcome. I'm Helen Years."

As she stepped into the foyer, Lara nodded at the door knocker. "That's lovely. Is it an antique?"

"Indeed it is. Dates back to Regency-era London." Helen looked delighted to share this information. "A bit of a splurge, I admit, but I just adore it. I've never understood the feminine obsession with shoes or handbags, but I can't resist Regency artifacts. Everybody has her vice, I suppose."

Though Mrs. Years was dressed stylishly in a cranberry blouse and black pants, her interior decorating tastes seemed to run more toward petticoats and pelisses. Looking around the living room, Lara felt as though she'd been transported back in time. Oil paintings hung next to brocade draperies, and small urns and statues crowded every available shelf. A large harp rested in one corner, and a small wooden instrument with ivory keys held a place of honor by the front window.

"Is that a piano?" Lara asked.

"Pianoforte," Helen replied.

"Wow, it's beautiful. Is that also an antique?"

"Technically, yes, but of course it's been restored. Some of the woodwork is very recent. My husband and I are Jane Austen enthusiasts. Jane-ites, if you will." Helen looked a tad defensive. "I know that seems odd to many people."

Lara shrugged. "Hey, I spent my entire paycheck last month on eye surgery for a dog named Mullet who hates my guts. I'm in no position to judge anybody else's hobbies."

"Well, not everyone shares your tolerance. My husband and I don't run in the same social circles as most of our neighbors—the country club circuit just isn't our cup of tea—and we've gotten a few cutting remarks over the years. This home was custom-built to our precise specifications. The exterior, of course, had to comply with the homeowner association standards. But the interior was mine to do with as I pleased, and I may have gotten a bit carried away. I wanted to capture the essence of a stately manor, like Pemberley or Delaford."

Lara nodded, trying to keep up.

"Those are the country estates of Mr. Darcy of *Pride and Prejudice* and Colonel Brandon of *Sense and Sensibility*," explained the tall, lanky man walking up behind Helen. He offered a slight bow, then a hearty handshake. "Frank Years."

Lara returned his smile. Everyone

jumped as another series of loud howls erupted down the halls.

"And that would be the dogs," Helen said with a sigh. "Frank, release the hounds."

Frank headed back down the hall, and a moment later Lara heard the *snick* of a door latch and the scrabble of claws against marble as two perfectly matched dogs hurtled toward her.

She braced for impact as the pair leapt and slobbered with pure, unadulterated joy.

"Off!" Helen cried, her tone high and pleading. "Off, off, off!"

The dogs ignored her and continued to accost Lara, nudging her hand for pats and banging their tails against her legs.

"Frederic, Elfrida," Frank said, his voice low and firm. Both dogs backed off slightly, still beaming up at Lara with wagging tails and glistening tongues. "We named them after two of the characters in Jane Austen's juvenilia," he explained. "*Elizabeth* and *Darcy* seemed too obvious."

"They're gorgeous," Lara said, admir-

ing their playful brown eyes, well-mus-
cled haunches, and glossy black, white,
and tan coats. "And very sweet."

"They're"—Helen cleared her throat—
"exuberant. Their energy simply knows
no bounds."

"How old are they?"

"Thirteen months."

Lara nodded. "Well, they'll mellow
with age."

"When?" Helen pressed.

"Um, in about six or seven years."
Lara had to laugh at Helen's horrified
expression. "I assume they're purebreds?"

"Oh yes," Frank assured her. "Fine
English hounds, just like Sir John Mid-
dleton's pack of hunting dogs."

"*Sense and Sensibility* again," Helen
whispered.

"Sherry and sport, that's what makes
a man." Frank planted his hands on his
hips, as though about to don a scarlet
coat and saddle his steed for a hunting
party.

"Well." Lara's eyebrows shot up. "I'm
not sure that I would consider foxhunt-

ing a *sport*, but it certainly required great stamina on the part of the dogs."

Helen reached over and patted Lara's arm reassuringly. "He doesn't actually hunt, dear. Though I'm sure if the home-owner association allowed it, he'd build stables in the backyard and bring in a team of Royal Hanoverian horses."

"Don't you start with me, Helen." Frank's voice held a note of warning.

Lara broke in. "Here's the deal: fox-hounds are very persistent and high-energy dogs, and while that's a big as-set in the field, it can be a bit of a problem if they're indoors all day."

"I told him." Helen threw up her hands. "I tried to make him see reason. 'We live in the suburbs,' I said. 'Get a pug,' I said."

"A pug!" Frank recoiled in disgust. "Like Lady Bertram in *Mansfield Park*! What kind of sissified fop do you take me for?"

"Pugs were very popular in Jane's day." Helen referred to the author as though she were a frequent dinner guest. "Pugs, Dalmatians, bulldogs. But no. He had to spend thousands of dollars on not one but two ungovernable English foxhound puppies, all in the name of masculine puffery."

"A few thousand dollars is a drop in the bucket compared to what you've spent on historically accurate dresses and jewelry," her husband retorted. "How many wide-brimmed bonnets have you specially commissioned? How many butterfly brooches and amber crosses and even diamond and emerald earbobs, when we both know that they were considered vulgar among the gentry?"

"My diamond and emerald earbobs have never gotten a complaint letter from the Mayfair Estates HOA," Helen shot back.

Lara was trying to figure out how to politely excuse herself when Frederic and Elfrida began to bay. The howls echoed off the high ceilings and the polished floor. Lara could have sworn she felt her bones actually vibrating.

The bickering ceased as Helen clapped her hands over her ears. Lara reached over, grabbed the dogs' collars, and gave each a swift sideways

tug. The dogs stopped baying and resumed panting and wagging their tails.

"Why must they do that?" Helen's
face remained twisted into a wince.

"What seems to set them off?" Lara
asked. "Tension? Arguments?"

"Everything." Frank shook his head in
despair. "The doorbell ringing. The clat-
ter of their food bowls. The recycling
truck passing by. The phone ringing."

"The TV," Helen added. "The alarm
clock. The sound of the bathroom fan."

"So it's probably just stress relief,"
Lara concluded. "It's self-rewarding for
them to howl."

"And it's going to get them banished
from the neighborhood." Frank's face
slackened into a weary frown. "I know it
was folly to buy them. I wasn't thinking
of their happiness; I was thinking of my
own. Jane certainly would not approve."

"But they're still young," Helen said.
"I'm sure they'll be very happy roaming
a ranch somewhere." She turned to
Lara, hopeful. "Perhaps you know
someone with a lot of acreage?"

Lara considered her response very

carefully. She looked at Helen, then looked at Frank, and said, "Let me ask you something. Do you *like* your dogs?"

Frank didn't hesitate. "Very much. I know they have their faults, but they're loyal and they wouldn't harm a fly."

She turned to Helen, who grumbled, "I'd like them a great deal more if they'd stop driving me deaf and insane. I'm trying to launch my own Jane Austen newsletter, and I need uninterrupted time to work."

Lara gave up on Helen and focused on Frank. "We can absolutely work with Frederic and Elfrida, but they need a job. You and I need to find a way to fulfill their instinct to work the field."

Frank's face lit up. "You're suggesting I go ahead with the stables and the horses?"

"No! I'm suggesting that the Regency era is about to collide with the real world. One of the vets I know was just telling me about a new urban sport: scent work. The dogs learn to identify certain smells and track them through buildings or cars. But one of you"—she shot Frank a pointed look—"will have to slgn on as handler and complete the training with them."

"Urban scent work." Frank looked excited. "Does that involve explosives, narcotics, and cadavers?"

Lara laughed. "More like birch and sage oils." She smiled down at the hounds, who were busy sniffing her purse. They had obviously scented the crumbs of dog biscuits buried in the Interior pockets. "I think your problem children are about to become prodigies."

Chapter 17

BRUNG finally lured Justine out of hiding. Lara knew, when she spelled out the word with her Scrabble tiles, that she was baiting the bear. But she hit the PLAY button anyway, chuckling to herself as she spooned up a bite of cereal at the kitchen table.

Exactly one second later, she heard an outraged howl that put Frederic and Elfrida to shame.

Then a door slammed as Justine burst out of the bedroom, clad in a navy cashmere robe and slippers and carrying her open laptop in both hands.

"Brung?" She slammed the computer down on the counter and pointed an accusatory finger at Lara. "Sixty-five points for *brung*? That's bullshit!"

Lara froze, her mouth wide-open and her spoon loaded with soggy shredded wheat.

"Well?" Justine stalked closer, her nostrils flared. "Explain yourself."

"I had sucky letters?" Lara tried. "And I wanted to build off *knob* and *tier*?"

"Brung is not a word!"

"According to the computer, it is," Lara said. "And with the double-word score and all the overlapping letters—"

"You cheated!"

"I did not." Lara found this amusing rather than offensive. "You're just mad because I might actually beat you for once."

A little vein popped out in Justine's forehead. "You're only beating me because you cheated!"

"Breathe, Mom. Breathe. Listen, *brung* may not be proper grammar, but it *is* a word. Don't hate the player; hate the game." Then Lara noticed the bulky bits of fabric visible below her mother's robe. "Are you wearing *sweatpants*?"

"Don't try to change the subject. I demand you retract *brung*."

"I didn't know you even owned sweatpants. Are they, like, Gucci sweatpants? Made with platinum thread and unicorn hair?"

Justine squinted in the full morning light like a disoriented woodland creature stumbling out into sunshine after months of hibernation. "Who did this to you?"

Lara glanced around, bewildered. "What?"

"Your highlights." Her mother strode across the room, took Lara's head in both her hands, and tilted her face forward to examine her hairline. "The glaze is so saturated, it's almost purple near the roots."

"Does this mean you're not going to cut me for playing *brung*?"

It was like Justine didn't even hear her. "This is unacceptable. Unforgivable."

Lara tried to regain control of her

head, but Justine maintained her vise-like grip. "Relax. It's just hair."

Justine finally released Lara's skull and narrowed her eyes. "I want a name. Who did your color that day after the TV interview?"

"I don't remember," Lara lied. "I swear."

"You realize I can easily call the salon and get answers."

"Then call." Lara jerked her chin toward the phone. "I'm not going to be an accomplice to some poor hairstylist's murder."

"Don't be absurd." Justine sniffed. "I'm not going to murder anybody." She smiled, her lips thin. "I'm just going to maim her. Slowly."

Lara went back to her cereal. "I'm hiding your car keys the next time you take one of your naps."

Justine pounced. "Aha! So you admit that your stylist was a 'her.'"

Lara choked on shredded wheat. "I admit nothing. Now will you please sit down and eat something?"

Her mother remained right where she

was, but conceded, "I suppose I could make coffee."

"Mom, no. You need actual nutrition. Name your poison. Eggs? Bagel? Quiche?"

Justine perked up. "We have quiche?"

"No, but I'll learn how to make it right now if you stop obsessing about my hair." Lara walked to the refrigerator and poured a glass of orange juice, which she served up along with a multivitamin. "Cheers."

Justine took a sip and swallowed the pill, but she waved away all offers of food and continued to circle Lara, examining her roots from various angles. "That color is entirely too warm for your skin tone and the ends of the front layers are shattered."

"Well, I thought it looked good. And they didn't charge me, so I guess we'll call it even."

"Get out here and sit down." Justine unlocked the door to the patio and stepped into the sunlight.

Lara held her breath, waiting to see if her mother would disintegrate like a vampire.

But no. Justine pulled out one of the padded teak chairs from the outdoor table. "This instant, young lady. I'm going to fix your hair."

"Right now? But you've been handling the business side of things for years. When's the last time you actually did a color and cut?"

"Sit down," Justine repeated.

Lara obeyed with a rebellious sigh, fidgeting and flinching as her mother ran her fingers through the layers of hair.

"I don't want anything drastic," Lara cautioned. "And nothing fancy. I don't blow-dry, I don't use product, and I don't own a straightening iron."

"I know, I know. You refuse to do anything to help yourself reach your full potential."

"I need a low-maintenance, wash-and-go style."

"Stop telling me how to do my job and be grateful. Do you have any idea how much I would charge for my services?" Justine finished her hands-on hair assessment, then commanded,

"Go shower, comb out your hair, and get back out here, stat."

When Lara returned, Justine gathered high-end styling supplies and set to work, lifting up sections of hair and letting the strands fall back against her scalp. Lara closed her eyes, stretched out her legs so she could feel the cool breeze on the tips of her toes, and thought about all the haircuts her mother had given her over the years. Justine would have died before letting her daughter out of the house with a bowl cut or uneven bangs. Every morning before elementary school, Lara used to sit on the toilet lid and yelp while her mother brushed out the tangles and tortured her limp brown locks into some semblance of style with a curling iron and shiny satin ribbons.

By the time Lara started middle school, she declared herself too cool to allow her mother to dictate her hairstyle. Thus began the dark and troubled era of hair spray and "tsunami bangs," which eventually gave way to the spiral perm (procured during a weekend at Gil's), the self-chopped bob (the only time she had ever seen Justine close to tears), and, finally, the sloppy ponytail she still favored today.

"Remember how you used to comb out my hair?" Lara asked, her eyes still closed.

Justine clicked her tongue. "How could I forget? You cried and carried on so much, I thought the neighbors would call CPS."

"What can I say? I never had your flair for fashion."

Justine poured some cold goo along Lara's scalp. "All your dogs, I notice, are perfectly groomed."

"So?"

"So why do you take better care of your pets than you do yourself?"

Lara was still trying to figure out how to respond when Justine put her squeeze bottle down and sank into the chair next to Lara's.

"I just got the salons' profit-and-loss statements for last week."

Lara opened her eyes just enough to peek at her mother though her eyelashes. "And?"

Her mother raised her hands to her

face and patted her splotchy cheeks and naked eyebrows, as if to check that they were still there. "And everything looks great. We're actually up from this month last year. The management team I put in place is working out beautifully."

"Well, that's great."

But Justine didn't sound happy. "I could retire permanently tomorrow, if I wanted to. I could sell the salons to the LA investment firm. They made me an outstanding offer." Justine went silent for a few moments. "And then what?"

"What do you mean?"

"If I'm not needed at my salons, then who am I? What will I do?"

"Well, you . . ." Lara shifted in her seat. "You'd have a boatload of cash, right?"

"Right."

"So I guess I'm not really seeing what the problem is."

"The problem is, two weeks ago I was the founder and president of Coterie Salons. I was a force to be reckoned with. And now I'll be just another Botoxed old lady wearing too much makeup and a wig." Justine's dark eyes were dull. "This house, the clothes in my closet . . . Who cares? Is this all I have to look forward to for the rest of my life? A shiny German car and a bunch of mail-order packages from Neiman Marcus? *That's* supposed to somehow validate my existence?"

"Mom."

"Not that running a chain of high-end salons was exactly on par with rescuing orphans or feeding the hungry." Justine raised her palm. "But at least I had a purpose. If I have to give that up, I'm . . ."

"Free," Lara suggested.

"Useless," Justine finished.

Mother and daughter sat side by side on the patio, soaking up the sun and watching the sprinklers water the green grass on the golf course beyond the pool.

Lara broke the silence first. "Know what you need?"

Justine shot her a warning look. "If you say 'a man,' you're out on the street."

"A dog. Let's go to the pound this afternoon and see if there's anyone you might click with." Lara tried to imagine what kind of dog would suit her mother. "But honestly, I bet you're going to end up with a pedigreed purebred. Something exotic and high-status, like a Cesky terrier."

"Let's make a deal: I'll get a dog when you get extensions and dye your hair ash blond."

"Or we could just have a few bowls of cereal and keep bickering about *brung*."

This time Justine's smile was genuine. "Sounds like a plan."

Chapter 18

Lara had never seen a Great Dane in a public restroom before. But then, she reflected as she washed her hands in the ladies' room at the agricultural exhibition area of the Arizona State Fairgrounds, she was going to experience a lot of firsts today. In thirty minutes she and Eskie would make their AKC conformation debut, vying for the Best in Breed ribbon against six other Bernese mountain dogs.

She'd arrived early today, long before Cherie, and after she checked in with the show administrators and put on her official armband, she'd spent some time scoping out the scene. Cherie had described this as a small show, so Lara had been surprised and somewhat intimidated by the number of participants and spectators. The parking lot was crammed with huge white utility vans and luxury RVs, each emblazoned with the name of a kennel. Vendors had set up booths selling pet food, toys, and specialty collars, and small children milled around, eating ice cream and popcorn.

All of the dogs here were so well behaved. That had been her first thought when she entered the arena, which smelled of wet fur and floral-scented shampoo. Hundreds of purebreds intermingled, everything from Jack Russell terriers to Scottish deerhounds, but the atmosphere was amazingly calm and quiet. No barking, no snarling or scrapping.

The huge harlequin Dane sat patiently outside one of the stall doors, ears perked up and body motionless. The dog gave Lara a quick glance when she walked in, then went right back to staring at the door latch.

Two toilets flushed and a pair of women emerged from the stalls, resuming a conversation. One was a redhead, the other a brunette, but both were sprinkled with black dog fur.

"Yeah, Westminster sucks," the brunette said. "We skipped it this year."

"Bench shows are hard," agreed the redhead. "Bismarck gets so stressed after all that time in his crate, he won't eat, and when a min pin skips a meal, you can tell."

Lara loitered by the paper-towel dispenser, eavesdropping. They glanced over at her, noted her handler armband and panicked expression, and smiled kindly.

"Did you go to Westminster this year?"

Lara swallowed audibly. "No. This is my first time handling, actually."

"You'll do great," the redhead assured her. "Which breed are you working with?"

"Bernese mountain dog."

The brunette glanced at Lara's tweedy

tan skirt. "The dog must have a great topline."

"How did you know?"

"Well, with dark breeds like Berners, sometimes the handler will wear a black skirt to help disguise a sloping spine. But if you want to show it off, you wear a light color."

"Who's judging your group?" asked the redhead.

Lara furrowed her brow and tried to recall the name. "Herb Faxon."

The other women laughed. "Pepe Le Pew."

"He douses himself in cologne," the brunette explained. "It spooks some of the dogs. Once, while he was examining my friend's Newfoundland puppy, the dog practically strangled himself with his slip collar trying to get away from the stench."

"When your aftershave can gag a Newfie, you know it's time to tone it down." They laughed again.

"Just be confident. Try to have fun and the dog will, too," the redhead advised. "And don't worry if something goes wrong. My very first show—I'll never forget—as soon as we got into the ring, my dog squatted right next to the judge and pooped. I thought I was going to die of humiliation."

"What happened?" Lara asked.

She shrugged. "I got a plastic bag and some baby wipes and cleaned it up. The judge was nice about it. She could've disqualified us, but she didn't."

The brunette shook her head. "How'd you score in that round?"

"I believe we finished dead last." They both cracked up and the Great Dane padded along behind them as they pulled the door open. "Good times, good times."

"Good times," Lara echoed weakly. Then she turned on the sink faucet full blast and splashed cold water on her face.

"Has Eskie pooped today?" Lara demanded when Cherie arrived at the fairgrounds in her spotless silver Mercedes SUV.

Cherie seemed taken aback by the question. "I believe so. She went out to

her usual spot in the yard after breakfast."

"Are you sure? Are you *positive*?"

Cherie leaned out the window and
pulled an errant strand of hair off Lara's
fitted, velvet-trimmed tweed jacket.
"You seem stressed, dear. What's the
matter?"

Lara recounted the tales from the ladies' room. "There are people here who
have been to Westminster and have
snarky little pet names for the judges!
I'm way out of my league. You should
have hired a certified handler who
knows what she's doing."

"Don't start panicking on me now."
Cherie remained irritatingly serene. "Today's just for practice. We've been over
this. Nobody expects you to take Best
in Show your first time out." She slid
out of the driver's seat and strutted on
stiletto black boots to the rear of the
SUV. "Now stop worrying and prepare
to be dazzled. Eskie spent all morning
getting beautiful."

Cherie popped the door hatch to release Eskie, who looked more dignified
than Lara had ever seen her. Her fur

gleamed in the sunlight and every trace of spittle had vanished from her muzzle.

"We just need one last finishing touch." Cherie produced a small plastic jar from the pocket of her coat and smeared the dog's nose with a thin layer of dark, sweet-scented ointment.

"What are you doing?" Lara asked.

"This is black Vaseline. You've never heard of it? It's actually for horses, but it helps keep her nose moist and shiny."

Lara noticed a bright red aerosol can labeled BIG SEXY HAIR rolling around the backseat. "Is that mousse?"

"Volumizing spray. To keep her coat nice and fluffy."

Lara paused for a moment before pointing out, "But the rule book says Berners are supposed to be shown with a 'natural coat.'"

Cherie laughed at this naïveté. "And everybody ignores that rule. I made some calls to groomers and got the inside scoop. Black Vaseline and volumizing spray is nothing. At least we're not dyeing her chest fur or chalking out the freckles on her muzzle."

"Oh, and someone pointed out that I

shouldn't be wearing a light-colored skirt if her topline is faulty in any way."

"Lucky for us, her topline is exemplary." Cherie beamed with pride. She pressed Eskie's leash into Lara's hand. "Don't worry about any of the cosmetic issues. It's my job to make her look good, and it's your job to make her shine like the little star she is."

And Lara tried. She let Eskie sniff around the parking lot and played a rousing five-minute game of fetch to burn off some of the excess exuberance. She made sure Eskie knew she had a generous stash of beef jerky in her blazer pocket, and they practiced standing, stacking, and dashing across a practice ring.

They arrived at their competition area just in time to see an imposing giant schnauzer win the veteran division for seven- to nine-year-olds. After a smattering of applause, the Bernese mountain dog trials began, starting with the puppy class for six- to twelve-month-olds.

"We're next," Cherie trilled, squeezing Lara's hand. Sure enough, the announcer called for dogs twelve to eighteen months, and there was no more time to be nervous.

After Lara took her place in the ring with Eskie, the judge nodded at the handlers and said, "Please stack your dogs." Everything after that was a blur of running, posing, and trying to keep the high-spirited ninety-pound "star" under control.

A few of the dogs seemed skittish and spooked by the pressure, but Eskie was in her element. She pranced alongside Lara, tossing her head and batting her big brown eyes at the audience.

By the end of the three-minute competition, Lara had stopped worrying about slipping on the slick cement floor and started to enjoy herself—just a little. She did notice, however, when the judge leaned in to examine Eskie's teeth, the overpowering smell of Old Spice.

While the judge stepped back to deliberate, Eskie lunged her front half into a play bow and tried to romp with the dog next to her. Lara was so busy trying to redirect Eskie that she didn't realize the final scores had been announced until the other contestants filed out of the ring and the judge handed her a third-place ribbon.

Third place out of six. Lara was mortified. All that work, all the training sessions, all those campaign photos and checks written . . .

But Cherie couldn't have been prouder if they had won Best in Show at the much-maligned Westminster.

"Here's a treat for my darling girl!" She gave Eskie a big kiss and a chunk of freeze-dried liver. Then she slipped a small package into Lara's pocket and winked. "And a treat for you, too."

"I can't help feeling a little bit like a prostitute," Lara said as she described the diamond-encrusted dog bone pendant to Kerry. "The working girl of the working group."

Kerry laughed on the other end of the phone. "Is it silver?"

"White gold. Possibly platinum. I can't tell."

"And you only got third place? Imagine what you'll get if you win."

Lara could hear Kerry soothing her fussy baby, but she thought she heard a chorus of other mewling infants in the background. "Where are you?"

"I'm in the waiting room of the gastroenterologist. My pediatrician thinks Cynthia might have severe acid reflux, so she sent us to get a second opinion and some tests."

"Oh my God. Is everything okay?"

"I hope so. The sad part is, at this point I'm actually hoping for reflux, because at least that would explain the constant screaming. Otherwise, I'm just a crappy mom and my kid hates me." Kerry sounded so heartbroken that Lara teared up in sympathy.

"You're a great mom and Cynthia loves you," she said firmly.

Cynthia wailed, as if in rebuttal.

"Hang on," Kerry said. Lara heard rustling and murmuring and then Kerry came back on the line. "Okay. So tell me more about your life as a kept woman."

Lara turned the little pendant over in her hand. "Cherie said it can be my lucky charm. And, I mean, I appreciate her generosity, but it makes me feel kind of weird. 'Here's a treat'? It's like I'm her bitch. Literally."

"Well, if it's too degrading for you, I'd be happy to take it off your hands."

"I couldn't give it to you even if I wanted to. She's going to expect me to wear it to every event I have with Eskie." Lara shook her head. "How did this happen? One minute I'm scrounging under the couch cushions for vet money; the next, I'm Mayfair Estates' answer to Cesar Millan."

"The Dog Doyenne," Kerry said. "Now with extra diamonds. So the regulars on the dog show circuit must have a ton of money, huh?"

"Oh yeah. You can spend a hundred grand a year just on campaigning," Lara replied. "Plus there's travel and hotel expenses, grooming, entry fees. . . . It's like raising racehorses, only without any of the payouts."

Kerry jumped right to the important question. "Any hot guys?"

"That would be a big negative. All the men I met at the show were either married, gay, or eligible for AARP membership." Lara sighed. "Besides, I'm not ready to meet anyone yet. I miss Evan. I know I shouldn't, but I do."

Kerry went into maternal lecture mode. "Nobody's saying you have to jump into a serious relationship, but you do have to move on. Just dip your toe back into the dating pool. Have a little fun."

"But where do I find somebody who shares my idea of fun? Face it—most guys don't want to spend their Saturday at a dog show, and they definitely don't want to share their bed with a slobbery Rottweiler. Or their couch with Mr. Squirrel. Exhibit A: Evan Walker."

"True," Kerry agreed. "You need to find yourself a guy like Richard—someone who will abandon you for weeks on end while he gets to have room service and eight-hour stretches of sleep in nice hotels." Every word dripped resentment.

"Uh-oh." Lara frowned. "What's going on?"

"Nothing."

"You lie."

"I lie. But I can't talk about it right now."

"I'll come over tonight," Lara offered. "We'll have dinner."

"No can do."

"Why not?"

"I'll tell you later. Oops, the reception-ist just called our name. I have to go. Congrats again on your big win."

"It was third place. Third out of six."

"Think positive: You're in the top fifti-eth percentile. Plus, you scored jewelry. Victory!"

"How was your day?" Justine asked when Lara sat down across the dinner table that night. Since Shelly was still on vacation and no one had been gro-cery shopping, they had scrounged up a nutritionally questionable meal of yo-gurt, fruit salad, and French bread for dinner. Lara had suggested going out to a restaurant, but Justine had refused. "And what is that look for?"

Lara blinked. "What look?"

"That ridiculous grin." As usual, her mother went on the defensive and as-sumed that she was the source of amusement. "Are you looking at my hair? My face?"

"Mom, no. I was just trying to remember when we last sat down to dinner together other than Thanksgiving or Christmas or some formal shindig at a four-star restaurant."

"I haven't the vaguest idea. What's your point?"

"Nothing. It's just nice to have a regular family meal, that's all."

Justine peeled the foil lid off her fat-free Yoplalt and placed the plastic carton on her bone china plate. "When have we ever been a regular family?"

"We could be. We could start now."

"Don't get your hopes up. I may be housebound and living in the suburbs, but if you're expecting me to start cooking meat loaf and vacuuming in high heels and pearls, you're going to be sorely disappointed."

Lara sat back and crossed her arms. "Why do you always have to be like that?"

"Like what? Don't be so sensitive. All I said was—"

"Never mind." Lara changed the subject. "Speaking of pearls, I got a new necklace today." She pulled her shirt collar open to show the diamond-studded dog bone. "Cherie Chadwick gave it to me after the conformation show."

She waited for Justine to go off on a rant about boundaries, etiquette, and the importance of appearances, but Justine barely glanced at the necklace. "Hmm. A little kitschy, but you can pull it off."

"Don't you think it's inappropriate?" Lara prompted.

"Why?"

"Because I barely know the woman and she's giving me expensive gifts and treating me like I'm her new puppy."

Justine shrugged. "You saw some of the gifts I brought home over the years. When I was still cutting hair, my regulars used to give me all sorts of things. Lots of them passed on books they'd enjoyed, and one woman even gave me her collection of vintage Hermès scarves. They trusted me with their hair, and hair is very personal."

"I guess," Lara said. "You've got your hands all over their heads."

"It's very intimate contact, when you think about it," Justine went on. "Women used to cry in my chair. They'd confess things they'd never told anyone else. Some of them didn't have anyone else in their life who would give them undivided attention. And I kept their secrets. I'll take it all to the grave."

"Ooh, that sounds juicy." Lara pushed aside her plate and leaned forward. "Give me some hints. You don't have to name names—you can make them blind items, like in the gossip columns."

"To the grave," Justine repeated. Then that faint smile reappeared. "Maybe, if you're lucky, I'll put a few blind items in my will."

"Okay, but the fact remains: I'm not cutting Cherie's hair."

"You're training and caring for her dog, which is arguably even more personal."

"Maybe. Eskie is like her baby."

"Keep the necklace. Don't give it a second thought. Remember: It's not about you. It's about how you make your clients feel." Justine refilled her iced tea. "Which reminds me: I assume you're getting your legal affairs in order? Incorporation, tax forms, all of that?"

Lara helped herself to a hunk of warm bread. "For what?"

"Your dog training business."

"I'd hardly call it a business. It's just a few little neighborhood side jobs."

"The IRS would beg to differ." Justine raised one of her penciled-in brows. "Are you at least documenting all of your income?"

"Sort of," Lara hedged.

Justine shook her head and raised her gaze heavenward. "Where have I gone wrong? Set aside a few hours tomorrow morning. We're going to go through your bank statement line by line. Good business starts with good organization."

"No can do. I have a bunch of new client consultations tomorrow morning. I'm booked solid until six p.m."

"Then we'll do it tomorrow night. I assume you have no plans?"

"Wide-open," Lara confessed. "My only dates these days are with dogs. I

think I may be a spinster in the making."

Justine's ruby-studded bangle flashed
in the fading light as she finished her
yogurt. "You say that like it's a bad
thing."

Lara noted the bracelet and decided
that in her mother's case, accessorizing
was a step in the right direction. She
could hear the dogs snuffling and whining down the hall, and then there was a
yip from the vicinity of the front door—
Ivory wanted company on her evening
rounds. "The wolf pack awaits. We're
off for a moonlight jog. Care to join us?"

Justine remained in her seat, gazing
at the window, which, in the darkness,
reflected the interior of the kitchen. "And
disrupt my busy schedule of Scrabble
and sleeping? I don't think so."

"You're going to have to get back out
there sometime. You can't put it off forever."

"Forever, no. For tonight, yes."

Chapter 19

"Thank God you're here." Melissa O'Brien, a petite, rosy-cheeked blonde, raked her fingers through her short, spiky coif. "My house is in shambles and my stepkids hate my guts. Help me—I'm begging you."

Lara took a step back from the front door of the sprawling Santa Fe–style house. She'd taken the initial phone call for this appointment while driving through a valley with spotty cell phone reception, but she could have sworn she'd heard "adopted dog" and not "adolescents." "Oh, I don't train kids, ma'am. That's not my jurisdiction."

"Wait! Please don't leave me." Melissa clutched Lara's hand in hers. She was shockingly strong for such a wee little woman. "The kids aren't the problem—not *your* problem, anyway." She pulled Lara into the entryway, where Lara immediately tripped over a skateboard lying on the floor.

"Robbie!" the sweet little blonde screeched, so loudly that Lara jumped. Melissa braced both hands on the newel post and continued yelling up the stairs. "I told you to pick up your crap. Get down here right now!"

No response from upstairs.

"Robbie!"

Lara covered her ears.

"Right! Now!"

"Omigod, could you please stop screaming?" A lilting, languorous voice drifted over from the family room, where a trio of leather couches surrounded a huge TV. "I'm trying to watch *Gossip Girl*."

"Portia, I thought I asked you to go

get dressed. You can't wear your pajamas all day."

Portia turned up the TV, and Lara could hear the rapid-fire click of nimble adolescent fingers texting.

Melissa maintained her sunny smile and kept hollering. *"Portia!"*

Lara's nerves couldn't take any more. She placed a hand on Melissa's shoulder and applied gentle pressure, the same technique she used when she needed to get Rufus or Maverick to focus. "Is this a bad time? I can come back later."

Melissa's voice dropped several decibels to a despairing whisper. "It's always a bad time."

Lara waited for her to explain.

Melissa glanced pointedly at the sullen teenager lounging in the next room and led Lara back to the kitchen. She grabbed the full carafe from the coffeemaker, poured two mugs, and gulped down half of her Colombian roast before Lara had taken a single sip. "When my husband and I started dating, the kids and I got along great. They told me everything that was going on at school with their friends; we went to the movies. I felt like the fun older sister. But six months ago Keith and I got married and, just like that, they started sulking and ignoring me. Fine. Blended families need an adjustment period. I get it." Melissa slugged down the rest of her coffee as if she were doing tequila shots at happy hour.

"I know I'm not their mother. I'm not *trying* to be their mother, but I have gone out of my way to be nice to them and I deserve a little respect. They're trying to break me and damn it, I'm broken!" Melissa looked so defeated that Lara knew she should comfort the poor woman.

She needed to say something wise and reassuring. Something soothing and heartwarming.

She had nothing. This was why she worked with dogs and not people.

Just before the silence started to get awkward, Lara spied a black-and-white dog staring at her through the French doors. She hurried toward the glass panes with a surge of relief.

"This must be the dog you called me about."

Melissa's frown deepened. "Ah, yes. Cleo."

"She's a cutie-pie. Border collie?"

"I'm not sure—we adopted her from the shelter. But yes, the vet thinks she's mostly Border collie, with maybe some beagle mixed in. The kids call her a 'be-gollie.'"

Lara laughed. "The latest designer breed."

"They said they wanted a dog." A tear slipped out of Melissa's right eye. "They begged for a dog. Keith and I talked to them about the responsibility—the feeding and the walking and the brushing and the vacuuming. They promised they'd help out."

Lara had heard this story countless times. "But the novelty wore off and now they're not holding up their end of the bargain?"

Melissa nodded. "They ignore me, they ignore the dog, and now it's like I have a third stepkid who won't listen to a word I say."

Lara got out her notepad and pen.

"Which of Cleo's behaviors, specifically, are causing problems?"

Melissa threw up her hands. "It would be easier to list the behaviors that *aren't* causing problems. If that dog isn't eating or sleeping, she's doing something bad. Barking, chewing, digging, puncturing the garden hose, pooping in the flower beds, stealing shoes off the doormat . . ."

Lara nodded. "You said you picked her out at the shelter. What was it about her that appealed to you?"

"Well, as you said, she's pretty. And she's very friendly. When we first saw her, she came right up to the wire mesh and stuck her nose through to say hello. The shelter workers said she was a high-energy dog, so I thought she'd be able to keep up with the kids."

"High energy," Lara repeated. "That's the key phrase right there. Border collies are kind of a polarizing breed—people tend to love them or be driven completely insane by them. They're very spirited, and they're also very smart. That can be a dicey combination if they're stuck in a backyard in the suburbs. If you don't keep them mentally and physically stimulated, they'll find a way to do it themselves, as you've discovered." She opened the door and stepped outside. "May I say hello?"

Cleo greeted Lara politely, sitting with her head tilted and her blue eyes sparkling. She was small and light-framed, with short legs, a smattering of black freckles on her white muzzle, and a fluffy "beard" on her chest.

"This is an act," Melissa declared. "Don't fall for it. Usually, she's tearing around out here like a squirrel on speed."

"A faker?" Lara grinned, remembering Linus's marathon naps. "I've got one of those at home."

"So, basically, I'm screwed." Melissa folded her arms. "If we keep her, she'll continue her campaign of terror on my rosebushes. If I hold the kids to their word and take her back to the pound because they aren't doing their part, she'll probably get put to sleep before someone else adopts her. No matter what I do or how nice I am, I'm the bad guy."

"Well, you called me, so that's a step

in the right direction." Lara waited a beat for Melissa to calm down. "Let me ask you this: Do you *like* Cleo?"

Melissa took her time before answering. "Not at the moment, no. But I think I could. I'm frustrated, but that's more about the situation I'm in with the kids."

"So she's caught in the emotional cross fire."

"Yes."

"I guarantee you she's picking up on that and it's contributing to her behavior," Lara said. "But that's okay. We can work as a team to change this."

Melissa looked skeptical. "Who's 'we'?"

"Everybody. You, your husband, Cleo, and the kids have to come together. You're all a team, and I'm your coach."

"Is this going to end with the whole family linking arms and singing up in the Alps, like *The Sound of Music*?"

Lara laughed. "We can only hope."

"Well, I'll be happy to wear a nun's habit and sew those kids costumes from the curtains if it'll save the sprinkler system. What's the plan?"

Lara figured that taming teenagers

and disciplining naughty dogs couldn't really be that different. "First of all, you need to stop worrying about being the bad guy. You tried being nice and the kids didn't respond, so you might as well get tough. Second, you have to stop yelling. Yelling's not going to get you what you want."

Melissa sighed. "It's not like they're listening, anyway."

"They're not listening because they don't have to. If you scream at them, and they blow you off, what do you do?"

"Scream louder," Melissa admitted with a lopsided smile. "Then they tell my husband what an evil hag I am, and my husband and I have a fight."

"Right. When someone comes to me with a puppy and asks for obedience tips, I tell them not to waste commands. Say it once and mean it."

"But what if they don't follow the command the first time?" Melissa asked.

"Then there are consequences. Clear, consistent consequences. That skateboard in the hallway? You ask Robbie politely to put it away. Once. Then you throw it out."

Melissa's forehead creased. "You mean hide it in the garage for a while and tell him I threw it out."

"No, I mean take it down to Goodwill and donate it." Lara did her best Maria von Trapp impersonation. "So long, farewell, *auf Wiedersehen*, good-bye."

The other woman's eyes widened. "But he'll freak."

"Probably." Lara shrugged. "But I'll bet that next time you ask him to put something away, he'll hop to."

Melissa considered this for a moment. Then her face fell. "He'll complain to his mother, though, and she'll just buy him another one and use the whole situation as ammunition against me."

"You can't control what his mother does. But you need to set up clear, consistent rules for your home, and everybody—including you—must follow them. Dogs and teenagers might act like they want to call the shots, but they don't. Being in charge is a big responsibility. They're not ready for it, no matter what they say."

"I see what you're saying. I do." Melissa twisted her lips into a worried little moue. "But don't you think Cleo needs more time to adjust? The poor thing starts slinking around whenever she sees a stick or a broom—what if she was abused as a puppy? I don't want to bully her."

"You're not bullying; you're setting up ground rules. Don't worry too much about the broom thing. There's no way to know what happened to Cleo before you got her, and honestly, it doesn't matter. Don't feel sorry for her, and don't try to compensate for her previous life. You have to have high expectations from the very beginning, and the dog will rise to meet them." Lara put away her notepad and prepared to get to work. "You got this dog to bring your new family together, right? So let's find an activity that everyone will enjoy. Something mentally, physically, and emotionally challenging."

"Unless you can figure out how teach Cleo to play Wii or try on clothes at the mall, I'm not optimistic."

"Get ready for rule number three: No more negativity. They don't call me the Dog Doyenne for nothing." Lara eyed the huge, shimmering swimming pool in the backyard, grabbed her cell phone, and dialed. "Hi, Kayla. How's it going with Roo? Another pound down? Good for you! Listen, do you guys feel like going for a swim?"

Nothing like a hot ex-model to shake up the family dynamic.

Kayla showed up in oversize sunglasses and a microscopic bikini, and Melissa's stepkids came around so fast, Lara nearly got whiplash.

Robbie abandoned his video games as soon as he realized there was a sultry brunette in the house, and Portia drifted out after him, having changed into a fairly skimpy bikini herself. The young girl watched Kayla with a mix of envy and admiration, and started subtly imitating Kayla's poses and speech patterns.

Lara left the humans to introduce themselves and got to work on Cleo and Roo. The "begollie" and the "flabrador" circled each other, sniffing and wagging, then began chasing each other around the yard.

"Okay," Lara called to Kayla and Melissa. "Have these guys been swimming before?"

Kayla nodded, but Melissa shook her head. "Cleo won't go in. Won't even go near the edge."

"Then, Kayla, I'd like you to please get in the shallow end with Roo. He's looking quite svelte, by the way."

Kayla beamed. "The lifestyle changes are helping a lot." She flicked back her hair, a bit embarrassed. "I call it a lifestyle change instead of a diet. It feels less harsh."

"I'm proud of you both." Lara patted Roo's side. "And you're both indulging in a weekly 'cheat,' right?"

"We're going to get frozen yogurt this afternoon." Kayla looked around, well aware of the effect she was having on her audience. "Hey, would you guys like to come, too?"

"I love this woman," Melissa muttered as Robbie and Portia nodded. "You could charge double your hourly rate, and it would be worth it."

"Thanks, but don't start celebrating just yet," Lara murmured back. "Bringing teenagers to heel is the easy part. A Border collie might be a bit more of a challenge." She turned to Kayla and handed her a tennis ball. "All right, Roo. Do your thing."

Kayla leaned *waaay* over to grab Roo's collar, and Robbie looked like he was having heart palpitations. Then the bronzed goddess tossed the ball into the water and the flabrador leapt in with a splash that drenched everyone on deck. The huge yellow beast started paddling around, his mouth open in a goofy dog grin, and Kayla lowered herself into the water. Portia strode toward the pool, determined not to be outdone.

"Come on, Cleo." She snapped her fingers at the Border collie and pulled on her collar. *"Come on."*

Cleo planted all four paws firmly on the deck and refused to budge.

"Don't force her." Lara pried Portia's fingers off the collar. "We want her to go in voluntarily."

"How?" Robbie's eyes were wild and

a bit desperate. "We have to get in there right now."

Lara hid her smile and urged patience. "I've used a life jacket in the past, but we don't have one handy, so we'll find something else that motivates her. Does she have any toys that might float?"

"She likes Frisbees," Robbie volunteered.

This was clearly news to Melissa. "She does?"

"Yeah. I was tossing it around in the backyard yesterday and she went bananas."

"And what's her favorite treat?"

"We gave her a Milk-Bone this morning, and she gobbled it down," Melissa said.

"Her favorite is dried blueberries," Portia informed them with world-weary authority. "I spilled the container when I was packing my lunch last week, and she loved them. I think she likes them even better than dog treats."

Lara couldn't hide her surprise. "Dried blueberries? Really?"

"Are those bad for her?" Melissa asked.

"No, they should be fine in moderation, but most dogs prefer meaty flavors."

"Not Cleo. She's totally healthy. I even used them to teach her a trick. Ready?" Portia's ennui finally cracked as she addressed the dog with mock dismay. "We're getting papped, Cleo!"

Cleo hit the deck and used both paws to cover her muzzle. Portia burst out laughing. "Good dog!"

Melissa and Lara exchanged a look. "What on earth is 'getting papped'?"

"You know, like celebrities with the paparazzi. She's trying to duck from photographers." Portia snapped her gum.

"How long did it take you to teach her that?" Melissa asked.

Portia shrugged. "Like half an hour. We worked on lying down first, then the part with her paws. It's amazing what you can do when you're procrastinating starting your geometry homework." Her cheeks flushed as she tried—and failed—to disguise how pleased she was with her dog training prowess.

Lara was impressed. No wonder Portia had picked out a Border collie at the shelter—they had so much in common. Both were deceptively fluffy and pretty on the outside, but clever and persistent underneath.

"We're in luck," Lara said, "because dried blueberries float. Would you mind grabbing the container from the kitchen?"

As Portia went into the house, Melissa shook her head in disbelief. "I can't believe she trained the dog. I swear to you, the only time I've seen her put her phone down is when Keith threatens to take it away at the dinner table."

"This is perfect," Lara said. "You want the dog to be mentally engaged, and you want the kids to be emotionally invested in training her." When Portia returned with a small tub of blueberries, Lara caught Cleo's attention and tossed a few into the pool. "Go get it."

Keeping her belly close to the ground, Cleo crept closer to the pool's edge.

"It's okay," Lara urged, tossing another blueberry in. "Go ahead."

Robbie groaned with impatience and started toward Cleo, but Lara stopped him with a stern look.

Cleo, who had evidently decided to milk this little melodrama for all it was worth, made a big display of inching ever closer to the water, then pulling back at the last second. Every time a drop of water hit her nose, she yelped as if burned by hot embers.

Portia rolled her eyes. "Omigod. Drama queen."

This went on for another ten minutes. Robbie waded into the shallow end and stared at Kayla. Roo paddled around, his big paws churning the water. Melissa, Lara, and Portia cooed and coaxed, and Cleo luxuriated in the attention.

Then Roo ate one of the blueberries.

Cleo barked, dashed to the steps, and submerged one dainty white paw.

Everyone paused, waiting.

Roo, who had snarfed up the first blueberry by accident while playfully snapping at the waves he'd created, needed a few seconds to process the joy and wonder of what had just happened. Then he spotted a second blueberry bobbing a few feet away and swam toward it.

Cleo jumped in and started flailing wildly.

"Portia!" Lara directed. "Put your hand under her belly and help support her until she figures out how to coordinate her legs."

Portia complied, and after a few moments of panic, Cleo calmed down and started to swim independently. She ignored Roo until she had tracked down and consumed every last blueberry in the pool.

Lara observed, "So she's smart, she can swim, and she's competitive. I see a bright future for her in the great sport of doggie dock diving."

"What's that?" asked Melissa.

"Basically, you train your dog to run full speed down a dock and jump into a long pool of water to retrieve a toy. It's fun, and bonus, it's a surefire way to exhaust the dog. The three of you could all train and compete with Cleo. I'll give you the name of the club president in Scottsdale and you can go to a practice or two to try it out."

Robbie turned to Kayla and blurted, "Roo likes to swim."

"Yeah, will you guys do it, too?" Portia asked.

Kayla glanced at Melissa and flashed her cover girl smile. "Sure, why not? It'll be a fun new lifestyle change for him."

"There you go. I'll shoot you an e-mail with the details." Lara stood up and wrung out her shirt hem. "Keep practicing, guys. I'll check in on your progress in a few days."

"You are a miracle worker." Melissa pressed a check into Lara's hands before giving her a hug.

Lara patted Melissa's back awkwardly and gasped for breath. "The hills are alive."

Chapter 20

"I need you to take Mullet." Kerry's eyes were red and swollen as she sat on her couch nursing the baby. Her body was slumped, her bare feet were swollen, and her customary spark had been completely extinguished. "I'm sorry. I just can't deal with all this anymore."

Lara stood in the family room, holding bags of takeout and baby supplies, and surveyed the chaos around her. Dogs wandered by, shaggy and panting. She noticed the water dish was empty, so she deposited her bags on the kitchen counter and refilled it. Then she poured a big glass of water for Kerry.

"You have to take care of yourself," she chided.

"Look who's talking."

Lara reached out and beckoned for Kerry to hand Cynthia over.

Kerry sipped her glass of water, then pulled a woolen throw blanket around her shoulders. "You know how judgmental I am of people who dump their dogs when they have a baby."

"I believe you may have mentioned it once or twice."

Kerry's lower lip trembled as she started to cry in earnest. "But this . . . I had no idea, Lara. I can't keep going like this. I'm so tired. She wants to eat every two hours, around the clock. And when she finally does take a nap, I'm so wired that I can't fall asleep. I just lie there, grinding my teeth, dreading the moment when she wakes up and starts screaming again."

Lara put her arm around Kerry shoulder, careful not to jostle the baby. "Oh, honey."

"We started medication for the reflux

issues, but it hasn't kicked in yet, and I'm not sure it's ever going to. Last night she cried for four hours straight. I am not exaggerating. I tried running the vacuum, the hair dryer, the fan. I put her in her car seat and drove around the block—and she just cried harder. I feel like such a failure."

"You're not a failure."

"Yes, I am. I'm a horrible mom. I want to run away to Mexico and not come back until she's sleeping through the night."

Lara smiled. "I'll go with you if you need a margarita buddy on the beach."

"No, listen, I'm serious. I'm at the point where leaving the country actually sounds like a sensible, viable option. Richard and my mom could do a better job than I'm doing. The *dogs* could do a better job."

Lara's worry intensified. "Have you talked to your doctor about this?"

"Yeah, and she said my hormone levels are plummeting and it's normal to feel moody. She told me to call back in a week or two if I'm not feeling better.

But I noticed she didn't dispute my claim that dogs could out-parent me."

Both women gazed down at the tiny pink newborn, snoozing so intently that her eyelids crinkled like an old lady's.

"That's just the sleep deprivation and the plummeting hormone levels talking," Lara said firmly. "I don't know much about babies, but this can't go on forever. The kid has to start sleeping eventually, right?"

"Maybe not." Kerry started sniffling again. "My neighbor dropped by with a casserole today and I asked her how old her daughters were when they started sleeping through the night, and do you know what she said? 'My youngest is two and a half and she *still* doesn't sleep through the night.'"

Lara gasped. "That's the meanest thing I've ever heard. Well, screw her. You need to take a nap and a shower and then get a pedicure or something."

"I'll get right on that, as soon as Cynthia graduates from high school."

"No more discussion." Lara stood up, cradling the baby as if she were a delicately wired explosive device. "Here's what's going to happen. I'm going to put Mullet in the car, and then I'm coming back for Cynthia and all her gear."

"Lara—"

"No more discussion."

"You don't have to do this."

"Too late. It's done." Lara glanced around at the spit-up-scented detritus. "Do you have some milk pumped?"

"Enough for one feeding."

"All right, then I'll take that, too." She handed Cynthia back to Kerry and started gathering Mullet's supplies.

"You have no idea what you're in for. She's going to scream the whole time."

"Not a problem. Auntie Lara has earplugs and a pacifier."

"But what about—"

Lara made the universal *zip it* gesture with her fingers. "If I were you, I'd spend less time arguing and more time sleeping." She scooped up Mullet, who immediately went limp in passive protest, and headed for the front door. "We're rescuers, right? This is what we do."

*   *   *

"Dear Lord, what is that screaming?" Justine looked appalled when she saw the baby in Lara's arms. "Don't tell me you're taking in foundlings from the street now?"

Lara had to pull out her earplugs and wait for a break between wails before replying. The high ceilings and long, varnished floors in Justine's house created a virtual echo chamber of colicky discontent.

"This is Kerry's new baby." Lara offered up the infant, and Justine retreated, shaking her head. "Her name's Cynthia, and she has the tiniest bit of colic."

"Colic?" Justine looked dubious. "She sounds possessed."

"Well, Kerry's completely burned out and I stepped in and told her to take a break for a few hours."

"Of course you did. Listen, I know I agreed to let you bring a ragtag pack of dogs over here, but I never agreed to small children. Babies are not in my repertoire, Lara. They're . . ." Justine trailed off, looking dismayed and a bit afraid.

"I feel exactly the same," Lara assured her. "Don't worry. This isn't going to be a regular thing. But Kerry's husband keeps leaving for business trips and her mom only stayed for a week, and she's completely overwhelmed."

Justine's eyes softened just a little. "It's hard being a new mother. Trial by fire."

"Was it overwhelming for you when I was a baby?" Lara knew the answer before she'd finished asking the question. Justine was never overwhelmed by anyone or anything. "Dad left when I was what? Two or three months old?"

Justine seemed to find this whole line of questioning offensive. "I didn't have the luxury of sitting around, analyzing my feelings. I just did what needed to be done. That's motherhood. That's life."

"Never mind." Lara sighed. "Forget I asked."

"I will say that I don't remember you screaming like this," Justine admitted. "But you certainly had your moments."

Lara started bouncing up and down on the soles of her feet, and Cynthia's cries turned to gurgles. Everybody visibly relaxed.

"Keep doing that," Justine instructed. "All day and all night, if necessary." She turned and started back down the hall with a great sense of purpose, so Lara called after her, "What are your plans today?"

"None of your business."

"I'll take that to mean more online Scrabble and TV."

Justine just kept walking. Lara glanced down at the baby, then glanced up at the clock, hoping that enough time had passed that she could return Cynthia to Kerry. It felt like she'd been pacing this hall for hours on end.

According to the clock, twenty minutes had passed.

"Hey, Mom," Lara called out. She heard Justine's footsteps stop. "If I ever had a baby, would you come and stay with me and help out?"

Justine reappeared around the corner. "I suppose it would depend on my schedule. But I can promise you this— I'll hire you the best night nurse money can buy."

Lara nodded, but her disappointment must have shown on her face because Justine put one hand on her hip.

"What?" she demanded.

"Nothing," Lara said. "I'm just a little hurt that you'd rather hire a nanny than be a grandma."

Justine's expression remained impassive. "Why must you always set me up for failure with your expectations?"

"I'm not—"

"Let me finish, please. A night nurse will be much more useful than I ever could be. And you should know better than anyone that I'm not very maternal."

"How can you say that?" Lara raised the baby to her shoulder and patted the warm little back. "You give me expensive handbags and free spa services. Most people would consider that an ideal mother."

"But not you. When did you ever come by the salon of your own free will, Lara? What do you do with those handbags?"

"Um . . ."

Justine's frown lines deepened. "You've

never wanted the things I had to give you."

"You're the normal one," Lara said. "It's not your fault you gave birth to a fashion-impaired dog lover. You have to know you were a good mom. A great mom. You made sure I had the best of everything."

"Except a real family." When Justine turned away, Lara could see patches of pale scalp showing through her hair. "I failed in the most fundamental aspect of parenting—I picked the wrong father for you."

Lara heard an undercurrent of doubt and self-reproach in Justine's voice that reminded her of Kerry.

"I don't see how you can blame yourself for Dad walking out. I mean, if we're going to blame anyone, we might as well blame me. Everything was hunky-dory until I was born."

Justine turned back to face her. She looked resolved again, harder. "That's not true."

"What are you saying? You never really loved him, even before I came along?"

"Oh, I loved him." Justine held her gaze, and Lara could see what it cost her mother to admit this. "I let myself go and fell completely in love even though I should have known better. I committed to the wrong man, and you're the one who's spent her whole life paying for it."

Lara wanted to hug her mother, but she didn't want to risk being rebuffed, so she stayed where she was. "But how could you have known? He can be very charming."

"Yes, he can."

"He called me a few weeks ago," Lara confided. "To have dinner."

Justine said nothing, just tilted her head and waited.

"He remembered my birthday this year, too. He gave me a Dyson vacuum cleaner." Lara lowered her voice and tried hard to sound cynical. "I think he wants something. Something big."

Part of her wanted her mother to jump in and confirm her worst suspicions, to pile on with criticisms and judgment. But Justine held her tongue.

"He's getting married, you know."

One of Justine's cheek muscles twitched. "I didn't."

"Yeah. She's young, but she seems really nice. I liked her. He says he wants to get together again soon." Lara was embarrassed to hear the hope in her own voice.

And still her mother didn't correct her.

"Why aren't you saying anything?" she finally demanded.

Justine got her cheek muscles under control and the twitching stopped. "Is there something you would like me to say?"

"Yes! Say, 'Don't be stupid!' Say, 'We all know how this is going to end.' Say, 'How many times have I warned you to never trust a man?'"

Justine finally registered a recognizable range of emotions: shock and outrage. "When did I ever tell you not to trust a man?"

"Gee, let me think." Lara gazed up at the ceiling, pretending to rack her brains. "Oh, that's right: All the time."

Justine shook her head. "I told you not to be *dependent* on a man. That's very different. Once you're self-reliant, you have the luxury of deciding whether to trust people. You should be with someone because you love him, not because you need him."

Lara considered this. "But with Evan, I felt like I loved him *and* I needed him. Right up until I flushed his engagement ring down the toilet."

Justine reached over and brushed Lara's hair back from her forehead. Lara was so startled by this spontaneous affection, it was all she could do not to flinch.

"You are astonishingly generous," her mother said. "It's the best thing about you, but also your fatal flaw because you're always willing to give people one more chance. Some people don't deserve one more chance."

Lara tried to decode the underlying message here. "So you're saying don't have lunch with Dad?"

"I'm saying that time is a precious resource—time and money and energy. *You* are a precious resource, and unless you start seeing yourself that way, you're going to deplete your reserves and have nothing left to give."

"But that sounds so . . . stingy."

"Only if you don't think you're worth taking care of." Justine nodded to indicate that this discussion was now at an end. "And by the way, there's spit-up all over your shoes and the floor. Please move to a carpeted area; stomach acid isn't good for the wood varnish."

"And you say you're not maternal." Lara had to laugh as she grabbed a dish towel and attempted to wipe up the vomit while continuing to soothe the baby. "Don't try to hide it, Mom. You're practically Mary Poppins."

Chapter 21

The alarm clock buzzed at six o'clock on Monday morning, jarring Lara out of a sound sleep. Her hand shot out from the warm cocoon of covers and smacked the snooze button. She knew she ought to get up, but she snuggled in for an extra ten minutes of rest. Justine might have her faults, but the woman knew how to decorate a guest bedroom. It was so dark in there, so cozy under the comforter, so quiet. . . .

Lara scrambled up to a sitting position. The room was absolutely silent. All she could hear was the faint rustle of the air moving through the ducts by the door to the bathroom.

No snuffling. No scratching. No snorting.

"Mullet?" she whispered, climbing out of bed.

Linus, sprawled out next to her on the mattress, lifted his head, then dropped it again and let out a long, rumbly sigh as he went back to sleep. Rufus and Raggs didn't even stir in their crates.

No matter how she strained her ears, she couldn't detect any of the surly Shih Tzu's wheezing or grunting.

Then she noticed the tiny sliver of pale light by the doorway. The door was ajar just enough to allow a stealthy little dog to slip out into forbidden territory.

The foyer floor.

Lara sprinted toward the grand entryway, her pulse roaring in her ears. She skidded to a stop and started examining the gleaming planks of wood and leather for scratches, teeth marks, or gouges.

"Lara?" her mother's voice called from the kitchen. "Is that you?"

"It's me." Lara swallowed hard as she followed the scent of freshly ground espresso beans. She rounded the corner to find her mother standing by the counter, stirring skim milk into her morning coffee. Mullet was sprawled in the middle of the floor with her tongue hanging out.

"I assume you're responsible for this"—Justine glanced down—"creature?"

Lara nodded, mute with horror.

"It showed up in my bed in the dead of night. On my face, actually. I've never been awakened by slobber, and it's an experience I hope never to repeat."

"I understand, Mom, and I am so sorry. I swear to you that we'll all be out of here soon—I'm going to go talk to a real estate agent this weekend—but I'll be more careful about closing the door to my bedroom."

"What did you say this unfortunate mongrel's name is?"

"Mullet. As in Billy Ray Cyrus."

"An affront to hairstylists everywhere." Justine kept staring. She appeared to be hypnotized by the sheer hideousness of Mullet's fur. "Why is it so be-draggled?"

"She's had a tough life," Lara said defensively. "Scarring and tangles so bad we have to shave her bald. And PS, it's a girl."

"Ah." Justine gave Mullet a wide berth as she walked around to Lara's side of the counter. Mullet struggled to her feet and flounced after Justine, snuffling and snorting all the way.

The two divas ignored each other in a truly awe-inspiring display of indifference.

Lara glanced at the microwave clock. "You're up early. Want to walk the dogs with me?"

"No, thank you."

"Oh, come on. It's still dark outside. No risk of sun damage, no chance of running into anyone you know. Let's get our sneakers on."

"Excuse me? Half the neighborhood is roaming the streets right now, jogging and power walking and driving to work. Forget it." Justine tucked a magazine under her arm and started back toward the master suite.

"Mom. Every time I try to get you to go out in public, you say no."

Justine continued her leisurely stroll. "Yet you persist in asking me."

"Well, I'm curious." Lara tagged after her. "What would it take to make you say yes?"

"There's nothing that would make me say yes."

"Sure, there is. According to you, everyone has a price."

Justine straightened her shoulders. "You're asking what would convince me to go out and expose myself to ridicule and pity from people I don't know and schadenfreude from people I do?"

"No. I'm asking what would convince you to go to the damn grocery store," Lara replied.

"Hmm." Justine pondered this over a few sips of coffee. "You know, maybe I do have a price. You're interested in finding a house, correct?"

"I am." Lara started to grin as she shared her good news. "And it's a nightmare trying to find a rental to take the dogs, but since I don't have much of a down payment, I thought buying was out of the question. Well, it turns out that Melissa O'Brien—she's the one with the dock-diving begollie, remember?"

"What on earth are you talking about?"

"Never mind. Anyway, her husband is a big muckety-muck at the bank, and they're going to help me qualify for a loan."

Justine's face remained carefully neutral. "Really."

"Really! And since I became the Dog Doyenne of Mayfair Estates, I make enough to cover a mortgage. It'll be cheaper than renting, actually. Check it out—I'm an entrepreneur, just like you."

Justine looked at Lara. Lara looked at Justine.

Finally Justine said, "Very well. If you let me go house hunting with you, I'll go grocery shopping afterward."

Lara narrowed her eyes. "Why do you want to go house hunting with me?"

"That's immaterial. You asked my price and I named it. Take it or leave it."

Lara wheedled and whined and stamped her foot. Then she gave in to the inevitable. "Fine. But you have to keep your opinions to yourself, and you are not going to pick out my house."

"We'll see." Justine smiled a victor's smile, then opened the door to her bedroom.

Lara heard the click of nails against floor tiles. Moving faster than Lara had ever seen her, Mullet skittered around the corner and darted through the door to the master suite. "Is she going in there with you?"

Justine scowled after the Shih Tzu. "I don't see why she would."

"Mullet!" Lara called. "Hey! It's walking time. Walk! Hello?"

All the other dogs came running, but Mullet ignored her.

"I'll let her out in the yard," Justine said. "But after that, she's going right back into your room. I won't be able to concentrate on my Scrabble game with all that snorting."

"Well, don't get attached," Lara warned. "She hates everyone."

"Perfect. So do I."

*   *   *

"I've got a new one for you," Jason said as soon as Lara walked into the clinic for her appointment with the office manager. "Female boxer mix, about two years old."

Lara braced herself. "Give me the bad news."

"No bad news." Jason spread out his hands, the picture of innocence. "She's young; she's healthy; she's even spayed."

"Uh-huh." Lara remained skeptical. "So what's the deal?"

"Owner surrender. It's a married couple, and the wife is jealous."

"Of the dog?"

"Yeah. She says they picked out the dog together, but now the dog only likes the husband and it's 'ruining the intimacy of their marriage.'"

"Are you kidding me?"

"I know—I could barely keep a straight face," Jason said.

"Must be some dog. Any aggression?"

"No, she's a sweetheart. She does seem to prefer men, though. I brought her by this morning to meet the staff, and she barely looked at the women."

"Uh-oh." Lara got a sinking feeling in her stomach. "Are we dealing with Mullet the Second?"

"No way." Jason had clearly succumbed to the boxer's charms. "She's just a guys' girl."

"Okay, I'll start working on her Web site bio." Lara created profiles for each dog in the rescue group's care. These featured flattering photos and read like personal ads: *Sweet-as-pie snuggle addict seeks confirmed bachelor for long runs in the park and lavish affection. Loyal to a fault.* "What's her name?"

"Lucy." Jason paused for dramatic effect. "Lucy Fur."

Lara burst out laughing. "You lie."

"The husband named her Lucy. The wife added the Fur. I couldn't make this stuff up."

"When do I get to meet this little femme fatale?"

"Want to do a playdate at the park tomorrow evening with Maverick and the spaniels?"

"No can do," Lara replied. "I've got another conformation competition coming up this weekend, so Eskie and I are doing two training sessions a day. Plus I've got personal training with Roo the flabrador, swim practice with Cleo the begollie, and urban scent training with the Jane Austen hounds. Oh, and house hunting with my mom. I'm booked solid."

"Swing by tomorrow at lunchtime," Jason suggested. "Fifteen minutes. Ten."

"I'll try," Lara promised. "But I'm so swamped right now that even one more obligation is going to push me over the edge."

Right on cue, her phone rang, and she answered against her better judgment.

"Hey, La-la." Her father sounded so excited and proud of himself that she had to smile. "What are you doing right now? We've got a surprise for you."

"Sorry I'm late." Lara used a tissue to blot the sweat from her forehead as she loped across the grassy library plaza toward her father. "My last appointment took forever, and then there was traffic. I hope you . . ." Her voice trailed off as she spied the black and tan puppy squirming in Trina's arms.

Gil rose from the bench and gave her a kiss on the cheek. "Meet the newest member of our family."

"This is Teddy," Trina announced with the pride of a new mother. "We just bought him yesterday."

Lara had lowered her face to receive puppy kisses, but she jerked back up when she heard this.

"He's a great dog," her father said, quickly and a bit too loudly. "But I read on the Internet that Rottweilers tend to be stubborn and willful, so I'm hoping you'll help us out with the obedience training."

Lara tucked her hair behind her ears and tried to hide her dismay. "I'm sorry. Did you say you *bought* him?"

Trina nodded, oblivious to the tension. "I saw him at the pet store at the mall and I just fell in love."

Her father smiled indulgently and rubbed Trina's back. "She had to have him."

"But . . ." Lara looked to her father,

bewildered. "I had no idea you wanted a dog. Why didn't you ask me?"

"I didn't know I wanted a dog until I saw Teddy." Trina nuzzled the little guy against her cheek. "And then he was the only one who would do."

"Don't get upset, honey," Gil soothed, returning his focus to Lara. "I know how you feel about pet store puppies."

"No," Lara said. "I really don't think you do."

"I know you're against them."

"Yes, but do you know *why*?" Lara prepared to launch into her lecture on the evils of puppy mills—the irresponsible breeding practices, inhumane living conditions, and resulting health and behavioral problems.

Then she saw Trina's blissful, adoring expression and decided to save her breath. Trina was not going to hear a word of her long-winded diatribe. Trina was strung out on soft puppy fur and sweet puppy smell.

Lara watched owner and dog interact, and she had to admit that it did seem to be a pretty good match. The chemistry was definitely there, even though Teddy was a little bit lacking in the looks department.

Perhaps Lara's recent stint in the dog show ring had made her hypercritical, but she couldn't help noticing that Teddy fell woefully short of the breed standard. His muzzle was too long and pointed, his eyes were close-set, and the bones and muscles in his shoulders were not aligned at the proper angle.

This roly-poly puppy was a genetic nightmare, and would probably develop painful and expensive orthopedic issues in the next few years.

But Lara didn't say any of that. She saw how happy Trina looked, and how happy her father looked, and she managed to squeak out, "Congratulations."

"Teddy's going to be in our wedding," Trina confided. "I asked the florist to make him a little wreath to wear around his neck." She paused, wrinkling her nose. "I just hope we can get him potty trained by then."

"Well, the wedding's not for months and months, right?" Lara asked. "You've got plenty of time."

"Actually, the wedding's going to be

any day now," her father announced. "We decided to skip the formal ceremony and fancy reception and all the hassle and just go for it."

"I don't care about any of that," Trina said, in a wistful voice that made Lara suspect that she had very much wanted the formal ceremony and fancy reception. "The marriage is what's important, not the wedding."

And now Lara recognized this puppy for what it was—a consolation prize. Gil had gotten his way with the wedding, but Trina was still going to feel as though her fiancé indulged her every whim.

"Are you going to get a great dress, at least?" Lara asked.

At the mention of dresses, Trina jerked out of her puppy reverie and plunged into her bridal reverie. "I found a gorgeous gown on sale last week. It's a cocktail dress, technically, but it's made of this flowy, creamy chiffon—"

"Don't encourage her or we'll end up with a veil, a six-foot train, and twelve bridesmaids." Gil chuckled. "We're just going to city hall and then inviting a few friends and family members to lunch.

Nothing fancy. We'd like you to be there, of course."

"Absolutely." Trina's smile got even wider and more sparkly. "And we have something to ask you."

Her father shook his head slightly at his fiancée.

"Is it about Teddy?" Lara asked.

"It's nothing that can't wait," her father said. "Let's focus on one thing at a time."

"Like potty training." Trina winced as Teddy started gnawing on her knuckle. "I really could use any tips you could give us."

"Tip number one: You can't let him do that." Lara reached over and gently pried the puppy's teeth off Trina's index finger. "He's going to grow up to be a big dog, not to mention a breed with a bad public relations rep, so you have to start teaching him bite inhibition right now. Nipping is not cute and it's not funny. It's unacceptable."

Trina nodded, her eyes huge. "How do I correct him?"

Lara yearned to reply that it was his mother's job to teach the puppy bite inhibition, but that Teddy's mama had probably been unable to do so due to premature separation from her litter. She restricted her response to: "You redirect him, firmly and consistently. Also, right now he's in a critical period for socialization, so you need to get him out and about every day. Expose him to a wide variety of experiences because his personality is going to get more rigid as he matures. If you want him to swim, start putting him in the pool now. If you want him to get along with other animals, start introducing him to cats ASAP."

"Okay." Trina stroked the puppy's head as he started mouthing her wrist again. "But how do I get him to stop peeing on the carpet?"

Lara sighed, reached over, and pried Teddy's mouth off Trina's skin. "Do you have a crate?"

"No." Gil smiled apologetically. "We were hoping we could borrow one from you."

"What are you feeding him?" Lara asked.

"Right now we're just using up the

little sample bags the store gave us," Trina said.

Lara rattled off a list of high-quality kibble brands, then said, "Rottweilers can be great dogs, but you have to be serious about training from the very beginning. Have you heard of the 'Nothing in Life Is Free' training theory?"

Blank looks all around.

"This whole thing was kind of a spur-of-the-moment decision," Gil said.

"Yeah, I can tell." Lara's annoyance must have showed, because her father shifted into his calming caretaker mode. "Don't stress—it'll be fine."

"It'll be fine for you because I'll take care of everything," she snapped. The words tumbled out of her mouth in a rush, and she immediately turned to Trina. "I'm sorry."

"Hey." Gil's smile never wavered, but his tone sharpened. "Take it easy, sweetie. It's just a puppy—no big deal. When did you get to be so type A?" He turned to Trina. "This is Justine's influence."

Lara stiffened. "Don't bring Mom into this, okay?"

"Good idea," Gil agreed. "Let's not fight. I'm on your side, kiddo. I'm the fun parent, remember?"

As he said this, Lara saw the hurt in his eyes. She glanced away, ashamed because she knew he had a point. Her father had always supported her decisions, and she'd never disappointed him because he'd never asked anything of her. He loved her unconditionally; didn't he deserve the same?

So she backed down and apologized again, and by the time she said good-bye and returned to the parking lot, she'd added a few more items to her type A to-do list: Find crate for Dad, recommend vet to Dad, carve out time for free training lessons with Dad, figure out how to potty train a Rottweiler puppy in seven days or less. . . .

For a "fun parent," he sure was a lot of work.

Chapter 22

When Lara came home from work on Friday, she was shocked to find her mother already dressed and waiting at the kitchen table.

"Hurry up—let's go." Justine stood up and collected her car keys and handbag as soon as Lara walked in. "We're late."

"Late for what?" Lara assumed the posture of a convict about to be frisked as her mother divested her of her black leather laptop case and started rolling a lint brush over her blazer and wool pants.

"I made an appointment with a real estate agent. We were supposed to be there five minutes ago." Justine straightened out Lara's pants leg and grabbed a dish towel to buff out a stain on her shoe. "It's terribly rude to keep people waiting."

"My last client meeting went long," Lara replied, automatically going on the defensive. "And I don't remember asking you to set up an appointment with anyone."

"Well, someone had to take charge. The first time you buy a house, you need an agent who knows what she's doing. Sandra helped me find this place, and she's a very good businesswoman. Detail-oriented. Not afraid to play hardball."

"But, Mom—" Lara began.

Justine grabbed her by the elbow, then marched her down the hall and into the garage. She opened the car door and slid on a pair of oversize designer sunglasses while the garage door purred open. As she ducked into the driver's seat, she gave Lara a warning look over the rim of her glasses. "Yes?"

Lara opened her mouth to protest being treated like a toddler and to list the many reasons why this situation was doomed to fail. Then she took a moment to watch her mother buckling her seat belt and tapping her nails on the leather-bound steering wheel.

Justine was about to leave the house for the first time in weeks, without a trace of bitterness or self-conscious- ness. At least temporarily, she was too preoccupied with micromanaging her daughter's life to wallow in her own.

"Nothing." Lara got into the passen- ger seat and clamped her lips together. "Let's go."

She stole sidelong glances as Justine eased the Mercedes out of the garage and into the driveway. But the bright af- ternoon sunlight didn't seem to faze her mother as she reentered the real world. She checked the street for oncoming traffic, then stomped on the accelera- tor.

"Now, remember," she warned Lara as they sped down the hill and waited for the tall wrought-iron gates at the community's main entrance to swing open. "Let me do the talking."

"So? What do you think?"

Lara planted her hands on her hips, gave the living room a thorough once-over, and nodded. "It's got potential."

Next to her, Justine scoffed. "Please. It's a dump."

"It is not! If I updated the lighting fixtures and slapped on a fresh coat of paint—"

"It'd still be a festering hellhole," Justine finished. She turned to Sandra, her tone icy. "You should hand out Hazmat suits along with the MLS details of this place."

Sandra retreated into the kitchen. "I'll give you two a moment to chat."

Lara shook her head. "Hey, Mom, know what's even ruder than keeping someone waiting? Snarking about Hazmat suits when they're showing you one of their property listings."

Justine waved this away. "This isn't her listing. Ugh. Sandra wouldn't be caught dead representing a seller of this caliber."

"Then why are we here?"

"Because the arbitrary lowball budget you insist on sticking to leaves her no other choice."

"My budget may be a little on the low side," Lara admitted, "but there's nothing arbitrary about it. I know how much I can spend on a mortgage every month, and I'm not going over that amount. I'm being financially responsible. You should be proud."

"You're being stingy," Justine countered. "If you'd just let me pitch in, you could afford a much nicer neighborhood and a much nicer home."

"I want to do this by myself. I appreciate your offer, I really do, but it's time I stood on my own two feet. You should understand that better than anyone."

"But this *hovel*!" Justine cringed as she noticed the popcorn ceiling overhead. "The carpet is ancient. Look at those stains. I shudder to think of the filth and bacteria, and I don't even want to imagine what might be behind the bathroom walls."

"It's not perfect, but it has potential."

"Potential to be condemned."

"Not everybody needs professional landscaping and silk wallpaper and a shower the size of a 7-Eleven to be happy."

"Yes, they do," Justine said with absolute certainty. "If they're honest with themselves."

They stared each other down for a moment. Lara could hear Sandra rustling papers from the safety of the kitchen.

Finally Justine stepped closer to Lara and lowered her voice to an urgent whisper. "I did not spend the last three decades pulling ninety-hour workweeks so that my only child could live"—she spread out her arms to encompass the perfectly serviceable living room—"like *this*."

"Yes, you did," Lara insisted, sticking out her chin. "You showed me every day how important it is to set goals and bust your ass to achieve them. You didn't expect things to be handed to you, and neither do I."

Justine pressed her index fingers

against her temples. "Why must you be so stubborn?"

"Can't help it. It's in my bloodline."

Sandra poked her head out. "Well, ladies? What's the verdict?"

"Let's put it on the 'maybe' list." Lara folded up the listing sheet and tucked it into her pocket.

"Unacceptable," Justine said. "We need something with more square footage, a better floor plan, and grass in the yard."

Sandra's gaze bounced from mother to daughter and back again before she made her decision and followed Justine's directions.

"Absolutely. I've got a place in mind. Just went on the market."

"Excellent," Justine said. "How many bathrooms?"

"Two and a half," Sandra reported.

"And the bathtubs—are they garden tubs or standard?"

Justine and Sandra led the way out of the starter home and climbed into the front seat of Sandra's sedan. Lara was relegated to the backseat, where she regressed to a slouchy, sullen adolescent. While the two older women in front discussed mortgage rates, equity, and desirable neighborhoods, Lara dug an ancient pack of Trident out of her bag and proceeded to blow bubbles.

But Justine was in her element, engaged and electrified with the prospect of ferreting out a bargain. Carpet stains and the promise of garden tubs had done what Lara herself could not— given her mother a reason to venture beyond the gates of silent, sheltered Mayfair Estates.

And that, Lara reflected, was worth a few wasted house tours.

Chapter 23

"We're going to win the blue ribbon to-day," Cherie Chadwick announced when she greeted Lara outside the convention center in Scottsdale. "I can feel it."

"We'll do our very best." Lara took Eskie's leash and scratched the bouncing Berner behind the ears. "Right, girl?"

"I sent out a card announcing our third-place finish to all the judges. I had it professionally designed."

"Which judges?" Lara asked. "The ones from the last competition?"

"No, no—the ones who will be judging today." When Cherie crouched down to kiss her dog, the massive diamond studs on her earlobes sparkled in the sunlight. "My darling girl looks especially radiant today, I must say. And so do you—this suit is smashing." She smoothed down the lapels of Lara's fringed blazer.

The smashing suit, featuring black, white, and turquoise bouclé, had cost upward of fifteen hundred dollars. Cherie had taken Lara to visit her personal shopper yesterday morning. Lara had nearly passed out in the dressing room when she glanced at the price tag, but Cherie insisted that she try it on, come out into the mirrored alcove between dressing rooms, and parade around like a show dog strutting her stuff for the judges.

And then Cherie had whipped out her credit card and purchased the suit without a second's hesitation. A suit that would hang unused in the closet, save for the few hours per month when Lara would put it on to trot around an arena with a dog. But that was the world of conformation shows. Ultimately, Lara knew, Eskie's scores depended more on good looks and the judge's personal preferences than structural perfection or obedience.

"Today is a winning day." Cherie practically sang as they waited at the edge of the parking lot for Eskie to complete her final pre-show potty break. "There's nothing like a blue ribbon to accessorize an outfit."

"Come on, girl." Lara took the leash and worked Eskie through a few basic commands and practice stacks. "Let's go get 'em."

And they did. Lara wasn't sure if it was the energy in the convention center or the way her suit skirt showed off Eskie's topline or the groomer's liberal application of Big Sexy Hair, but everything seemed to fall into place. Eskie picked up on Lara's quiet intensity, and instead of trying to play with the other dogs in the ring and say hi to every living being that wandered by, she focused on the judges. She pranced and preened and showed her teeth in a demure little canine smile.

"Good girl," Lara murmured as they awaited the judge's scoring. She rewarded the dog with an extra bit of beef jerky.

The judge must have liked what he saw, because he awarded first place to Eskie. Lara beamed as she shook his hand and then filed out of the ring.

"Mission accomplished." She handed over the blue ribbon to Cherie, who handed back a sealed envelope, no doubt containing another "treat."

"I knew it! I knew my baby was a winner, and I knew you were the right one to handle her." Cherie threw her arms around Eskie and kissed every inch of the dog's fuzzy white muzzle. "Oh, I love being right! And now we're going to sweep the Best in Group title, too, and go on to Best in Show. My darling's going to be a national champion."

"One thing at a time," Lara cautioned.

"I can't wait to tell everyone. Here, go back in the ring and pose with the judge. I need to take some photos for the next campaign ad." Lara and Eskie smiled for the camera while Cherie snapped pictures and complimented the judge on his exquisite taste.

Because the Best in Group title

couldn't be awarded until all the working breeds finished showing, they had an hour of downtime. Cherie took Eskie back to the car for brushing and black Vaseline application, then handed the dog back to Lara.

"You should take her for a while," she said, looking a bit sheepish. "I'm all keyed up, and I think it's making her nervous."

"No problem." Lara picked up Eskie's leash and strolled around the perimeter of the arena. At first Eskie did seem a bit stressed, panting and drooling, but soon she relaxed enough to start sniffing the ground and licking the sides of trash cans.

As Lara watched a group of Belgian Malinois compete, she noticed a man smiling at her from across the ring. He was so good-looking and gazing at her so intently, it was all she could do not to whip her head around to see if some hottie was standing behind her.

And then she realized: *Oh, he's checking Eskie out.* In a crowd like this, a beautiful Bernese mountain dog caused more of a stir than any supermodel.

But no, the guy kept glancing directly at her. Once she made eye contact, he started toward her.

Flustered, she wiped her palms on her skirt and said a quick prayer of thanks that Justine had refused to let her leave the house without mascara, lipstick, and powder.

She felt a bit fluttery, but her excitement was tempered with little pangs of disappointment and disloyalty. She didn't want to be thinking about Evan at a time like this.

But she was.

As the stranger strode up, tall and broad-shouldered with a boyish dimple in one cheek, Lara returned his smile.

Before either of them could say a word, Eskie inserted herself between them, sitting directly on the guy's shoes and leaning against his shins.

He stumbled backward but laughed as he righted himself.

"Sorry." Lara guided the dog back into a sit-stay. "This is Eskie. She must like you—I've never seen her do that before."

"She's very pretty." He bent to pet

her, then glanced at Lara for permission. "May I?"

"Go ahead. She loves meeting new people." This proved to be an understatement. Eskie reared back on her hind legs, placed her paws in his hands, and lunged forward to swipe at his face with her tongue.

To his credit, he neither retreated nor grimaced in disgust. He let Eskie down easy, one paw at a time.

Lara reinstated the sit-stay, pulled a tissue out of her jacket pocket, and reached up to dab at his cheek. "Well, now you know my secret: I'm the worst dog trainer ever."

"On the contrary." His fingers grazed hers as he took the tissue and finished drying his face. "I can see that she respects and fears you."

Lara had to laugh, and while Eskie didn't launch another full frontal assault, she wagged her tail and lifted one paw in an offer to shake hands with her new crush. Lara could practically see the red cartoon hearts in place of her eyeballs.

"I'm Tim." Much to Eskie's dismay, he opted to shake with Lara instead.

"Hi, Tim. I'm Lara." She put her hand in his and they both held on just a moment longer than necessary. "Is your dog showing today?"

"No, I'm here with my sister. She's showing a couple of her Jack Russell terriers. I was helping her out with the grunt work like setting up crates and keeping an eye on the dogs who aren't in the ring." He flexed his bicep. "I'm the Jack Russell roadie."

"What a nice brother."

"Well, I still owe her for scalping all her Barbies when we were kids. But we're done for the afternoon, and . . ." For the first time, he seemed unsure of himself. "There's no witty way to say this, so I'll just come right out with it. Is there any chance I could take you and Eskie to dinner?"

Lara had never been very good at flirting. She kind of laughed and sighed simultaneously, then said, "I'd love to, but we have to stick around for the Best in Group judging."

"How about tomorrow, then?"

Lara hesitated. She knew she should say yes. "Well . . ."

"Next week?" He grinned again, flashing that dimple. "Stop me if I start to sound desperate."

"You sound delightful," she said. "I have to ask you one question, though. Are you a dog person?"

"Absolutely," he replied, without a moment's hesitation. "Love dogs. Don't have one currently, but that's just because of recent changes in my life."

Lara leaned in. "What kind of changes?"

"Let me give you my card. Call me if you want to get together and talk."

He pressed a card into her fingers with another lingering squeeze, then patted Eskie and walked away.

Lara and Eskie watched him go, both of them drooling slightly.

She felt a slow, stunned smile spreading across her face.

Evan who?

Oh my God, it's Evan Walker!

On Sunday afternoon, Lara agreed to

attend an urban scent class with Helen and Frank Years and their two fox-hounds. The class was held in a public park next to a big outdoor shopping center, and the parking lot was crowded with weekend shoppers. Lara had to circle Target, Petco, and Home Depot until she finally found a spot. As she hurried across the asphalt, she noticed a man matching her stride in the next aisle of cars. A man who looked a lot like Evan.

She stopped in her tracks, trying to determine if it was really him.

It was.

Her whole body froze up, and she inhaled sharply, so loudly that the guy— the guy she'd been living with and sleeping with and planning a future with until Squirrelgate—glanced her way.

Evan froze up for a moment, too. Then he ducked and covered and ran back to his car like he was fleeing sniper fire.

Lara kept her gaze straight ahead and her facial muscles locked into what she hoped was a neutral expression. But her initial humiliation quickly twisted into red-hot rage. How dare he ignore her? And *flee*? After all they'd been through together, she didn't deserve to be treated like—

"Lara?" She heard his voice behind her. He sounded slightly out of breath and teeth-gratingly jovial. "What are you doing here?"

She refused to turn around. "I'm on my way to a dog training class. You?"

"Home Depot run."

She couldn't resist. "Need a few plumbing supplies?"

He tried to laugh this off. "No. Just fixing some drywall."

She closed her eyes and waited for some pointed comment about how he was still repairing all the damage *her* dogs had done to *his* house, but he surprised her by changing the subject.

"How've you been?"

"Great," she said, matching his cheery tone. "I'm thinking of buying a house."

"Really?" He didn't sound quite so jolly anymore. "Good for you. It's a great time to buy." He hesitated, then asked, "Are you staying with Kerry?"

Lara shook her head. "My mom."

"How's *that* going?"

She bristled at his tone. "Fine, actually. We're bonding."

"You? And your mother? Are bonding?"

"That's right. I'm staying in her guest room until I find my own place. Somehow, I've become the neighborhood Dog Doyenne."

He laughed. "What's a Dog Doyenne?"

"Everything. You name it, I do it." She finally turned to face him and chronicled some of her more colorful house calls.

He braced a hand on a lamppost and listened, really listened, his eyes locked on hers while she talked. They both laughed at the same places in the story.

"You should call that TV producer back and tell her you need your own show," he said when she finished.

They inched closer together in the fading sunlight, smiling at each other. When a cool breeze blew Lara's hair across her face, Evan reached out and brushed the strands back, his hand lingering on her cheek.

Her phone beeped and they jumped apart, startled and self-conscious.

"Ignore it," she murmured.

But Evan cleared his throat. "Go ahead and answer it."

She tucked the rest of her hair back behind her ear. "No, no. It can wait."

"Lara, come on. It's probably a new litter of pit bull puppies or a sheltie fresh out of surgery who popped a stitch or some other dog emergency." He gave her a knowing look. "Am I getting warm?"

She narrowed her eyes. "Are you *trying* to pick a fight?"

"No, I'm just telling you to live your life." He stuck his hands in his pockets and shrugged. "You don't have to feel guilty now. We broke up. You can do whatever you want."

"Yes, I'm aware of that."

"Then why do you look so pissed off?"

She wasn't buying his bewildered-and-innocent act. "You sound very sure of what I'm doing these days. But what about you? What are you doing with all your free time?"

His face reddened. "Oh, you know, just working. Getting ready for midterms. The usual."

She nodded. "You did a very thorough job of cleaning every last molecule of my belongings out of your house."

He misinterpreted this as a compliment. "You're welcome."

"And you changed the locks." She paused. "I take it you're already interviewing replacement candidates?"

He stared at her. She stared back.

Slowly, carefully, he said, "Let's not have this conversation."

"Too late," she informed him. "You didn't hang up the phone the last time we talked."

His horrified expression confirmed all her darkest suspicions. "What did you hear?"

"Enough to know that you either found someone else with lightning speed or you were cheating on me while we were still involved." She crossed her arms. "So which is it?"

"You know I wouldn't cheat on you."

"No, I do not know that. I didn't know that you were so angry with me. I didn't know that you hate dogs. I didn't really know you at all, apparently."

He finally flinched. "Let's just leave the dogs out of this, all right?"

"You said you loved me, Evan. You said you wanted to get married. How the hell can you go out and replace me just like that?" She snapped her fingers.

"You didn't want me," he pointed out. "You flushed my ring down the toilet." He shoved his hand deeper into his pockets and addressed the gum wrapper at his feet. "So what do you care if I have someone new in my life? You want me to spend the rest of my life pining away, miserable without you?"

"No." *Yes.* "Not forever, but how about a decent mourning period?"

His head jerked back up. "Maybe I'm not sad."

"Well, maybe I'm not, either," she shot back.

"Good."

"Great."

They both pivoted and went their separate ways, Lara unzipping her handbag as she went.

"Wait!" he called after her.

She slowed and turned around, cursing herself for the little spark of hope that kindled in her heart.

"Can I . . ." He raked his hands through his hair. "Can we . . ."

She looked him straight in the eye. "Before you finish that sentence, think about the 'honey' you already replaced me with."

He froze, speechless and stricken. When he recovered his composure, he stammered, "I'm not . . ."

"Can't finish that one, either?" She gave him one more moment before walking away. "Good-bye, Evan."

She ransacked the purse's pockets until she found the business card she'd tucked away a few days ago. When she arrived at the park, she tamped down all her rage and regret and dialed her phone with shaking fingers.

"Hi, Tim, it's Lara. Listen, I've been thinking about your invitation, and I'd love to have dinner with you. How's Saturday night?"

Chapter 24

"I have a date on Saturday," Lara informed her mother as they drove to the grocery store for Justine's second official public outing. "With a guy I met at a dog show last weekend."

She could tell from her mother's shallow breathing and tightly curled fingers that Justine was on the verge of a panic attack, and she hoped that opening up her love life for criticism would help distract her.

The ploy worked like a charm. As soon as Lara uttered the word *date*, Justine relaxed and shifted her focus.

"Oh, Lara, no. Now that you're finally having some success with your training business, you're going to derail yourself again with 'love' and 'romance'?" Justine used one hand to make air quotes. "Did you learn nothing from your last relationship?"

"Please note that I didn't say I was having a *relationship* on Saturday." She wanted to keep her mother talking as they turned into the grocery store parking lot. "I'm not *moving in* with the guy I met at the dog show. I just have a date. A revenge date, actually."

"What's a revenge date?"

"It's a prearranged social meeting with a hot guy to prove to your ex that you are able to upgrade and enjoy life to the fullest and are therefore winning while he is losing."

"I see. Well, that certainly does sound promising."

"Doesn't it?" Lara unbuckled her seat belt. "Okay. Let's go."

Justine didn't move. "I'm not ready for this."

"Sure you are. We're just running in for salad. It's not like we're going spend an hour restocking your pantry. We'll be in and out in five minutes."

"Tell you what—I'll give you my order, and you can go in and make my salad for me." Justine nodded toward the designer handbag tucked in the backseat. "Take my wallet. Whatever you need."

"Nice try." Instead of reaching for Justine's bag, Lara plucked the keys out of the ignition and pocketed them. "But bribery's not going to get you out of this. You made me go house hunting with you, so now you're going salad shopping with me."

"When did you get so pushy?" Justine checked her lipstick in the rearview mirror for the twentieth time, put on her sunglasses, wrapped an Italian silk scarf around her head, and opened the car door. "Be honest. How do I look?"

"Like a very glamorous international spy in desperate need of arugula and sliced radishes."

Justine huddled behind Lara as they stepped into the clean, organic, fair-trade-certified, and exorbitantly expensive supermarket. They had timed the trip for midafternoon to avoid the lunch rush and the pre-dinner crowd. The produce aisles were practically deserted, except for a few young moms pushing toddlers in carts. Once Justine had ascertained that she was in no danger of being recognized, she took off her glasses and started unwinding her headscarf.

"Ooh." Lara stopped to admire a display of exotic fruits. "Mangoes."

Justine nudged her toward the salad bar at the far wall. "Move along. We're not here to browse."

Lara laughed. "This right here? This is how I got pushy."

They collected their little plastic bowls and started spooning up lettuce, olives, and feta cheese. Justine used a pair of plastic tongs to inspect a slice of carrot, then wrinkled her nose and placed the wilted garnish back in its bin.

And that was when Lara noticed the man staring at her mother.

"Psst." She sidled up to her mother.

Justine shooed her away. "Don't crowd me, Lara. You'll get your turn with the tofu soon enough."

Lara kept right on nudging. "That guy over there is checking you out."

"What?"

"Hot prospect, nine o'clock."

Justine's head shot up. "Where?"

"Don't look!" Lara hissed. When Justine returned her attention to the produce, Lara murmured, "The guy over by the deli counter. With the leather jacket and the chiseled jawline."

"That guy?" Justine's sharp eyes swept over the man in a critical, two-second assessment. "He's not tall enough for me."

"He's got to be six feet."

"I prefer six-two or above."

"You know, I used to wonder if anything would ever be good enough for you, ever. And now I have my answer: *No.*" Lara sucked in her breath as the guy made his way toward them. "He's moving in. I'll head over to the dairy aisle and let you two have a moment alone."

Justine gasped. "Don't you dare desert me. We had a deal!"

"Too late." Lara darted off toward the

Greek yogurt, flashing the guy an encouraging smile as she went.

Two minutes later, she heard the unmistakable *click-clack* of Justine's high heels, and her mother rounded the corner holding a black-edged business card.

Lara clapped her hands together. "Well?"

Justine put her sunglasses back on. "His name is Dale, and he's a lawyer who just bought a house in the neighborhood."

"And he asked you out!" Her jubilation faded as she took in her mother's expression. "Uh-oh. He didn't ask you out?"

Justine whipped out her scarf and strode toward the exit. "He's a personal injury attorney, Lara. And no, he didn't ask me out. He wanted to know what happened to my face and if there's someone we could sue."

"Calm down, Mom. Let's not overreact here." Lara chased after Justine, through the garage and into the house. On the way to the kitchen, she opened the door to her bedroom and let the dogs out.

"I'm not overreacting." Instead of stowing her handbag carefully in a closet, Justine tossed it onto the counter. "I'm merely making a call."

"Who are you calling?" Lara asked, her eyes wide.

"The investment group in LA. I'm selling the salons."

"Mom!"

"No, Lara, I'm done. When people are pulling you aside in the grocery store to ask who they can sue about your face, it's time to get out of the beauty business."

"This is insane. You can't sell the salons."

"Watch me."

Lara opened the fridge, grabbed a bottle of white wine, and poured two glasses. "But the salon is your life's work. It's your baby."

"*Was* my baby." Justine plucked a tissue out of the box and started wiping off lipstick. She accepted the wine Lara offered and drank deeply. "The management team is doing just fine without me. They don't need me anymore."

"You don't have to decide this right away. Think it over. Twenty-four hours."

Justine shot her a glare over the rim of her wineglass. "I don't recall asking your opinion."

Lara gave Linus a warning look as the big red dog placed one paw on the foyer floor. Chastened, he ducked his head and U-turned back into the kitchen. "I swear to you, Mom, your face really isn't—"

"Save it, Lara. I know exactly how I look."

Lara couldn't think of anything more to say, so she reached over and covered her mother's hand with her own.

"I'm sorry," she said softly. "I shouldn't have made you go to the store."

"Please." Justine tossed her head. The glossy black strands of her wig gleamed under the kitchen lights. "You can't *make* me do anything."

"Yeah, but I got all pushy and told you to talk to Dale—"

Justine finally snapped. "This isn't about a man. Don't you see that?" She slammed her glass goblet down so hard, the base cracked. "Who cares about some random jackass at the supermarket? This is about *me*." She pivoted and strode off toward her bedroom.

Lara called after her, "If you feel like talking later—"

"I won't."

"Okay, well, it's your turn in Scrabble."

Justine didn't reply. She didn't slam her bedroom door, either, but she closed it with such a firm, definitive click that Lara knew better than to go knocking.

Not ten seconds later, Lara heard an outraged scream from the master suite: "Why is this animal always on my bed?"

A quick head count of the dogs confirmed what she already knew: Mullet had slipped away and made herself comfortable in the other alpha bitch's bed.

Lara waited, listening for the sound of the door opening and Mullet being forcibly evicted, but there was nothing.

She cleaned up the wineglass and took care of the household chores: wiping down the counters, bringing in the garbage and recycling containers from the curb, heating up the last batch of Shelly's frozen soup for dinner.

At six thirty, there was a bark at the front door. Ivory had arrived to join everyone for a walk.

After a tiring three-mile trek up and down the narrow, hilly streets, Lara settled back on the sofa and maintained a vigil, waiting for any sign from Justine.

Finally, at ten o'clock, her phone buzzed.

Justine had made her move: TUNIC for a whopping forty-four points.

Sighing with relief, Lara studied her letter tiles and strategized her next word, knowing even as she did so that it was futile. Her mother was going to clobber her. Without a moment's hesitation or a single shred of mercy.

All was right with the world.

"I'm in love," Kerry gushed.

Lara put her cell phone on speaker and double-checked her directions to the restaurant. She was en route to her dinner date with Tim, and she'd answered Kerry's call expecting tears, sleep deprivation, despair . . . pretty much anything except Kerry's actual announcement.

"You are?"

"Totally, blissfully, head over heels in love."

"Well, good for you." It was so good to hear Kerry's usual moxie back in her voice. "What happened? Did Richard come back early from his trip and whisk you away for a romantic weekend?"

"Oh, him?" Kerry asked, as if she could barely pick this Richard fellow out of a lineup. "No. He won't be back till next week, but that doesn't matter. I have everything I need right here."

Lara turned right at a stoplight. "What's going on? Do I have to remind you to stay away from the craigslist personal ads?"

Kerry laughed. "I'm in love with Cynthia. She's perfect. Not to mention unlawfully cute. My sweet little girl is delectable."

"Wow." Lara whistled, impressed.

"So those acid reflux meds finally kicked in, huh?"

"Yep. I think my hormones leveled out, too. I don't know what happened, and I don't care." Kerry sounded strung out on either endorphins or illegal substances. "I feel like . . . Remember your first love in high school, how the feelings totally consumed you? You wanted to stay up all night talking and watch the sunrise and the euphoria was seriously like a drug?"

Lara tried to think past her recent romantic disaster in the Home Depot parking lot. "Vaguely."

"Well, that's what this is like. I am *in love* with this baby."

"I'm so happy to hear you say that."

"Don't get me wrong—I'm still tired and the house is a war zone and I may never wear a shirt without spit-up stains again, but somehow none of that matters anymore." Kerry made a little noise that was half coo, half sigh. "I could watch her sleep for hours. Her little nose, her little fingers, and her cheeks, my God, her cheeks . . ."

Lara almost said, *That's just how I*

feel when I get a new puppy, but censored herself just in time. "Sounds like
somebody's bonding."

"Like Super Glue." Kerry stopped
crooning and got down to business.
"Listen, all that complaining I did, all the
crying jags and crazy talk about moving to Mexico?"

"Yes?"

"None of that ever happened, okay?
Erase the past few weeks from your
mind."

"Consider it erased." Braking for a
red light, Lara adjusted the rearview
mirror and dabbed on an extra layer of
lip gloss. She had let Justine style her—
hair, makeup, and wardrobe—and she
barely recognized her own glamorous
reflection.

"Great. And by the way, you should
totally go out and get knocked up.
Motherhood is the best thing ever."

"Now you're scaring me. Are you going to show up on my doorstep, trying
to convert me with informational literature from your Mommy and Me group?"

"Resistance is futile." Kerry let out an
evil little cackle.

"I'm going to have to call you back—I'm pulling up to the restaurant."

"Wait—what restaurant?"

Lara grabbed her tin of breath mints out of the glove compartment. "That would be the restaurant where I'm meeting my date tonight."

"Lara Madigan! You've been holding out on me!"

"How could my paltry first date possibly compete with you finding the true love of your life?" Lara provided a two-minute summary of meeting Tim as she maneuvered the station wagon past the valet stand and into one of the plebeian parking spots.

"Well, this guy sounds perfect."

Lara made a face. "They always seem perfect in the beginning."

"Okay there, Justine."

"Ouch."

"I'm just saying, keep an open mind."

"I'll try," Lara promised as she turned off the car.

"And have fun."

"I'm planning to."

Kerry paused. "And don't forget to ask him if he wants kids."

"I have to go."

"I'm telling you, I could just sit here smelling her head for hours."

"Look into baby rehab, you junkie."

Lara was still grinning when she walked into the restaurant.

And there he was, waiting for her, impeccably dressed and right on time: the perfect man.

Chapter 25

"This is lovely." Lara settled back against the plush banquette and took a sip of her sparkling water. "I haven't been out in forever."

As soon as the words left her mouth, she wanted to cringe. Nothing like opening a first date by talking about your lack of a social life.

Tim, exuding *GQ* debonair in a tailored shirt and tie, looked even more handsome by candlelight. "I find that hard to believe, with all the guys you must meet at shows and training classes."

"You'd be surprised. Most of the men I work with only call me because their wives or girlfriends make them." Lara smoothed her hair, which had been relentlessly conditioned, blown dry, and straightened. "As a rule, guys don't seek out a female trainer."

He shot her an arch smile. "They can't handle an alpha female?"

Lara smiled back. "Something like that, I guess. So did you enjoy the dog show?"

"I've never seen anything like it. My sister has been breeding dogs for years, and I kept promising to come to a show. I'm glad I finally showed up." He beckoned Lara in and confided, "I met a cute brunette by the Belgian Malinois."

Lara tilted her head. "Good chemistry?"

"Great chemistry. Even her Bernese mountain dog couldn't keep her paws off me."

Lara pretended to be scandalized. "Shameless hussy."

"Hey, there's nothing wrong with being direct." They paused as the server stopped by the table to recite the specials.

Tim gave the menu a cursory glance, then returned his focus to Lara. "What looks good?"

Lara felt her face suffuse with heat, but managed to maintain eye contact. "Everything."

The server took this as his cue to depart for a few minutes.

This is great, Lara told herself. *We're having fun; we're flirting; we have good chemistry. . . .*

Sort of.

The fun and the flirting were definitely present and accounted for, but the chemistry was a bit more elusive. Which made no sense. This guy was attractive, confident, funny, smart—she *had* to be attracted to him. And she would be, she assured herself, once the initial first-date jitters wore off.

"So did you grow up with Jack Russells?" she asked.

"Nah. I've always had mutts. Up until last year, I had a husky mix named Uno."

"As in the card game?"

"As in public enemy number one. He was a pain in the ass sometimes, and the shedding was unreal, but he was a great dog."

"What happened to him?" Lara held her breath, praying that Tim wouldn't reply, "I couldn't deal with the fur and the squeaky toys so I dumped him at the pound."

"He got cancer. I spent a ridiculous amount of money on chemo and medication, but in the end, the poor guy was in too much pain. I had to let him go. Sometimes I think about getting another pet, but Uno kind of spoiled me for your average dog."

"I understand," Lara said. "My first dog was a Chihuahua named Beacon, and I haven't been able to find another dog that I click with the same way."

"A Chihuahua? Interesting. I don't see you as a Chihuahua kind of girl."

"I'm not," she admitted. "Usually, I gravitate toward big, lazy lugs like hounds, but Beacon was one of a kind."

They traded dog stories for a few minutes, and then the conversation ventured into more personal territory.

Lara couldn't help herself. She asked, "Have you ever gone out with someone who didn't get along with your dog?"

Tim adjusted his shirt cuff, looking a bit embarrassed. "It hasn't been an issue, since I haven't really dated in a long time."

Finding this sudden shyness adorable, Lara teased, "So you don't normally troll the dog parks, picking up Berners and the brunettes who love them?"

He glanced back down at the menu. "I was married for five years. This is my first foray back into the social scene."

Lara's smile faded. "How long ago was the divorce?"

"No divorce." He swallowed hard. "My wife died just over a year ago. A month before Uno, actually."

"Oh my God. I'm so sorry."

He nodded, accepting her condolences. "It still sounds strange to me, saying that. Valerie was sick for a long time, but somehow I never expected her to actually die."

A note of strain and exhaustion crept into his voice. Lara didn't push for details, but he seemed to feel compelled to provide them.

"Leukemia," he said simply. "We found out a month before our wedding, but we were so sure she would beat it. And she did, for a long time. She hung on until the day after our fifth wedding anniversary."

Lara hadn't realized she'd raised her hand to cover her lips until she tried to talk. "That's . . . I . . ."

He squared his shoulders and forced a smile. "Oh, man. I swore I wouldn't do this—play the grieving widower card. My sister gave me strict instructions not to mention Val's name during dinner tonight. I was offended that she thought she had to point that out. And yet here I am."

"Don't worry," Lara said. "Your sister will never know. It'll be our little secret."

"That's what they all say in the beginning." He rubbed his face with his palms. "Then, next thing I know, you're blackmailing me for my roadie services, dog grooming, nail clipping. . . . Where will it end?"

"Hey." Lara sat back but nudged his

foot with hers under the table. "Just think of this as a practice run."

"But I don't want to practice." He nudged her back. "I spent the last year falling apart, and it's time to start putting my life back together. I miss Valerie, of course, but it's more abstract now. I'm trying to readjust to being single, but it's tough to remember all the rules. Rules like 'Don't talk about your dead wife on first dates.'"

"You're doing great," Lara assured him.

He chuckled. "If I was doing great, you wouldn't have to tell me 'you're doing great.' You'd be too busy trying to suppress the urge to rip my clothes off."

Lara made a big show of sitting on her hands, and they both laughed, but the romantic atmosphere had converted to one of camaraderie. So she relaxed, settled in, and shifted from date mode to friend mode.

"So you're not enjoying the single life?" she asked after she'd flagged down the server and ordered an appetizer.

One side of his mouth tugged up. "I

was never that great at dating, to be honest."

"What are you talking about?" She practically slugged him on the bicep. "You're, like, the perfect guy."

He also seemed to sense that the nature of this dinner had changed and he adjusted accordingly, loosening his tie and ordering a beer. "Playing the field was never my thing. I liked being married. Everyone warned me that it was going to be boring, but it wasn't. Val and I had a great time curled up on the couch on Friday nights, watching *The Bourne Identity* for the eighteenth time."

"You two were big Robert Ludlum fans?"

"I was a Robert Ludlum fan. I think she was more of a Matt Damon fan." He grinned. "What about you? Have you ever been married?"

"Almost." She stalled, taking another sip of water. "My last relationship was pretty serious, but it didn't work out."

"What was the problem?"

"Well, he wanted to get married."

"What an asshole," Tim deadpanned. "No wonder you broke up."

"I wanted to get married, too. At first. And then we moved in together and everything fell apart in a matter of weeks."

He leaned forward, intrigued. "But you still love him."

Lara choked on her water. "What? I do not!"

"Yeah, you do. You should see your face when you talk about him. You look like Eskie with those big sad eyes."

She had to stop hacking before she could reply. "Now you're comparing me to a dog? That's not very gentlemanly."

"Just your eyes," he corrected. "And so what if you're still in love with your ex-boyfriend? It's nothing to be ashamed of. Hey, I'm still in love with my dead wife. At least you still have a shot at getting back together with your guy." Before the conversation got somber again, he pushed his plate aside and started talking strategy. "So I guess you're going to have to be the one to propose next time, huh?"

"Oh, I don't think there's going to be a next time. We're finished."

"You don't sound finished to me."

Lara twisted the napkin in her lap. "At this point, it doesn't really matter whether I'm finished or not—he's finished enough for both of us."

"I can't believe that. You're so pretty, so charming. . . ."

"I flushed the engagement ring down the toilet."

His jaw dropped.

"He drove me to it." She provided a quick rundown of Squirrelgate. "Still think I should propose to him?"

"I think you're hot enough to pull it off, so yeah."

She blushed. "You say that because you haven't had to deal with me bringing home a bunch of sick strays or using our vacation fund for emergency canine surgery."

"Wait. Did he hate the dogs, or did he hate the way the rescue stuff sucked up all your time and energy?"

Lara furrowed her brow. "I'm not sure. He said I never knew when enough was enough. He said I was never willing to draw a line."

Tim rolled the beer glass between his palms. "Was he right?"

Lara took her time, finishing off her entire glass of water before admitting, "Kind of." She had to laugh. "This is the worst first date in history."

"Yeah, but we're having a good time." He looked wistful. "I miss this. Just the companionship, you know? I miss having someone there in bed with me at night. I miss having someone to eat cereal with in the morning."

Lara nodded, thinking of Evan. And then she looked back at Tim, a strong man struggling to recover from a devastating loss. A man in need of a lifeline. "You know, Tim, you're a great guy—"

"Oh no." He groaned. "Don't say that. 'You're a great guy' means I'm not even going to get to kiss you good night."

Lara gave him an exasperated look. "We just spent our candlelit dinner date deciding that I'm still hung up on my ex and you're still grieving for your wife. Why do you even *want* to kiss me good night?"

"Because I'm a guy."

She had to give him points for honesty. "Fine, you can kiss me good night."

He held up his hand for a high five.

"On the cheek."

He withdrew his high-five offer.

"But I can promise you that you'll never have to worry about sleeping solo or eating your cereal alone again." She smiled, thinking about Lucy Fur's silky brown coat and lack of tolerance for girlfriends. "I may not be the right woman for you, but I've got the perfect dog."

Chapter 26

Lara didn't go to her father's wedding. Nobody did, except Gil, Trina, and Trina's parents, since the civil ceremony was held midmorning on a Wednesday. But she met everyone at the celebratory luncheon—Trina's family, her college roommate, and a few close coworkers.

The groom's side of the invite list included only Lara, as far as she could tell. Her paternal grandparents had both died, and Gil wasn't close to his brother, who lived in Oregon.

Trina's family would become Gil's

family, Lara could see. He would spend his future holidays at his in-laws' dinner table; he would attend barbecues and New Year's Eve parties with people his wife had known for years.

Gil officially had a new life now, and much to Lara's surprise, she didn't feel shut out. Instead, she was grateful. Because she could finally stop worrying about him, and wondering if he would ever settle into a steady, normal routine.

Trina sat to the right of Gil at the meal, and Lara sat to his left. She laughed at all his jokes and raised her glass for every toast, but she did not make a speech of her own. She hugged him as she finished dessert and prepared to slip away and let him go until the next time he felt like connecting.

But her father grabbed her hand as she pushed back her chair.

"Wait," he said. "I need to talk to you."

She heard the expectation and determination in his voice and wanted to race for the exit, but she stayed.

She stayed because he asked and she couldn't say no.

And when the meal was over and the

guests had departed, Gil guided Lara outside to a whitewashed wooden bench on the restaurant patio. He sat with his back to the sun, leaving her shading her eyes with her hand and squinting while his new bride stood behind him, plucking at the skirt of the understated cream cocktail dress she'd settled for in lieu of a frothy white wedding gown.

"I love you, La-la." Gil smiled at her and slung one arm across the back of the bench.

"I . . . love you, too," she said slowly.

He took a deep breath and launched into his pitch. "Do you remember how, growing up, you always used to beg for a sibling?"

"So, you know my dad," Lara said to Kerry that evening as they tossed tennis balls for the dogs in Kerry's backyard while Richard—home for twenty-four hours between business trips—gave Cynthia a bath.

"No, not really," Kerry said.

"Okay, well, you know *of* my dad."

Lara knelt to accept the slobber-soaked green ball Linus offered, then stood up and lobbed it as far as she could. Linus streaked off after it, surprisingly speedy for a dog built like a tank.

"I know that you have a father, yes."

"Well, he got married today."

"On a Wednesday?"

"It was a simple civil ceremony, no frills. Anyway, we all had lunch afterward, and he pulled me aside to tell me that he and Trina, his new wife, want to have kids."

"Oh boy. Isn't she, like, your age?"

"Yeah, but that's not the problematic part. Just wait for it." Lara had to wait a few moments herself. Repeating all of this to Kerry was making the whole thing a little too real. "Trina can't carry a baby to term. I don't remember all the gory details, but something about ovarian irregularities and cysts."

"This story better not be going where I think it's going."

"Wait for it," Lara repeated. "So since the doctor says it's unlikely she'll be able to carry a baby to term—"

"Shut up! He wants you to be their surrogate?"

"No." Lara closed her eyes. "That would be an easy call: hell, no. I might be a pushover, but even I draw the line at hormone injections and carrying somebody else's baby. Especially after seeing you deliver Cynthia."

"Painful, exhausting, and a bit fluid-y for my tastes," Kerry agreed. "But worth every moment."

"You're just saying that because you're high on hormones. Anyway, here's the deal: He and Trina are looking into adoption, and they want me to write them a letter of recommendation that will go out to the caseworkers, potential birth moms, whoever. They want me to spend at least two pages raving about what a great father my dad is."

Kerry shot her a sidelong glance. "So they're asking you to lie."

"Kind of, I guess."

"What do you mean, *you guess*?" Kerry practically spit out her gum in outrage. "Your dad wasn't around for eighty percent of your childhood. I've been your best friend for five years, and I've never even met the man."

"True."

"And when he does bother to see you, it's always on his timetable and usually at the last minute."

"Also true. But that doesn't mean he's a bad person. He's just"—Lara searched for the right word—"limited."

"Yeah, and you're the one who suffers for his limitations." Kerry scooped up the tennis ball and hucked it for Maverick, who tripped over his own paws in his haste to retrieve it. "He's unreliable and he makes promises he has no intention of keeping."

"To be fair, I think he does *intend* to keep them." Lara sighed. "Anyway, I want to believe in his potential. I really do. He's starting a new life, and Trina seems great, and, well . . . what if he's changed?"

Kerry just looked at her.

"What? It could happen. Isn't that why we founded Lucky Dog? Because we believe in the potential for growth and second chances?"

"For wayward Westies. Not for grown

men who walk away from their families just because they're not feeling it. From what you've told me, it sounds like he was your buddy who would help you break curfew or whatever once a month, then disappear whenever the going got tough."

"He did let me get my belly button pierced. Oh, and he paid for my spiral perm, although I think that was just a passive-aggressive dig at my mom." Lara had started to notice that she couldn't have even a short discussion about her father without overusing the word *but*. "But there are a lot of kids out there who need a good home. And who am I to judge?"

"You're the kid he's already parented," Kerry pointed out. "I'd say that makes you uniquely qualified to judge."

"But what if he really has changed this time?"

Kerry tossed a rope chew to Rufus and Maverick so they could play tug-of-war. "Okay, have it your way. What if he has?"

Lara watched the dogs for a minute, then reclaimed the tennis ball from Linus and held it up. "The whole thing with my dad is kind of like me, Linus, and this tennis ball. My dad is me, and I'm Linus."

"Who's the tennis ball?" Kerry asked.

"He always acts like he's about to throw the ball, but every time he fakes me out." Lara pulled her right arm back into a pitcher's stance, then reared forward, but held on to the ball. Linus galloped off toward the back gate in crazed pursuit of the ball that was still clutched in Lara's hand. "And after all these years, I still go for it every time. I'm even dumber than Linus."

"Well, let's not get carried away. *No one* is dumber than Linus." Kerry got serious when she saw Lara's expression. "You're not dumb; you just want to trust your dad. That's completely normal."

"I want to believe that he's different now. I want to believe that he's capable of being a more involved parent, even if it takes a different child to get him there." Lara nibbled her lower lip. "Plus, I don't think he'll take it very well if I say no."

Kerry mulled this over for a bit. "Let me ask you something: If your father wanted to adopt one of our dogs, would you approve his application?"

Lara called Linus back from his frantic, fruitless search and handed over the tennis ball. "I wouldn't have a choice."

"Really? You'd send him on his way with Linus here, and sleep well at night? You'd feel confident that your dad would keep up with vet appointments, heartworm preventatives, excellent nutrition?" Kerry cupped her hand to her ear. "I don't hear a *yes*."

"Children and dogs aren't the same thing," Lara protested.

"Yeah, babies are way more work-intensive and emotionally draining," Kerry reminded her. "And they get colic and reflux and they don't potty train till they're three years old. So if you can't say in good conscience that you'd trust your dad with a puppy, then I don't see how you could even consider endorsing him for a human being."

"Yes, but . . ." Lara went through all

the automatic objections to Kerry's argument.

What if he really has changed, like, really for real this time?

And if he hasn't, isn't it enough to have a great mom even if the dad's unreliable?

And how dare I dictate what's best for other people's families when I can't commit to one of my own?

In the end, she simply admitted the truth: "But if I don't do what he wants, he's going to drop out of my life again, and this time he might not ever come back."

Lara screamed when she saw the foyer floor. She couldn't help it. The planks of leather and hardwood by Justine's front door had been scratched, deeply scored with tiny, close-set hatch marks that unmistakably matched the sharp claws of a Shih Tzu hell-bent on destruction.

Her mother was going to die. Her mother was going to kill. Her mother was going to—

"Good Lord, Lara, must you shriek like that?"

Her mother was in the kitchen, about to step out and see the architectural carnage.

Lara threw herself in her mother's path, trying to block Justine's view by wrestling her into a bear hug.

"Oof." Justine gasped for breath. "Get off me."

"I love you, Mom."

"Then stop assaulting me." Justine wriggled out of Lara's grasp and sniffed her daughter's breath. "Are you drunk?"

"No."

"Then what's going on with you? You've been acting strangely ever since you went to your father's wedding."

"I didn't go to his wedding," Lara said. "Just the lunch afterward."

Justine was in no mood to equivocate. "Pull yourself together, young lady. I've answered three calls for you just this morning from neighbors requesting your services. Apparently, Cherie Chadwick and Melissa O'Brien have been singing your praises at the country club."

"And people are calling you?"

"Cherie and Melissa told everyone you're staying with me." She smiled with a certain grim satisfaction. "I haven't even reviewed the official offer of purchase for Coterie and already I'm being dragged back into the work world as your secretary and business manager."

"Come on, Mom. We both know you'll never sell the salons."

Justine's smile went from grim to diabolical. "No one knows *what* I'll do. It keeps life interesting."

"Well, thank you for passing along the messages," Lara said. "But I really don't need a business manager. I'm fine. Truly."

"I beg to differ." Justine frowned down at her cuticles. "And by the way, your hourly rate just doubled."

"Mother!" That was when Lara noticed that Justine was wearing real clothes—not pajamas masquerading as "loungewear"—and appeared alert and well rested. She didn't look glamorous, but she did look content.

So Lara swallowed her objections. "Thank you."

"You're welcome." Justine glanced over her shoulder toward the foyer floor. "Now let's go back to the kitchen and sit down for a minute, shall we? I need to speak with you."

That was when Lara realized how quiet the house was. "What did you do to Mullet? Where is she, Mom?"

"Calm down. All the dogs are safely tucked away in the laundry room."

"The laundry room?" Lara cried, as if the laundry room were a rotting third-world prison instead of a clean, bright area so spacious it could practically double as a dog park.

"Yes. Or, as I like to call it, the holding cell. Now *sit*."

Lara felt the blood drain from her face as she followed her mother to the table and took a seat.

Justine took her time pouring a glass of water and arranging herself in the chair across from Lara. "I want you to admit that you've overextended yourself with these dogs."

Oh God. It was going to be Squirrelgate, Part II.

"Go on," Justine commanded. "I want

to hear you say it: 'I have too many dogs.'"

"I . . ." Lara's voice lapsed into a wheeze.

"Have too many dogs," her mother prompted.

Lara repeated the words, mumbling low and almost unintelligibly.

"You have overcommitted yourself, and as a result, you are stressed and the dogs are stressed. And Mullet in particular is acting out. Things cannot go on as they have been."

"I know," Lara told the gleaming granite tabletop. "I know, and I'm so sorry. I'll pay to have the floor refinished."

Justine sighed with impatience. "I should have known you weren't going to make this easy on me."

Lara screwed her eyes shut and waited for the ultimatum: *Get rid of the dogs or get out of my house*.

"You want me to beg? Fine." Her mother shifted in her chair. "I'd like to formally adopt her."

"Who?" Lara's eyes flew open. "*Mullet?* But you hate each other."

"We do not." As if on cue, Mullet

strolled into the kitchen, gave Lara a filthy look, and sank down next to Justine's chair with a phlegmy snort. Instead of petting the dog, Justine sort of nudged her with her foot. Mullet kicked right back.

Lara watched this exchange in disbelief. "Yeah, you do. I've never seen so much stone-cold bitchery in my life. From both of you. And how the hell did she break out of the laundry room?"

"She's very resourceful. Have you ever considered that the reason you have so many problems with her is that you constantly underestimate her?"

"No. I definitely have not considered that."

"Well, I'll have you know that Mewlay is extremely bright. Temperamental, yes, but—"

Lara did a double take. "What did you just say?"

"Mew-lay," Justine repeated. "Her name."

"Is she French now? Are we going the way of calling Target 'Tar-jay'?"

"She's a dignified dog who deserves a dignified name. Honestly, Lara, *Mul-*

let? Can you blame her for being out of sorts?"

Lara looked down at the furry little thug with the squashed-in face and the permanent sneer. "Are you going to start painting her toenails pink and dolling her up in a diamond tiara, too?"

"Of course not. That wouldn't be dignified, either."

"Let me tell you something about your precious Mew-lay. She's impossible to please. She's rejected at least five potential adopters."

"I would expect nothing less from my little Muumuu." Justine beamed with pride. "She adheres to the highest standards. She was holding out for the right owner, and here I am."

Lara gagged. " 'Muumuu'?"

"Your jealousy is painfully transparent and frankly unbecoming." Justine sniffed. "There's no reason to feel threatened by the bond I have with a helpless dog saved from certain death at the pound. You're still my daughter."

Lara gave up. "And she's your soul mate."

"She is." Her mother nodded. "I thought you wanted me to be happy."

Lara kneaded her face in her hands for a moment, then looked up as the realization struck. "I know why you like her so much—she's a cat."

Mullet stuck out her tongue.

"In all the ways that count, she's more feline than canine," Lara said. "The open disdain for humans, the blatant manipulation and sky-high self-esteem . . . Mew-lay should meow."

Justine exchanged a look of cliquish superiority with the Shih Tzu. "She has self-respect and dignity, like me. I could never respect a dog who would debase herself for a bowl of commercially processed food."

"But that's every dog in the world! Debasing themselves is what they do!"

"Not mine." Now Justine was just flat-out bragging. "Really, don't be jealous. Green's not your best color." She tapped one finger on the table. "Although I feel compelled to point out that you've been slacking in the Scrabble department. You haven't played a new word in days."

"I've been busy."

"I'm just saying, literacy and opposable thumbs are clearly an advantage in this ugly episode of sibling rivalry. If I were you, I'd put them to use."

"So now you're pitting my own foster dog against me to manipulate me to play Scrabble?" Lara *tsk-tsk*ed Justine. "You're unbelievable." She turned to Mullet. "And you're a traitor. After all I've done for you . . ."

Mullet flopped over on her side, stretched out her legs, and started snoring.

Lara got up from the table. "You two deserve each other."

As she stalked out of the kitchen, she could have sworn she heard her mother chuckling.

Chapter 27

On Saturday morning, at the latest of what was shaping up to be an endless season of conformation trials, Eskie once again snagged Best in Breed and moved on to the Best in Group competition. Midway through the show, Lara discovered a ruthless competitive streak she'd never realized she had. After years of opening her heart, arms, and wallet to the most filthy, matted, and gimpy dogs in Arizona, she found herself suddenly channeling her inner Justine, hyperaware of cosmetic flaws and dismissive of anything less than perfection.

No dog could possibly live up to her standards . . . except, of course, Eskie.

"Look at the snout on that mastiff," she whispered to Cherie as they scoped out the competition. "Disgraceful. And that schnauzer's gait is so bouncy."

Cherie tilted her head and joined in. "That Newfoundland is frizzy. And the styling on the Kuvasz? *Not* cute."

When the Best in Group judging began, Lara and Eskie bounded into the ring, full of confidence.

"Second," the judge announced, moving on to award the blue ribbon to a young fawn boxer so energetic he appeared to be spring-loaded.

Lara hurried over to the boxer's handler, offered up a handshake and a totally insincere round of congratulations, but started fuming the second she left the show ring.

"We were robbed," she hissed, covering Eskie's ears to shield the sweet, innocent pup from the harsh truths of the pageant world.

"Robbed," Cherie agreed, giving her a pat on the shoulder. "This is nothing but breed discrimination, pure and simple. If you'd been up against all those schlumpy sheepdogs in the herding group, we'd have won hands down, but the working group is so cutthroat. Everyone knows it's practically impossible to beat a boxer."

"We'll get 'em next time," Lara promised Eskie, who was too busy trying to play with a Brussels griffon puppy to hear her.

"You have an admirer," Cherie whispered in Lara's ear as she pressed another post-competition "treat" from Tiffany & Co. into her palm.

Lara followed Cherie's gaze to a stocky, fortyish guy in a baseball cap across the ring. When he caught her eye, he waved and walked toward her with a brisk, purposeful stride.

"Oh boy." Lara shoved the beribboned blue box into her bag, handed Eskie's leash to Cherie, and edged toward the exit. "I better go."

Cherie grabbed her wrist. "Don't run away. What if he's nice?" Her eyes gleamed. "What if he's loaded?"

And before Lara could make her escape, he was upon them.

"You're Lara Madigan?" he asked, his gaze disconcertingly direct.

Lara nodded.

The guy nodded down at Eskie. "This your dog?"

"Actually, she's mine," Cherie volunteered. "Swiss Star's Evening Escapade. Isn't she a beauty?"

The guy sort of grunted by way of agreement, then returned his focus to Lara.

"You have excellent handling skills. How long have you two been showing together?"

"Just a few weeks," Lara said. "Believe it or not, Eskie only learned to stack a month ago. She's a natural."

"Berners in general aren't known for their brainpower, but Eskie's smart as a whip!" Cherie crowed. Eskie panted up at them, looking sweet but vapid.

"Mm-hmm." The man didn't spare the dog another glance. "I'm Harold Jenkins, and I'm involved with a production company shooting a feature film here in town." He handed Lara a business card. "We're scheduled to shoot a few scenes featuring a dog, and our trainer dropped out of the project unexpectedly. We've been using the same animal-handling agency for the last few years, but they can't get us a replacement on such short notice. I'd like to talk to you about the possibility of working with us over the next couple of weeks."

"Oh, wow," Lara said. "I actually did an internship with a studio trainer when I was in college. What did you have in mind?"

"Well, it's an outdoor scene that requires the dog to run up to a picnic table, grab a hamburger, and run away. We're slated to shoot in about ten days. I know that's not much time to train—"

"Especially since she's booked every Saturday morning," Cherie interjected.

Lara stepped between the film producer and the socialite, feeling absurdly like the prom queen trying to juggle two varsity-football-playing suitors.

"That's going to be tight, but it *might* be doable, given the right dog," she told Harold. To Cherie, she said, "And you know I would never let another job sidetrack me from Eskie."

Harold checked his watch and held out his hand. "Great. So if you could just give me your contact information, I'll have my people start drafting the offer."

Lara fished a pen out of her bag. "How did you find me, anyway?"

"I called everyone I knew out here who's in the TV and film business, and one of them recommended you. Claudia Brightling, from the local news affiliate."

"Oh, right. She just interviewed me about my rescue group."

"Yeah, she raved about you and passed along your number. When I called, your mother answered and told me you were working the show here." He launched into a rapid-fire explanation of script demands, call times, per diem salary rates, and something about force-adding Lara to a union, but Lara was thinking about only one thing: "Do you have a dog in mind for the role?"

He shook his head. "We don't need a specific breed, but we're hoping to find a scrappy little terrier."

Lara started to smile. "A scrappy little terrier."

"Yeah. Any chance you could dig up one of those? Already trained and ready to work?"

"I'll see what I can do." She walked Cherie and Eskie back to their car, reassured Cherie that she was still Lara's first and most favored client, then got in touch with a guy who knew what it felt like to root for the underdog.

"Hi, Peter. It's Lara. How's everything going with Murphy? Great, I'm so glad to hear it. Listen, is there any chance I could borrow my old buddy for a few days?"

"I have a new job," Lara announced as soon as Justine walked through the side door. She'd rushed home from the conformation show to find the huge house empty, and had been waiting (and practicing her online Scrabble game) for more than an hour.

"I'm aware." Justine took off her sunglasses and winced slightly as she pried off her wig. Mullet sauntered in behind her with the air of a tragically hip high schooler forced to be seen in public with her parent. "Congratulations."

"Thanks. By the way, what's up with answering my cell phone?"

Justine peered into the hall mirror, examining the arch of her penciled-in brows. "I got my start working the salon phones. What did you expect?"

"I'm going to make a ton of money on this job," Lara informed her. "I get a per diem, the dog gets a per diem, and they said if this goes well, they'll recommend me to the other production companies that film commercials and movies out here." She glanced down at the trio of shopping bags in Justine's hand. "Where have you been?"

"Oh, Mew-lay and I hit up some of the boutiques in Old Town. I needed to find her a leash and collar better suited to her personality, and it's just so hard to tell what things really look like on the Internet."

"How'd it go?"

Justine puckered her lips and dabbed on another coat of gloss. "Oh, fine, except there was a bit of a scrap with a wretched little Yorkie."

"That sounds about right."

"It was entirely the other dog's fault. Mew-lay was just minding her own business."

"I'm sure." But Lara shot the snotty little Shih Tzu a look of thanks. She had motivated Justine to leave the house without bribery, coercion, or bloodshed. "Anyway, this whole film thing is very exciting because I know exactly what I'm going to do when I get paid."

Justine put the cap back on her lipstick with a perfunctory *click*. "Buy a house in a gated neighborhood with great mountain views and a steam shower?"

"I'm going to officially incorporate the Lucky Dog rescue group as a nonprofit."

"That's your financial priority?" Her mother threw up her hands. "What's the rush? You can do all that after you've gotten another few jobs under your belt and closed escrow on a stylish bachelorette pad. In fact, I was talking to one of the boutique owners about a loft that just went up for sale. Great location, right by the river."

"No, thanks." Lara stood firm. "I'm not a *House Beautiful* kind of girl, and I never will be. You were right when you said I've overextended myself with the dogs. I have, and so has Kerry. I'm going to file the legal paperwork, find some kennel space, update our Web site, and get a more organized support system in place."

" 'File the legal paperwork,' she says." Justine snorted. "Do you have any idea how much effort is involved in setting up a nonprofit? It's a full-time job in itself. Tax forms and bureaucracy and fund-raising and publicity . . ."

"I can handle it," Lara assured her.

"You say that now, but you don't know what you're getting into. Trust me, I learned the hard way when I first started my business."

Instead of getting defensive, Lara smiled sweetly. "Well, it sounds like I'll need a partner who can stay on top of all the administrative duties. Would you like to apply for the job?"

Justine froze, mid-pore inspection.

"I'm serious," Lara said. "You know everyone who's anyone and you said yourself the salon doesn't need you anymore. So why don't you apply to be the Lucky Dog president? Or director? Whatever you want to call the position." She flipped her hair back over her shoulder. "I'll technically be your boss, though. And you'll be taking, like, a ninety-nine percent pay cut. Can you handle that?"

Justine folded her arms. "I'm sorry— did you just say I'll need to *apply*?"

"Well, I can't just up and hire you without an interview. Don't want to be accused of nepotism. You'll need excellent references, of course. And Mullet doesn't count."

Justine appeared to be torn between maternal pride and indignant outrage. "Tell you what. We'll start a new game of Scrabble tonight. If I beat you, I get the job."

"Deal," Lara agreed.

Her mother paused a moment, her wry smile fading. "And by the way, the film producer wasn't the only one who called while you were out this morning.

Your father called, too, and asked that you call him back as soon as possible."

Lara was almost afraid to ask. "What does he want?"

"I don't know. But he said it's urgent."

Chapter 28

"Lara, finally! Where have you been?" Her father's voice was frantic. "We've been trying to reach you for hours."

"I was working all morning and I left my phone at home." Lara wedged herself down on the bed between Rufus and Raggs. "What's wrong?"

"It's Teddy. He's sick. He's throwing up; he's lying around all lethargic; he's not eating. . . ."

"Okay, well, if he's throwing up you need to stop offering food." Lara pushed up her sleeves and tried to think about the most obvious diagnoses. "What does the vomit look like? Maybe he ate something he shouldn't have."

"It's kind of clear and foamy," Gil said. "I don't see food chunks or anything in it."

"Take him to the vet," Lara said. "Right now."

"But it's Saturday. Our vet's office is closed till Monday."

Lara could hear Trina crying on Gil's end of the connection.

"Get in the car and drive to the emergency clinic." Lara jumped up and grabbed her keys. "I'll meet you there. He's over twelve weeks old now, right? Is he up-to-date on his vaccinations?"

"Yeah."

She pulled on her coat, switching the phone from ear to ear as she did so. "Well, did the vet see anything unusual at his last visit?"

Her father hesitated. "No."

Lara heard Trina's voice again, and then Gil confessed, "We didn't take him to the vet for his twelve-week visit. We read online that we could buy the shots at a feed store and do it ourselves, so we figured we'd save the sixty-dollar checkup fee—it costs a fortune just to walk in the damn door—"

"You spent fifteen hundred dollars buying a dog on a whim, but you couldn't spare sixty for a checkup?" Lara forced herself to stop yelling and take deep breaths. "So what happened when you gave him the injections?"

"Everything was fine." Her father sounded huffy. "If there's a problem, it's because the manufacturer screwed up, not me."

Lara turned this information over and over in her mind until something finally clicked. "Did you keep the shots cold?"

More murmuring on his end of the line. "What do you mean?"

"Did you put them in the refrigerator after you bought them?"

"I don't know. You'll have to ask Trina. Why? What's wrong with him?"

Lara was already halfway to the garage. "I hope I'm wrong, but it could be parvo."

*   *   *

"It's parvo," the emergency vet reported, taking off her eyeglasses and tucking them into her jacket pocket as she scanned the results of her lab work. "And it's progressed pretty far. He's severely dehydrated and the lining of his intestinal tract is sloughing off."

Trina, who had spent the short, tense appointment sniffling into the front of Gil's shirt, completely broke down at this news. She covered her face and burst into wet, heaving sobs.

Gil wrapped his new bride in both arms and continued his conversation with the doctor. "But I don't understand," he kept saying. "We gave him his shot."

The vet stole a quick glance at Lara before replying. "If the syringe isn't stored at the proper temperature, it loses its effectiveness."

Lara kept her mouth closed and her expression as neutral as possible.

"How did he get sick?" Gil demanded. "Is this because we got him at the pet store?"

The vet put aside her paperwork and addressed Gil with quiet compassion.

"Parvo is rampant in Arizona. The little guy could have picked it up anywhere."

"You can fix it, right?" Gil bent his head to give Trina a kiss. "Tell me you can fix it."

Lara and the vet exchanged another sidelong glance. "We can try," the doctor said. "I've started him on antibiotics for the secondary infections, and we'll push fluids, but parvo itself is a virus and there's really not a lot we can do. Some dogs get through it, but he's so young and his immune system is still developing." She reached out and patted Trina's back. "We'll have to wait and see."

As they trooped out of the exam room and into the waiting area, Lara tried to comfort Trina, whose agonized sobs had lapsed into shuddery gasps for breath.

"He'll be fine," her father insisted. "He's a fighter. You'll see."

They sat in the waiting room for the next four hours, watching the cable news channel blaring from the TV in the corner and flipping through the old magazines scattered across the metal chairs. The vet techs came out with an update every half hour, and every time, the news was worse.

But every time, Gil's response was the same. "He'll rally. Don't worry."

Finally, as the sun started to set, Lara pulled her father aside and tried to make him understand. "It's time to let him go," she said. "He's just too young to get through this."

Anger flashed in Gil's blue eyes. "But the vet said—"

"She said they'd try. And they did. But he's getting worse." Lara looked away as tears stung her eyes. She'd been on the receiving end of this lecture with sick and injured foster dogs more times than she cared to recall. "I know it's hard, Dad. But if you wait for him to die on his own, he's going to suffer even more than he already has."

He jerked his thumb toward Trina. "What am I supposed to tell her?"

"Tell her the truth," Lara said. "They're doing everything they can, but it isn't enough."

Her father stalled for a few more minutes, then knelt down next to Trina's chair and started speaking to her in a low, soothing tone.

"No," Trina sobbed. "I can't."

When he tried to reason with her, she stood up, shoved past him, and ran out to the car. Lara let her go and remained with her father. She saw the receptionist watching them, waiting for them to make a decision.

"This is awful," Gil said, staring down at his limp, empty hands.

"I know." Lara pulled a tissue out of her coat pocket.

Her father sighed and rubbed the back of his neck. "And it's my own fault."

Lara didn't argue.

"If only I'd . . ." But then he stopped himself. "Well, maybe it's for the best." He glanced over at her with a mix of shame and hope. "I didn't want to say this in front of Trina, but after everything you said about puppy mills . . . If he was going to grow up with lots of painful joint problems and whatnot, maybe it's better that we let him go now."

Lara knew he was waiting for her to

absolve him, to hug him and tell him he couldn't have known any better. It was her turn to let him off the hook the way he'd let her off the hook so many times. But she couldn't force herself to move or speak.

When he realized she wasn't going to respond, he crossed the room and gazed out at Trina in the parking lot. He said, almost to himself, "We'll get another puppy and start fresh. Next time, we'll know better."

He nodded, shaking off his guilt. When the vet came out with a somber expression, Lara stepped forward to deliver their decision.

"Would you like to come in and hold Teddy?" the vet asked gently.

Lara looked to Gil, who stared back at her, once again waiting for her to intervene and offer absolution.

This time, she didn't disappoint him.

"I'll go," she said, her heart numb. "It'll be fine. Go take care of Trina."

Her father's whole body relaxed. "Okay. Thanks, La-la. I knew I could count on you to do the right thing."

Lara felt the burst of cold air ruffle

her hair as her father walked out the door. Then she followed the vet into the exam room and gathered Teddy's limp, warm little body into her arms.

Chapter 29

"He's never going to change," Lara said to her mother the next morning as the two of them took Mullet on a walk—or, more accurately, a waddle—around the neighborhood.

Beside her, Justine sighed and slid her sunglasses higher on her nose. "I know that."

"I mean, I sat there and held his dying puppy while he went out to the parking lot and made plans for his next foray into dog ownership." Lara balled up her fists inside her jacket pockets.

"I understand you're frustrated, but are you honestly surprised?"

"Yes! And that pisses me off even more because it just goes to show how stupid I am."

"You're not stupid." Justine ignored the friendly waves from a pair of passing power walkers. "You want to believe the best of your father. That's understandable."

"But I mean, people *are* capable of change, right?" Lara scowled up at the sun. "Otherwise, what is the point of living?"

"Stop trying to make him change and change yourself instead," Justine advised. "Adjust your expectations. Set limits and stick to them."

"That's exactly what Evan used to say."

Justine tugged on Mullet's black patent leather leash. "I've scheduled a meeting with my business lawyer for Tuesday at four o'clock. He'll be going over the basics for setting up the nonprofit and registering with the IRS. Then, of course, we'll have to see my accountant to set up the bookkeeping system and a checking account for the foundation."

"How much does your business lawyer charge?" Lara asked.

"Three hundred dollars an hour."

"Ouch."

"But we've had a long, lucrative relationship, so he's agreed to help out with Lucky Dog pro bono," Justine continued. "Now, we also need to think about leasing some office space and, as you said, finding or constructing a kennel for the dogs. . . ."

"Yeah, about that. Once I actually sat down and started crunching numbers, I realized that my movie check's not going to go as far as I thought."

"No," Justine agreed. "We'll need a lot of capital for start-up costs. I'm thinking we should host a big benefit event, although I'm still debating between a formal ball and a more casual luncheon. I've already put in some calls to my former clients." She adjusted her wide-brimmed straw hat as they started up the steep hill toward Cherie's estate.

"We can invite all my clients from the neighborhood, too," Lara said. "And

Claudia Brightling might give us a mention on the morning show. Ooh, maybe we could hit up some of the local pet boutiques and put on a dog fashion show. How about that?"

"Nauseating," Justine declared. "But a sure crowd-pleaser."

"We could let owners walk their dogs down the runway," Lara said. "Cherie and Eskie would be first in line."

"Make her pay for the privilege," Justine said.

"Isn't that kind of tacky?"

"It's for a good cause, plus it's tax-deductible. It would be tacky if she didn't donate."

Mullet, who had been lagging behind them and making it clear that every step was a chore, suddenly picked up speed and raced to the front of the pack.

Lara spotted a familiar little white pooch a few houses down. But for once, Ivory wasn't making the rounds by herself. Today, she was being walked by a tall, broad-shouldered gentleman with ruddy cheeks and a shock of white hair. With his khaki pants and navy plaid wool jacket, he looked like a catalog photo for Brooks Brothers casual wear.

Suddenly the sullen little Shih Tzu was bouncing and snuffling and towing Justine across the street to meet her new friend.

Lara watched in amazement, then hurried to catch up. Ivory trotted over to greet her, and Lara gave the Maltese a few pats before she introduced herself to the older man in khakis.

"You're Ivory's owner?" she asked.

"I am now." He offered up a hearty handshake. "Jay Bexner." He looked perplexed as Ivory scampered around Lara's feet, begging for treats and affection. "Do you two know each other?"

"Ivory's a neighborhood celebrity," Lara said. "I see her greeting her loyal subjects every morning when I walk my dogs, and she's been tagging along on our evening jogs."

"She's an escape artist, all right. I couldn't figure out how she was managing it for ages. Then I finally found the tunnel she'd dug under the fence. Little devil dug the hole right by the rosebush so she wouldn't get caught."

"Mew-lay, come back here immediately!" Justine seemed a bit alarmed that her dog would deign to socialize with anyone else, canine or human. "Muumuu!"

But Mullet ignored her. The Shih Tzu was too busy frolicking with the Maltese, both of them chasing after birds and tangling their leashes together.

Justine tried to regain control of the situation, but Mullet refused to be contained.

"That's quite a collar." Justine pointed out Ivory's pink rhinestone–studded little band of ribbon. "Did you pick it out yourself?"

Jay looked amused, but not abashed. "Nah, my daughter has a thing for pink. A few months ago, she left for graduate school at the London School of Economics. Now that she's gone and my son took a job out east, I needed someone to fill up the house."

Lara noticed he hadn't mentioned a wife.

Jay shrugged. "I know her name's a little froufrou, too, but it fits her. I didn't have the heart to make her answer to Buddy or Butch."

"Ivory's perfect for her," Lara said, but Jay had shifted all his attention to her mother.

"You're Justine Madigan," he said.

"I am." Justine admitted this grudgingly. "Have we met?"

"Not officially, but I've seen you around. Is that your dog?" Mullet was lying on her back, pedaling all four feet in the air while Ivory pranced around snapping at flies.

"Yes. She's not usually so undignified."

"They sure seem to get on together. Maybe we could take them to the park and let them play sometime."

Lara flashed Justine a thumbs-up. Justine ignored her.

"I don't think so. I'm starting a new business, and as you can imagine, my schedule is jam-packed."

He nodded, undeterred. "Still have to walk your dog, though." He checked his watch. "You usually come out with her around this time?"

"Yes," Lara interjected, before Justine

had time to make up any more excuses. "She and Mullet will be out tomorrow at eight."

"See you then." He kept looking at Justine. "Nice to finally meet you."

"Nice to meet you," Lara replied. She waited until Jay and Ivory turned the corner, then rounded on her mother. "What is wrong with you? He was so sweet."

"Ugh." Justine wrinkled her nose. "Sweet just complicates things. I told you once and I meant it: I don't want a man. And you!" She shook her head at Mullet. "What a traitor."

"I told you so."

Lara clipped Murphy's leash on, walked the little dog out to her car, and opened the back gate of the station wagon so he could clamber into one of the padded crates.

He turned around three times, then collapsed on top of his Nylabone and immediately closed his eyes. Lara wasn't surprised he was tired. The scruffy little dynamo had spent the whole day running across a soundstage, hitting his "mark"—the built-in bench on a picnic table—and snatching a hamburger from an actress before running back to Lara, who was standing on the sidelines, giving hand signals and doling out treats. She'd spent the past week training him to perform the behaviors on cue, then devoted this morning to rehearsing on-set.

As she'd predicted, Murphy had enjoyed every minute of the job. He was clever and outgoing, with an incredible work ethic, and he definitely had "star quality." He knew that he'd done his job well, and he practically glowed with pride. Even the director had commented on the terrier's charisma.

"I think today is the beginning of a long and successful show biz career," Lara told the tired pooch.

Cleo the dock-diving begollie might have a cameo or two in her future as well. While Lara had gathered up Murphy's gear, one of the producers had approached her and asked if she'd be interested in booking a commercial for a flea-and-tick preventative.

"We need a dog who will run across a wooden dock and jump into a lake," the producer explained. "Do you work with any who can do that?"

"I do," Lara replied. "But you'll have to pay her in blueberries."

She backed out of the parking lot and checked the directions to Peter's house. He'd been delighted to send Murphy out for the job; he couldn't have been prouder if a talent scout had offered *him* a movie role.

Fifteen minutes later, as she was preparing to turn right at a busy intersection near the mall, a huge brown dog darted across the street directly in front of her car. She slammed on the brakes, missing the animal by inches.

For a split second, she closed her eyes, her heart slamming in her chest. Then she turned on her hazard lights and jumped out of the car.

The dog was ducking and weaving through four lanes of traffic, panicking. Lara waited for the light to change again, called out in her most authoritative tone to get the dog's attention, and headed for the safety of the sidewalk while clapping loudly. The dog's chase instinct kicked in, and it bounded after Lara, relieved to have a pack leader to follow.

"Good job." Lara wrapped her fingers around the dog's green leather collar.

The poor thing was wild-eyed and panting heavily, so Lara crouched down next to it and murmured in low tones while she moved her palms in wide, slow circles around its shoulders. This achieved the desired calming effect, but it also set off a river of drool, which hung down from the dog's jowls in stringy white loops.

"You look like a bloodhound," Lara told the dog. "And you drool like one, too."

She led the way back to her car, where Murphy was still sacked out in his crate, unaware that anything had happened.

"Come on. Let's get you a nice cool drink and we'll see if we can find your owner."

She poured bottled water into one of the collapsible canvas dishes tucked in the seat pocket, then twisted the green collar around to examine the brass tag attached to the buckle.

Sure enough, the tag listed a phone number and address.

A phone number and address that she recognized.

She sat back and stared at the massive, drool-drenched bloodhound. "You have *got* to be kidding me."

Chapter 30

"It's so good to talk to you, La-la. Come have lunch with me." Her father's voice on the phone was conciliatory. He knew she was angry, but he was pretending he didn't.

"Dad, I can't." She sat in Peter's driveway, waving good-bye to Murphy and keeping a close eye on the bloodhound, who'd spattered the back windows of the station wagon with speckles of drool.

"Come meet your pops for dinner," Gil said. "Just you and me."

"Can't," Lara said.

"Important work appointment?"

"Bloodhound in the backseat."

He paused, unsure how to interpret this. Then he tried again. "Just have a quick drink with me. I'm at the place where they have the iced tea you like. We'll sit on the patio so you can bring the dog, if you like."

Because Peter was still standing on his front porch, holding up Murphy and waving to her with his little yellow paw, Lara kept a smile on her face. "Dad . . ."

"One glass of iced tea," he pleaded. "Half a glass. That's all I ask."

Lara gave in, started the ignition, and unwrapped the square of dark chocolate she kept in her handbag for emotional emergencies. "If only that were true."

"I ordered for you," her father announced before she even sat down at the restaurant's wrought-iron bistro table. "Cup of clam chowder and the ahi appetizer."

She watched in dismay as a server approached, carrying a tray of hot food. "I told you, I can't stay. I have a random dog sleeping in my car." By the time she'd arrived at the restaurant, the bloodhound had crashed out in the back of the station wagon, so she'd parked near the patio, rolled down the windows, and let the poor thing nap.

"Calm down," Gil chided. "You can make time to slurp a bowl of soup."

Lara stopped protesting and simply pushed the steaming mug of soup away. This conversational merry-go-round could keep circling indefinitely if she didn't force a direct confrontation. "I think I know why you want to speak with me."

"You do?"

"Yes. About the adoption letter." She kept her gaze fixed on the wisps of steam rising from the chowder. The opening lines of her rehearsed little speech were lodged in her throat. It was one thing to make a decision in her own mind, but to give voice to these words, to actually come right out and say, *I can't endorse you as a parent*, seemed so harsh.

But she had no choice. There was no way she could sit down and write the recommendation, and so the end result would be the same.

She could dash his hopes with a quick, devastating assault or with a slow trickle of empty promises and strategic emotional retreat.

After years of chasing after a man in emotional retreat, Lara knew the direct approach was kinder.

So she would get straight to the point. Just as soon as she recovered from her panic attack.

"Sweetie." Gil touched her wrist. "Are you all right?"

Her airway closed up. She felt as though she was literally, physically choking.

"I'm all right," she finally managed. "Sorry. I guess the iced tea went down the wrong way."

He offered her a sip of his water. "Better now?"

"Better." She inhaled deeply. "So about the adoption recommendation. I can't."

Her father pulled away from her. "Lara." His voice was layered with surprise and raw, undisguised pain.

She started shredding the empty straw wrapper by her glass. Anything she could say now would only make things worse. Any defense would be systematically dismantled.

He waited.

She waited.

The silence between them stretched into a standoff.

Finally Gill sighed and gave in. "I know you're upset about Teddy. The pet store, the injections, everything. We screwed up—*I* screwed up. I admit it."

"This isn't about the puppy." She remembered the feel of Teddy's soft, warm body starting to cool in her arms. "It isn't just about the puppy."

"I know how you feel about dogs, but a puppy is not the same as a baby. Even you have to admit that."

"I do." She remembered Kerry's teary, bloodshot eyes as she paced with her infant and pleaded for help. She imagined first her mother, then Trina, experiencing that same exhausted desperation all alone.

Her father's eyes went dark with sorrow and disappointment. "I've changed, Lara. You underestimate my potential."

She nodded. "Maybe."

"I deserve another chance from you."

"I'll give you another chance," she said softly. "I'll always give you another chance, whether I want to or not. You're my dad and I love you. But I can't do this for you."

He glanced down at the floor, then took her hand again. "Don't you see how important this is to me? I can fix my mistakes, make up for all the time I lost with you. . . ."

For a nanosecond, she considered saying that it must be nice to apply for a do-over child and where could she apply for a do-over father?

But she knew he was hurting, maybe even worse than she was. He would never see himself clearly, never recognize his own failings, and it was not her responsibility to make him. Her job was to accept him for who he was and to allow herself to start grieving for the relationship she would never share with him. So she kept her mouth shut and her head down and weathered the guilt trip without comment.

When he realized she wasn't going to engage in his debate, he concluded with "I'm disappointed in you."

Lara was shocked to realize how much these words stung, how deeply she still craved his approval. Even though she was an adult who told herself she'd given up on him long ago, it hurt to think that he would give up on her, too.

"We're going to go ahead with the adoption anyway," he informed her, his tone defiant.

She nodded. "I know."

"I'm still going to get what I want."

"I know."

"Then why do you have to keep punishing me for things I can't change?"

"I'm not, Dad. I . . ." But she couldn't explain herself. More to the point, she didn't want to.

"Are you're saying I'm a bad father now? Is that what you're saying?"

"No."

"Then why can't you just let it go?"

Lara looked up and decided to do

exactly that. She gathered her coat and bag. "I'm leaving."

"You're just going to take off in the middle like this?"

"I have a lost dog to deliver."

"If you walk out of here, you're making a choice," he threatened.

She put down cash for her share of the meal and left.

She'd finally done it: set her limit, stuck to her boundary. And while she knew her father was upset, she couldn't worry about him anymore. All she could think about right now was the bloodhound waiting to be reunited with its owner.

Ten minutes later, she pulled up in front of a well-kept house in a quiet middle-class neighborhood. She strode across the lawn, taking care not to trip on the hose lying in the walkway.

When she reached the front stoop, she jabbed the doorbell, tapped her foot, then jabbed it again.

She heard faint sounds of life from

the other side of the door—muffled footfalls and the drone of a televised sportscaster.

"Give it up," she yelled through the thick wooden panels. "I know you're in there. I can hear ESPN." She turned her fist sideways and pounded on the door, SWAT-team style. "I'm not leaving until I get some answers."

She heard the locks unbolting, and then the door swung inward just far enough for Evan to stick his head out.

For a moment, Lara drew back and took in his bloodshot eyes and thicket-like cheek stubble. He looked as tired and despairing as Kerry had a few weeks ago.

"What are you doing here?" he asked.

Lara tried to tamp down her instinctive pangs of sympathy as she gave him a thorough once-over. Then she reached out and plucked a single strand of chestnut-colored fur off the collar of his white T-shirt. "Aha! What's the meaning of this?"

He ducked back into the house and tried to shut the door, but she blocked it with her sneaker.

"I don't have to explain anything to you," he said.

"You don't have to," she allowed, "but you will. I've got something in my car that belongs to you. Or should I say *someone*."

Chapter 31

"You found Honey?" The door swung wide again, and Evan stepped out onto the welcome mat.

"I did." Lara dangled her key fob in front of his face. "But before I unlock the car, you'll have to start talking."

He ducked his head. "Why bother? It sounds like you already know everything."

"All I know is that I damn near ran over a giant bloodhound near Scottsdale and Sixty-fourth, and—"

"Oh my God." His face went ashen. "She was running in the street?"

"—and when I coaxed her into my car, I checked her tag. Guess whose address and phone number were inscribed on it."

At this, a note of pride crept into his voice. "I got her microchipped, too. You always say dogs should have identification on them at all times."

"I do say that." Lara leaned against the tan stucco wall, confused and sad and angry all at once. "But I thought you weren't a dog person."

Evan's expression went from shocked to sheepish. "That's what I thought, too. But I guess I just hadn't met the right one."

She took a moment to absorb this. "So you and . . ."

"Honey," Evan supplied.

"You and Honey have been together for how long now?"

"A few weeks. She showed up in the backyard one morning, same as the pit bull puppies." He kind of slurred this last sentence together, the conversational equivalent of speeding past a perilous patch of road. "I wanted to call you to take her, or drop her off at the shelter, or something, but she kept looking at me with those eyes, and then I brought her with me to a soccer game, and next thing you know, we were going for a run every morning and watching the Super Bowl together."

Lara still couldn't believe what she was hearing. "You. Got a dog."

"I had no choice." He raked a hand through his hair. "She liked me. She wouldn't leave."

"And you like her, too."

"Yes, okay? Fine. I admit it. I like my dog."

"And if she ate a cake off your kitchen counter?" Lara pressed.

"I'd still like her."

"What's different about her?" Lara glanced back at her car, where the back window was spattered in Jackson Pollock–like dribbles of drool. "Is she perfectly behaved?"

"No, she's just as bad as all the rest." Evan chuckled, apparently amused by Honey's criminal tendencies. "Worse, really, because of all the drooling. It's unreal. We're talking rivers of drool."

"I can see that."

He ran his hand through his thick brown hair. "Plus, I'm pretty sure she has a death wish. The third day she was here, she ate a bunch of the neighbor kid's crayons, which gave her kidney stones, and I had to drop twenty-six hundred dollars at the vet's."

"And you're fine with all that?"

Evan shrugged. "I can't explain it. She's just special. After you left, this whole place was too quiet and empty. I missed you, and it was nice to have someone to come home to after work. I guess"—now he looked *really* embarrassed—"you know how you're always saying every dog is a lifeline?"

Lara nodded.

"Well, she's mine."

A few weeks ago, Lara would have felt vindicated at this admission, but now she just felt deflated.

"So you broke up with me and replaced me with a dog," she said. "Harsh, but fitting."

"Lara, I could never replace you. Never. While you were out looking for a new house and becoming the Dog Doyenne, I was sitting around on the couch in my old track shorts, eating bad take-out and thinking about what a jackass I'd been. In fact, the night I saw you by Petco, I was trying to—"

"Petco?" Lara pushed off the wall and put her hands on her hips. "You told me you were coming out of Home Depot!"

"What else could I say? When you first saw me, I was carrying a bag full of treats and toys and a stuffed squirrel exactly like the one I, uh, had issues with previously. I had to hide it in my car before I could talk to you."

She tucked her hair behind her ear. "So what were you trying to say that night? It seemed like you had a lot of unfinished questions."

He reached out to touch her cheek. "I wanted to ask: Can I see you again? Can we start over? I wanted to tell you I'm not seeing anyone else." His thumb traced her jawline. "What about you?"

Lara took a breath, then confessed, "I went out on one date. But it didn't work out."

"Jerk didn't like dogs?" Evan guessed.

"No, he liked dogs," Lara said, sidling forward a bit.

He took another step toward her, frowning slightly. "Couldn't bake you a cake?"

She threw him a devilish little grin. "Oh, he probably would have made me a cake eventually."

He leaned forward, his voice deepening. "I'm positive he couldn't love you as much as I do."

"Mr. Squirrel and all?"

He tilted his face until his mouth almost brushed hers. "You're perfect for me. Exactly the way you are."

"Then yes. Yes to everything. Yes, you can see me again. Yes, we can start over." She wrapped her arms around his neck and gave him a sweet, seductive, first-date kind of kiss. He responded with a hot, demanding, third-date kind of kiss, which left her no choice but to up the ante with a positively scorching fifth-date kiss. But then, before she got entirely carried away, she pulled back and said, "Not so fast. What about the white VW with the sparkly pink heart sticker?"

Thankfully, he was too busy trying to slide his hand under the hem of her shirt to ask how she knew about the white car. "The dog walker." His face darkened. "*Ex*–dog walker. I should have known better than to trust some flighty undergrad. I told her a million times to pay attention on walks and hold the leash with both hands, but *noooo*. She decided to let Honey off-leash 'just for two minutes' to show her friends how Honey can play soccer. I've been searching for two days, calling vets, posting flyers."

"Honey can play soccer?"

"She's the canine version of David Beckham. We'll discuss it later." He drew her inside the house and kicked the door shut behind them. They stumbled across the living room, kissing and kissing until they fell back onto the sofa cushions, eliciting a loud squeak from a dog toy buried underneath.

*   *   *

"Admit it," Lara said, swinging one bare foot lazily in the air as she sprawled across Evan's bare chest. "I've dragged you down to my level."

He ran his index finger along the curve of her back. "You have. I'm officially a member of the Cult of Dog. Pass the Kool-Aid."

She tucked her head under his chin. "So what are we going to do now?"

"I vote for more of what we just did. As long as we're both down at your level, we might as well wallow."

"You silver-tongued devil." She gave him a playful pinch, then got serious. "Can I ask you something?"

"You can do anything you want to me."

She shifted her weight on the sofa, setting off a fresh set of squeaks. "What does this mean?" She nibbled her lower lip. "For us. Does it mean anything?"

He took so long to reply that she finally lifted her head to see what he was doing. As soon as she made eye contact, he said, "It means so much that it's all I can do not to start asking dangerous questions."

She unleashed another fifth-date kiss. "What kind of questions?"

He cupped her cheek in his palm and shot her a warning look. "You know exactly what question."

"So ask," she dared.

When he hesitated, she took matters into her own hands. "Okay, well, if you won't ask, I will. Evan, will you—"

He pressed his hand over her mouth. "Hey! Stop. I'm the guy. I get to ask."

"Don't be sexist. We'll do it together," Lara suggested. "Okay?"

"Okay. On the count of three."

"One, two, three," they chanted, their voices jumbling together. "Will you marry me?"

"Jinx," she said. "You owe me a Coke."

"How about I give you a ring instead?" He got up, went back to the bedroom, and returned with the diamond ring, which was still encased in the plastic sandwich bag.

"I love it." She couldn't have been more thrilled if it had been presented in a little blue box with a bow. "But can we dip it in boiling water before I put it on?"

After they both threw on their clothes, Lara padded into the kitchen to fill a pot at the faucet and turn the stove burner on while Evan brought in Honey.

The jowly brown hound bounced between Lara and Evan, sniffing and wagging and drooling for joy.

Then she looked right at Lara and did a clumsy sideways stagger, almost like a four-footed canine jazz square.

"Did you see that? She's dancing."

"I told you, she's got moves." Evan used a pair of metal tongs to retrieve the ring from the plastic bag. "You should see her on the soccer field."

Honey opened her mouth in a dopey doggie grin and did it again. She tripped over her huge paws and careened face-first into her water dish, then lurched back onto her belly, whereupon she crossed her front paws daintily and waited for applause.

Lara looked into Honey's droopy eyes and fell deeply in love. It wasn't rational and it wasn't what she expected, but it was undeniable.

At long last, she'd met her new soul mate. And as luck would have it, her new soul mate just happened to be a package deal with the love of her life.

Chapter 32

"So you're getting married." Justine nodded in resignation when Lara broke the news over dinner at the house in Mayfair Estates. "I always knew you would."

Lara was through apologizing for her choices. "That's right. I'm getting married, I'm blissfully happy, and guess what? I don't care if you approve."

"Good. You're a grown woman. You don't need anyone's permission." Her mother paused just long enough to torture Lara. "I do approve, though."

"You do?"

"Why does that shock you?"

"What about all those warnings about the pitfalls of letting your guard down and trusting a man?"

"*I* am the one who will never fully trust a man again. *I* am the one who can't let her guard down. You are not me. You have your own path." Justine reached for her BlackBerry and snapped into business mode. "My calendar is filling up for the next twelve months, so we'd better nail down a date immediately. Are you thinking about a spring wedding, or summer?"

Lara waved one hand dismissively. "We're just going down to city hall. Nothing fancy. But don't worry, we'll find a time when you can come."

Justine went very still. "Excuse me?"

Lara knew she was in trouble, but she couldn't figure out why. "What? You *don't* want me to find a time when you can come?"

"You are not going to city hall, so rid yourself of that ridiculous notion right now." Justine brandished her butter knife like a shiv. "I will disown you if you go to city hall."

"I thought you just said I had to make my own path."

"You can find your path *after* I throw the wedding of the year." Justine gulped her white wine. "City hall? Bite your tongue, you ungrateful child. Let me spell this out for you so there's no misunderstanding: We are throwing a wedding. A big, extravagant, black-tie affair with crystal and caviar and a twelve-piece band. You are going to wear a couture gown and you're going to like it."

Lara groaned. "Mo-om, no."

"Yes." Her mother's tone left no room for debate.

Lara tried to debate anyway. "Formal affairs make me sweat. And I'm pretty sure white lace gives me hives."

"You're the bride. All you have to do is glide around looking pretty."

"Evan's not into all this stuff, either."

"Evan?" Justine craned forward as if she couldn't possibly have heard this correctly. "He's just the groom. He doesn't get a vote."

"And all that expense for one day? It's such a waste."

"It's not your money, so don't you worry your pretty little head about that."

"There's no point in arguing with you, is there?"

Justine scooped Mullet up from the floor and started feeding her scraps of salmon from her plate. "None whatso-ever."

"Well, if I'm going to have a fancy, formal wedding full of people I barely know—"

"You are."

"—then all the guests will get to bring a date, right?"

"Of course."

"Then you have to bring one, too."

Justine didn't miss a beat. "I have a plus-one." She scratched the top of Mullet's head.

"No, you have to bring a human date. Did you go out with Ivory's owner yet? What was his name?"

"Jay. And you know very well that I don't date."

"So you shot him down in cold blood?"

Justine hemmed and hawed and

rolled her eyes before admitting, "We met for dinner at the country club on Saturday, but I made it abundantly clear that it wasn't a date."

"Whatever. How'd it go?"

Justine lifted one shoulder. "I didn't have the urge to disembowel myself with a steak knife."

"All right! We'll call that progress."

"Don't make more of this than it is. Jay and I enjoyed a lovely tasting menu along with reasonably entertaining conversation. The end. I know you refuse to believe it, but that's all I'm interested in at this point in my life."

"I do refuse to believe it."

"That's because you're an incurable matchmaker. But the truth is, not everyone has to be paired off to be happy. I like my life the way it is. After so many years by myself, I'd be completely unsuitable for cohabitation with a man. The snoring, the blobs of shaving cream in the sink, the obsession with golfing and sports cars . . ." Justine grimaced. "No, thank you."

Lara laughed. "So you and Miss

Mew-lay are going to live happily ever after?"

Justine nuzzled the contrary little mutt, who went limp and played dead. "She may hog the covers, but she never contradicts me or whines about my work schedule."

Then Lara heard it: the distinctive *bing* from the laptop open on the counter.

"Hey, what was that?" she asked.

Justine toyed with her gold watch. "I believe that was my computer letting me know that it's my turn in Scrabble."

Lara's jaw dropped. "You're playing Scrabble with someone else?"

Justine's cheeks flushed. "Yes."

"But I'm your online Scrabble buddy!"

"Calm down. You're still my Scrabble partner. But you're busy, and you're only going to get busier as we start planning your big day and moving forward with the nonprofit. I'm allowed to have more than one game in progress."

"Who's your opponent?" Lara demanded.

"I'm not sure that's any of your business."

But living with Justine had taught Lara a few things about playing hardball during negotiations. "Spill your guts or I elope to Vegas."

Justine gasped. "You wouldn't."

"Try me. I've got a three-day weekend coming up and a hankering to say my vows to Elvis."

After a two-second standoff, Justine caved. "Jay," she choked out in a dramatic whisper.

"First the tasting menu, now Scrabble." Lara rubbed her palms together. "The plot thickens."

"We play Othello, too." She sounded so mortified that Lara had to tease her just a little.

"Maybe *you* should be the one picking out a wedding dress."

"When hell freezes over. Now, let's get down to business." Justine, still cradling Mullet, stood up and crossed to her laptop, where she started pulling up wedding Web sites. "Tomorrow morning I'll call the bridal salon at Neiman Marcus and make an appointment. Do you prefer a mermaid silhou-

ette or A-line? Silk satin or silk char-
meuse?"

Lara tuned out the second she heard
the words *bridal salon*. She gave her
mother a blank look. "Whatever you
think. You have great taste."

"Oh, I'm so glad you're going to be
agreeable about this." Justine clapped
her hands together. "I'll start interviewing event planners, and we'll need to
come up with a head count estimate as
soon as possible so we can book a location. I'm thinking the Four Seasons or
the Biltmore."

"Should I invite Dad?" Lara asked.
"He's still not speaking to me or ac-
knowledging my existence in any way."

"Yes," Justine said firmly. "He's your
father; you have to invite him. It's up to
him whether he attends or not."

"He won't come," Lara predicted.
"He's teaching me a lesson."

"And I'd say you're better off for having learned it, wouldn't you?"

Lara picked at her cuticle, then
dropped her hand when she noticed
Justine's frown. "I guess we'll just skip
the traditional father-daughter dance."

Justine came back across the room and covered Lara's broken, unvarnished nails with her own flawless manicure. "Oh, sweetheart. I'll dance with you."

"A mother-daughter dance?" Lara looked up, surprised. "I don't think that's Emily Post–approved. What will people think?"

"I don't give a damn what people think."

"But appearances matter, you know. I have it on high authority."

"My daughter matters more. I'm the hostess, and I'll dance if I want to."

"What will our song be?" Lara tried to come up with an appropriate theme song for her mother. "'Independent Women' by Destiny's Child? 'I'm Every Woman' by Chaka Khan?"

"It's a *wedding*, Lara. The song should be meaningful. It needs to say something about who you are and what having you in my life has meant to me."

"If you say 'Butterfly Kisses,' I swear to you I'm going to the justice of the peace at nine a.m. tomorrow morning."

"I was thinking something a little more

upbeat. Something to get everyone out on the dance floor." Justine paused, a mischievous glint in her eye. "'Who Let the Dogs Out?'"

Chapter 33

"Happy zeroeth anniversary." Lara kissed her groom. "Happy zeroeth anniversary to you, too, although I'm not sure such a thing really exists."

"It's less cheesy than saying the first day of the rest of our lives."

"It is, and I appreciate that." Evan closed and locked the door of the riverside cabin they'd booked for their honeymoon in Sedona. Although the little bungalow's exterior looked rustic, the interior was all French cotton sheets and bedside Belgian truffles.

"My feet are killing me." Lara grimaced as she struggled with the tiny bejeweled gold buckle on her ivory stiletto sandals. "I will never understand why brides are expected to spend the whole day running around in shoes that effectively hobble you."

Evan leaned down and kissed the nape of her neck. "Hobbled or not, you looked amazing today."

"Thanks. My mom picked out the gown." Lara yelped as she felt a cold, wet nose replace Evan's warm lips. "Gah! Honey, off."

She heard the click of nails against hardwood as Honey scuttled off and leapt up onto the bed.

In addition to selecting Lara's gown, Justine had also selected Kerry's maid of honor dress, the venue, the flower arrangements, the invitations, the menu, and most of the guest list. The result had been a gala worthy of a five-page spread in *Martha Stewart Weddings*.

Lara looked up at Evan and smiled. "I think today was the happiest day of my mom's life."

"But she doesn't believe in marriage."

"Exactly. This was her chance to

throw the wedding of her dreams without having to bother with any of that pesky commitment." She held out her arms and examined her freshly paraffined skin. For the last five days, she'd reported to the Coterie salon in Scottsdale every morning like it was her job, checking in at nine a.m. and clocking out promptly at five. She'd been buffed, waxed, plucked, polished, exfoliated, and slathered with acetone until the staff deemed her suitably transformed. "I think I finally lived up to her expectations."

"Your mom's proud of you. You know she is."

"She has to be—I'm her employer now. But I'm proud of her, too." Justine hadn't tried to hide behind a scarf or a veiled hat at the reception. She'd selected a fashion-forward pale green suit, put on a light layer of makeup, and made the rounds, personally greeting every guest along with her date. "Did you like Mullet's new 'do?"

The Shih Tzu had also been subjected to the full spa treatment, and was almost unrecognizable after having her hair trimmed, shaped, and subtly high-lighted to complement Justine's gold jewelry. Lara had administered the fin-ishing touches this morning, adding vol-ume around the muzzle and ears with a few well-placed spritzes of Big Sexy Hair.

Evan loosened his tie and went to work on his shirt cuffs. "I have to tell you, I didn't even notice Mullet."

"Too busy staring at your hot new wife?"

"Pretty much."

"But surely you noticed that Honey looked even prettier than usual." While her mother had obsessed over every detail of the event planning, Lara had focused her energy on training the bloodhound to walk down the aisle on a white rose-entwined leash in prepara-tion for her role as ring bearer.

Honey had hit her marks perfectly, holding a ten-minute sit-stay while Lara and Evan exchanged their vows, and coating the rings with only the bare minimum of drool when Evan untied them from her collar. But when the groom kissed his bride, Honey had raised her muzzle and let loose with a roof-raising howl that would have done Frederic and Elfrida proud. And Kerry's baby girl had joined in as well.

In the spirit of joy and new beginnings, Justine had let Honey live, but she'd been banished to the back room during the reception. (Mullet, of course, had a seat of honor at the head table.) Everything else had been picture-perfect—with one notable exception. The father of the bride hadn't shown up. Gil and Trina had sent their regrets, along with one of the bone china place settings that Lara (or, more accurately, Justine) had registered for.

Evan kicked off his shoes and flopped back on the enormous four-poster. Lara joined him, curling up against his chest.

Not to be left behind, Honey wriggled her way into the embrace and collapsed across her humans' feet and shins.

"How can such a skinny dog weigh so much?" Evan marveled. "I swear, her bones are made of iron."

"It's a bloodhound thing," Lara explained. "They have freakishly dense skeletons."

"I can't move my legs."

"Luckily, the phone is in reach. We can dial room service."

"Works for me." He reached across the bed and grabbed an extra pillow for Lara. "In fact, I may never leave this cabin again. Everything I need in life is right here."

"Me, too. I would like to change out of this dress eventually, though. It's kind of binding."

"Don't worry. That dress is coming off soon enough." But his words ended in a yawn.

"Big talk from a man who's losing consciousness." Lara listened to his heart beat and let her eyes close. "I'm so glad the wedding's over and we can get back to our real lives."

"I'm so glad we're finally taking a vacation."

"I'm so glad we found a four-star resort that takes pets."

They started to kiss, then broke apart, laughing, as the lace hem of Lara's gown got trapped under Honey's paw and ripped.

"I love you."

"I love you."

"Woof."

Acknowledgments

A big, slobber-drenched thank-you to . . .

Shawna Swanson, who let me tag along to dog shows and shared stories about competing, rescuing, and dating in the dog world. If you live in the Phoenix area and need a trainer, seriously, contact her right this minute: www.MaverickDogTraining.com.

Kresley Cole, amazing author, dear friend, and girl genius, who continues to make my life "easy peasy lemon squeezy."

My mom, who routinely kicks my ass at online Scrabble and will swear with her dying breath that "brung" is a word.

Jeannette Viteri and, of course, Etienne, Aiden, and Bella, without whom this book would probably still not be finished. I'll be over with a batch of M&M cookies directly.

Danielle Perez and Ivory, Kathie Galotti and Eskie, Erica Ashcroft and Petty, and all the Facebook fans who nominated their dogs for cameos in the story. (I'm still laughing about "Lucy Fur." You guys are the best!)

And of course, my own darling dogs, Roxie and Friday, who keep my feet warm and my entire wardrobe covered in fur.

After growing up with a purebred Bernese mountain dog, **Beth Kendrick** fell in love with a scruffy stray terrier named Murphy and has been a sucker for rescue dogs ever since. She lives in Arizona with her family and two rambunctious red mutts. Despite owning three vacuum cleaners, she is constantly covered in dog hair.